SAVING ARIANNA

Dot Com Wolves 2

ALISA WOODS

Cover Design by Steven Novak

ISBN-13: 9781095557990

***Saving Arianna* (Dot Com Wolves 2)**
Formerly published as *Dark Alpha*

Jak is the bodyguard for a woman captured and mated against her will. He owes his alpha his life—and his dot-com job—but he can't just watch her get hurt. When an attack lands her in his arms, he wonders if breaking an unbreakable magic bond will destroy them both.

Chapter One

If only she weren't so beautiful, it might not hurt so much to watch.

Jak guarded Arianna's backpack while she skipped around University of Washington's Red Square—although the red brick paving of the central plaza was mostly covered by the colorful fall leaves that Arianna was kicking up as she twirled around, arms flung wide. Her smile was big enough to garner smirks from the passing students who had to dodge her little freedom dance, but she didn't seem to care. The mountain was "out" today—the normal dreary drip of Seattle had parted to reveal brilliant blue skies and Mount Rainier shining in the distance. It was gorgeous and breathtaking and far, far out of reach… like Arianna in every way.

She spun closer then stopped and fixed him with her blue-dazzle eyes. “What are the chances, Jak?” Her breath made a small puff in the cool fall air, and her smile was infectious.

He grinned. “The chances of you being late to class? Getting better all the time.”

She lunged over and hit him. Not hard, of course. A slap on the shoulder for daring to remind her why they were here. But it was the first time she had ever touched him, and it brought a whiff of her natural scent over the backdrop of fall leaves: his shifter-enhanced senses detected a hint of musk under her blackberry-and-lavender soap. The earthy scent might be arousal… or it might just be the plain joy clear on her face. Either way, it speared through his heart. He had to force himself to keep the grin in place.

“No, Mr. Bodyguard!” She grinned again, and the noontime sun played with her hair. “What are the chances we would have such glorious weather for my first day back at school?” She tipped her head back, arms flung wide again as if to embrace the sky. Her cascading brown hair picked up red and gold tints from the leaves. “It’s a sign!” she declared to the heavens.

His grin was more natural again. "A sign of what? That you've been cooped up in Mace's house too long?" His grin faltered as he realized how bitter the words sounded out in the air, not just in his head. Mace was her alpha… but he might as well be her jailer. As far as Jak could tell, Arianna hadn't left the Red pack estate since she'd been brought there, nearly six months ago. Jak lived in the main house, with the rest of the unmated wolves, and while he could see Mace's house from his window, he rarely saw Arianna… and then only when she haunted the windows like a pale wraith imprisoned in the suburban-style home. Mace didn't let her even step foot on the lawn outside without an armed guard.

Which made sense, given Mace had basically kidnapped her.

But, for some reason Jak wasn't privy to, Mace had decided to allow her to return to school. And today, for Arianna's first day of freedom, Jak had pulled guard detail—probably because he was a recent alum of UDub himself. Or maybe because Mace was still angry with his own betas about the run-in over the summer with the Sparks pack. But whatever twist of fate that allowed Jak the right to escort Arianna out into the world again, it was a duty that both twisted his stomach and enlivened every other part of his body.

Arianna had sobered with his words as well and now gazed at him with those big blue eyes. "Can I tell you something, Jak?" She was only twenty-one, a few years younger than him, but in that moment, she seemed much older… yet still innocent at the same time. She was as winsome as a barely-grown girl, yet already burdened by the many things life had thrown at her.

Jak understood that feeling. "I am an excellent keeper of secrets." His mouth twitched with a repressed smile. If she only knew how many times she had filled his nighttime thoughts… and not always in an innocent concern for her safety.

Some of the glow left her face. "I haven't felt this alive since…" She blinked. "Since my alpha claimed me." And like *that* she was a ghost again, an empty shell where life used to be.

The lump in Jak's throat refused to budge.

A stray wisp of cloud drifted over the sun, and a shadow fell on her face. It was as if the light had gone out of the world. Arianna shrunk back a little and glanced at the red-bricked buildings encircling the central plaza.

"Mace doesn't really want me here." Her shoulder twitched.

Jak swallowed the lump and reached out to her, gripping her shoulders with both hands. He could feel her quake through the thin jacket she wore, and his inner wolf growled: not at her, but at the idea that anyone would make her feel afraid. Least of all, her own alpha.

"Everyone in the pack is expected to contribute," he said, "and the best way to do that is to join the company. Your alpha knows that. And you won't be much use to Red Wolf, Inc. until you have a degree in *something.* It's only logical for you to go back to school, now that you've… settled in." *Given up running away. Become used to being a captive. Had your spirit broken.* Those were the words he wanted to say… but he never would be able to, no matter how many times he pictured himself sneaking over to Mace's house and wrenching her free of his magical hold. Like that was even possible. Jak had managed to free one girl from Mace's grasp—all without Mace ever realizing Jak helped her escape—but that was *before* she became his mate. Mace still blamed his betas for the loss of the Sparks pack female. But Jak knew he was beyond lucky to have gotten away with something like that. The universe wasn't kind enough to let him get away with it a second time. Besides, Arianna was beyond saving: the mating bond was for life.

You can't save them all, he told himself. Again and again. It really didn't help.

Arianna's face remained clouded. "What if I can't… what if I'm not good enough? UDub is so much *bigger.* Bellevue was just a community college. And I didn't even finish my second year before… before coming here."

Before being kidnapped. Jak's inner wolf growled, and this time it almost reached his lips. "You'll do just fine." He tipped his head to the nearby buildings. "Although not if you don't attend your classes."

She gave a short nod, and he could see a steely resolve take hold as she squared her shoulders and marched off toward Kane Hall. She only had Business Finance today, but it was an upper-level class. One he'd taken and passed easily, in spite of his major being in technology… but he hadn't been ripped from his home and essentially imprisoned for half a year like Arianna had. Although Jak did know something about being uprooted and thrust into the middle of a new pack. Only in Jak's case, his alpha was saving him, not stealing him away. He owed his life to Gage Crittenden, and not just the part where Gage rescued him from being torn into small bloody pieces in the Olympic mountains. His alpha had welcomed him into the Red pack and put him through school. If only Mace Crittenden were half the wolf his brother was, maybe Jak's inner beast wouldn't bang against his skin and fantasize about saving Arianna from her fate every time Jak looked her way.

He watched Arianna ascend the broad, concrete steps of Kane Hall, her jeans hugging low on her hips as they swayed in a dance that spoke directly to his cock. Who was he kidding? He and every other wolf in the Red pack fantasized about Arianna's curves in exquisite detail, including how and where they'd like to put their paws on her.

It was the idea of *Mace* putting his hands on her that brought Jak's snarling wolf to life.

She's too good for him. And Mace was no good for any female.

Jak sucked in a breath and tried to rein in the slow-boil anger that thought raised. He and Arianna passed through the tall concrete pillars that lined the boxy modern building of Kane Hall. Inside was a little warmer than the cool fall air.

Arianna shucked off her gray jacket and held out a hand for her backpack. He gave it over.

A tiny frown wrinkled her forehead. "Sorry you're stuck babysitting me while I'm in class."

Jak slipped his phone from his back pocket and wagged it at her. "I've got plenty of work to do, no worries." He lifted his chin toward the classroom door where students were already filing in. "Go kick some ass in there. Show them UDub's got nothing on Bellevue."

A smile burst onto her face, and it stirred something around inside him that almost hurt. Like a physical ache, a pressure that needed release. It made his smile in return falter.

She turned and disappeared inside the lecture hall. Her sudden absence from his view left a weird kind of hollowness in his chest, a deepening of the ache that had sprung up from nothing more than her smile.

Goddamn Mace. The fact that a female like Arianna was mated to a dark alpha like him was proof that the world was essentially cruel.

His steaming hatred was jarred by a soft giggle down the hall. A trio of college girls—all bared legs and revealing midriffs even in the cool weather—strolled down the corridor, biting their lips and running appraising looks over him. He smirked and raked an appreciative gaze over their toned bodies and perky breasts. He could have all of that he wanted—human girls responded to his inner wolf without even knowing he was a shifter, and his wolf had a taste for the doe-eyed brunettes that Seattle seemed to possess in abundance.

But tasting was all he could have with them. Shifters mated with shifters—Jak may have come from a small pack in the country, but every pack-raised wolf knew that much. Which was great, except for the fact that female wolves were relatively more rare than males. A lot of wolves like him would forever be living in bachelor pads… or have to settle for marrying humans.

Even marrying outside their breed didn't help—other shifters didn't experience the same magical bond that wolves did. It was like nothing else. Jak felt a shadow of that bond each month when he submitted to his alpha. The magic of their blood linked in a way that went beyond brotherhood. Beyond love. It was an unshakable force that bound them together.

It made them *pack*. It was the sense of *belonging* that every wolf yearned for from the time he was a pup. And it was a bond he could never share with a human or non-wolf shifter.

But Jak was only a beta and could never compete with an alpha like Mace for a mate—especially not anyone near the caliber of Arianna—a fact that only twisted the knife a little more. His inner beast whined at the injustice, but his human side really couldn't complain. He had a fantastic job as a tech analyst at Red Wolf, one of the fastest growing dot-com investment companies in the Seattle area. He had quickly risen to become beta to Gage Crittenden, an alpha second only to Mr. Crittenden Senior in the Red pack hierarchy. And he was free to screw any woman in Seattle who chose to join him in his bed. And there were plenty who chose that on a regular basis.

The Ariannas of the world were simply never meant to be his.

She's not meant for Mace, either. Jak backhanded that thought to the dark recesses of his mind. It had no place in his world. He pulled in a breath and leaned against the cool stone wall opposite the classroom door, dragging his mind away from all the flavors of temptation of Arianna and focusing on his phone. A dozen messages and fifty new emails fought for his attention, and he was soon immersed in them.

Gage had a line on a new tech startup—something in data storage on quantum chips with some new laser accessing that looked promising. Jak set up an appointment to meet with the founders, which consisted of a professor and two graduate students working a side business. But that was often where the best startups came from. Scanning their bios, he saw the professor had done time at Google, so there were even more hints of promise there. He would definitely have to dig into the tech, see if they really had the goods, but there was a reason Red Wolf had doubled their portfolio every year for the last ten. The Crittendens were keen investors and quick to jump on promising leads. And the strength of the pack helped keep smaller investors, at least ones run by shifter packs like Red Wolf, out of the running. The Sparks pack were the only ones who gave them any competition at all, and since the run-in over the summer, even they had been keeping their distance.

Jak was buried in spreadsheets and halfway through a fifty-page report thick with graphs and mathematics when movement at the periphery of his vision caught his notice. He dragged his attention away from his phone only to find the hallway was *filled* with students. His heart spasmed as he flit his gaze across the moving sea of backpacks being slung and jackets being donned… but he didn't see her. Then, at the very end of the hallway: Arianna was standing at the corner, staring right at him. Then she slipped out of sight.

Oh shit.

He took off, shoving his phone in his back pocket as he fought his way past the mass exodus from the classroom. He muttered apologies but picked up the pace further until he was practically running when he reached the end of the hall. His boots screeched on the polished wooden floor as he took the corner. He barely saw her curvy rear end before it disappeared around another corner.

Goddamit. He couldn't believe he had let her slip past him. If she made a run for it while he was supposed to be watching her… Mace would literally have his throat for it. Although, honestly, that wasn't what really concerned him. He was more worried about what would happen to *her* if she escaped… only to be caught again. He couldn't let that happen—he couldn't let whatever punishment Mace might dish out be *his* fault. He would much rather have Mace's fangs sunk into his neck than see him lay a hand on Arianna.

Jak dashed down the hall, rounding the second corner, only to see she had doubled back… he barely caught the flutter of her gray jacket slipping out the door of Kane Hall. His heart rate skyrocketed. She was outside. There was no end of places she could run, hide… hell, get lost for all he knew. She was a shifter: he wasn't concerned about anyone in the human population giving her any real trouble. UDub students didn't exactly pack concealed weapons. But she was young, inexperienced, and completely on her own. And UDub wasn't Bellevue, where she likely had friends and family watching out for her most of the time. If she wandered off campus, she might find trouble in the shape of something more sinister than a frat boy trying to make moves on her.

Jak burst out into the sun-drenched Red Square. It was crisscrossed with students traveling and lunching and strolling, but it wasn't hard to find her. She was the thin girl with long brown hair hauling ass across the plaza. Breath heaving, he hesitated on the outside steps. One lone girl sprinting across a plaza was someone late for class. A girl running like her hair was on fire with a six-foot over-muscled guy on her tail… that was someone being *chased.* A dozen cell phones would document the whole thing before you could say *Twitter,* and campus police would almost certainly reach her before he did.

He kept his gaze glued to her quickly-receding back and strode as fast as he could in her general direction without actually running. She was making a beeline toward the main drag on campus—he judged he could cut through the library and maybe head her off. If he could just get ahead of her, let her know he was on to her, maybe he could keep her from bolting altogether. He hated the idea of losing sight of her, but unless he picked up the pace, he was going to lose her anyway.

She ran pretty damn fast for a girl on house arrest for six months.

He sprinted toward Suzzallo, the gorgeous library he knew intimately well from hundreds of hours spent studying, researching, and on more than one occasion, screwing a hot date in the "access-only" stacks. Jak flew up the majestic stone steps, through circulation and reference, and out the Allen library side door in the back. Since he wasn't chasing anything obvious, he only garnered a glare and a couple of turned heads. Between the two libraries now, he saw her sprint past, still too far away for him to catch her eye, but he was about even with her now.

She was headed for the giant circular fountain in the middle of campus, a hallmark that had to draw her eye if nothing else. He dashed in that direction, all while keeping the commons hall between them so she wouldn't see him. He pumped his legs so hard, they were starting to scream… but he rounded Mary Gates Hall and reached the fountain before her. He stood there, chest heaving and arms crossed, appearing casual as she sprinted toward him, throwing looks over her shoulder, where she no doubt expected to find him chasing after her. When she finally turned to face the fountain, dodging the few people scattered across the vast open area around the concrete-rimmed pool, it still took a moment before she recognized him.

He expected her to screech to a stop. Or dash off to the side. Or at least look surprised.

Instead, she simply grinned and barreled toward him. She didn't even slow down before grabbing his hand and hauling him closer to the fountain. The plumes were in full spray, and the wind was picking up… which meant Jak was covered in a fine mist before he could even begin to think about what was happening.

Arianna laughed in a breathy, hysterical way, doubled over and gulping in air, like being spritzed with pond water was the height of hilarity. When she stood straight, her laughs turned into hiccups. She hit him again and again, dull smacking thuds against his chest. He stood and took it, mostly because he couldn't think of what else to do.

She was crazy. "You're crazy, you know that?" He was still breathing hard from the run. "What the hell—do you *know* how much trouble I would be in if you got lost?" But his anger had no bite: she was safe and laughing, and most importantly, no longer running away.

She coughed through her last laugh then left one hand resting on his shoulder, bracing herself against him. He liked the solidity of her touch. The fact that she was close and breathing hard and that fine strands of her long brown hair were sticking to the sides of her face, plastered by the mist that was steadily falling on them both.

Her nearness made his mouth water.

She didn't seem to notice he was staring at her.

She grinned up into the falling droplets. "It just felt so *good.*"

"What felt good?" His voice was lower now, intimate. He wanted to pull her close, but that was ridiculous and out of the question. He just hoped she wouldn't move away.

She pulled her blue eyes down from the heavens and peered into his. The two of them were close now—the kind of close where puffs of breath reached each other and caressed their faces.

"Running," she said softly. "I haven't run in so long."

He nodded, even though she had scared the shit of out him. She *should* be able to run—anywhere, any damn time she chose. She should be *free.* That ache in his chest reached up and choked him for a moment, holding his breath as his gaze never left hers. She flashed a smile, then it grew shy, and she dropped her hand from his shoulder.

"You're getting wet," she said.

"I'll live."

She snuck a smile at him again but then turned away and stepped out of the misting zone next to the fountain. That smile held him in place, riveted. It meant something, that smile, he could feel it inside… he just didn't know what it was.

Maybe… could she be *flirting* with him?

He blew out that breath he'd been holding and laughed. Then he smacked the water off his face and joined her outside the spray zone. The last thing in the world Arianna Stefan would do, on this or any other day, would be to flirt with *him.*

"Ready to head back?" He meant the Red pack estate, not the classroom. She only had one class today. He didn't know if he would pull guard duty again, but eventually, probably… there were only so many wolves in the pack, and Crittenden kept them all busy. But Jak was already counting the probabilities in his head, rounding out the numbers, deciding how long it might be until this could happen again. This moment. Alone. Together.

Arianna pulled in a deep breath, chin tipped up to the sky. "We're coming back tomorrow, right?"

"We?"

She whipped her head toward him and frowned. "You will be my guard again, won't you?"

There it was again—a look that meant more than she was saying. He hesitated, struggling for words. Finally, he said, "Not my call."

She nodded gravely then looked back to the fountain. The sadness stole up on her again. Her entire face drew down with it. He wanted to say something to put a smile back on her face, but he didn't know what that would be. Without another word, she straightened her shoulders and turned back toward the plaza parking garage and his car.

The whole ride home, she was silent. He kept starting conversations with her in his head, but each died a death of awkwardness and stupidity before they left his mouth. She grew more withdrawn, pulling in on herself as they neared the compound. By the time he dropped her at Mace's house along the circle drive inside the estate, she barely had a nod of goodbye for him.

He felt as if he had let her down in some horrible way he didn't understand, and it was tearing him up inside. But he let her go without a word. When she reached the door of the house, Mace pulled her inside, his hands and lips already on her before she had crossed the threshold.

It was the middle of the day.

He should be at work.

He was waiting for her.

Arianna. Jak's wolf whined for her, even though he had no right. No claim.

She was another wolf's mate, the brother of his alpha. There were no less than a hundred reasons, including pack law and an unbreakable magic bond, as to why she didn't belong to him. And never would.

That didn't stop him from wanting her all the same.

Chapter Two

Mace took her from behind, as he normally did.

It pleased him, this position, and he was her alpha: pleasing him was her highest concern. As soon as she entered the house, she knew he had been waiting for her with pleasure on his mind. And she was his *mate*, the one he chose to care for and protect for the rest of her life… pleasure was a small thing in comparison to that, and the least she owed him.

But she couldn't help noticing how much stronger her bond to Mace was once she was back in his domain. *His territory.* It was her home now, but his presence filled the house and settled on her mind as soon as she crossed the threshold. The

UDub campus had seemed so bright and full of life by comparison—it wasn't just the blue skies, but the absence of that heavy weight, that haze on her mind, that happened when she was with her alpha.

It was the magic in her blood, she was sure. The bond from that first claiming, bolstered by every one since then. It was a heavy wool blanket that draped over her body and mind whenever he was near.

Mace's hands gripped her hips, holding her firmly against his steady thrusts. She moaned because he liked that too, but she kept it low. They had only started a few minutes ago, and she would need to moan and scream and grip the white comforter she was kneeling upon even more by the end: she had to build up to it slowly. Otherwise, her alpha wouldn't enjoy their lovemaking as much. He had shown his dissatisfaction before, early on, when she hadn't understood how she was supposed to respond. She had been a virgin when Mace claimed her the first time and too lost in the haze of the submission bond to control her reactions. Now she had over six months of practice, every night, in pleasing her alpha.

She was getting much better at it.

That thought pleased her, although it left a

hollowness in her stomach. When she tried to think about what that meant, the haze grew stronger, blotting out everything but Mace and his cock driving into her.

His grunts grew louder and his thrusts deeper. His claws came out, carving into the flesh of her hips. She stifled the cry that welled up—of course, the cuts would heal quickly, as soon as he was done. She was a shifter, after all, and it took a lot to kill one. But that didn't mean the pain wasn't there.

She moaned again, channeling some of the pain. It helped.

"You like that, don't you, baby?" Mace asked, breathless with his pleasure.

"Yes, oh yes. Oh god, Mace." He didn't always talk during their lovemaking, but when he did, it gave her alpha pleasure to hear her talk back. Only certain words, though. She had to be careful there. He liked hearing his own name, so that was usually safe.

"Oh yeah, baby." His claws retracted, easing the pain. He still held one hip with his hand, but he ran the other over her backside, caressing her. His hand felt slick against her, warm. She thought maybe it was her blood that he was wiping away. Strangely, it reminded her of the fountain at UDub, and Jak standing there, getting wet with spray, and with such a look of surprise on his face that it made her laugh and laugh. She hadn't laughed in so long, it nearly choked her.

A smile crept on her face. Jak was… *different.* Kind. She could tell by the sadness in his eyes. And funny. He had only chastised her a little for running like a wild thing like she had back in the time before… before Mace… before her alpha had come for her…

She tried to picture it—Bellevue College, her brothers, her mother—but it was like a fuzzy video from a dream someone else had. She couldn't make it sharpen at the edges. All she could grab onto was the sense that it was *brighter*… like today at school with Jak. A sunnier time. But her life had moved on from that. She'd grown up and mated.

This was her life now.

A sudden tug on her head wrenched it back: Mace had grabbed hold of her hair while she was daydreaming about times that didn't exist anymore. He still was thrusting into her, his one hand in her hair, the other gripping her breast almost painfully below her.

"You're mine, Arianna." His breath was hot on her back. "All mine. Always." It was his wolf speaking, and the way he was holding her head to the side, exposing her neck, she knew what was coming next: the claiming.

"Oh God, oh God, Mace," she panted in a rush. He didn't claim her every time they made love, but when he did, he wanted her shrieking with it. "Please, Mace. Please." He especially liked it when she begged.

He moaned and thrust deep just as his fangs bit into her shoulder. She cried out for real—with the pain of the bite, but also the fire that quickly flushed through her body, his saliva mixing with her blood, bonding her to him with a magic that started from the first time he claimed her and built with every bite since. She had a myriad of tiny white scars on her shoulder from them, along with the razor-thin lines on her hips.

Mace groaned and stilled. She could feel his cock twitch inside her, reaching his climax and spilling his seed. Someday she would bear her alpha's pups as well, but Mace didn't want the burden of a family just yet.

His mouth and cock left her at the same time, and she sighed in relief, flopping down on the bed next to him. She dared a peek at his face, but his eyes were closed, and his pleasure was clear. That relieved her even more, and she let her body truly relax on the bed next to him.

He was almost always more gentle afterward.

Mace's hand drifted over to stroke her breast. She didn't move, not sure if he was just fondling her or possibly readying for another run. She knew shifters were legendary lovers, but she suspected her alpha had more stamina than most. He often took her two or three times in a day, never seeming to stay satisfied for long.

"This is how I want you, Arianna." But his voice was calm, not charged with passion. "Every day. In my bed. You belong to me."

"Of course, I belong to you," she said. "You're my alpha."

"It was my father's idea to send you to school, not mine."

She stayed silent because she knew he disapproved, and she wanted nothing more than to keep going to class. No matter what his father said, Mace didn't have to allow it. So he must see a good reason for it, just as Jak had said. If she were lucky, Jak would be her bodyguard again tomorrow. She could ask him more about what he thought: about Mace, about school, about… *everything.* They could talk about anything, and it would be easy and simple.

No worries about what to say or not say. That thought warmed the aching parts of her body, the ones still tender from Mace's lovemaking.

Maces pinched her nipple, just short of being painful. "Don't embarrass me with this college business, Arianna."

Her heart pounded. "I… I don't know what you mean."

"If my father wants you to finish school, then I expect you to excel."

She sighed in relief. "The class today was easy. I don't think it will be a problem."

He gave her nipple a twist then released it. "Make sure that it's not."

"I won't embarrass you, Mace. I promise." And she fully intended to keep that promise. She wasn't lying about the class being relatively easy. And she would work hard at it, just for the chance to keep going back. A picture of Jak's future approving nod when she aced her classes at the end of the semester brought another flush of warmth to her sore nether regions.

"My father's going to make me managing partner next year," Mace said.

"That's wonderful, Mace!" Arianna propped herself up on her elbows. She didn't have to fake her enthusiasm—becoming partner, like his brother Gage, had been Mace's burning desire for as long as he'd been her alpha. Longer, the way he talked about it. And when Mace got what Mace wanted, her heart beat gladder for it. Not to mention that he was more gentle with her when he was in a good mood.

"Yes, well, it hasn't happened yet." He turned to glower at her. "And I don't want anything messing it up."

She frowned. Over the summer, there had been a disastrous encounter with another pack. She wasn't sure of everything that happened, but there was another female that Mace desired to make his mate as well… only it hadn't worked out. Mace had captured the girl, just like he had taken Arianna from her pack, but the girl's family came for her before Mace could sink his fangs and magic into her.

Arianna had always thought that the claiming would mean a forever love between just *two* people in a mating… not three. Or more. But she was a child then and didn't understand how the world really worked. The Senior Mr. Crittenden had two mates, and he seemed to protect both of them equally. Even Mace's older brother Gage had two.

That was part of why Mace desired another mate so strongly… if his brother and father had something, of course Mace needed to have it too. Arianna almost wished he had been able to claim the girl… if only so that Arianna would finally have a friend in the house. And possibly someone else to help slake Mace's vigorous sexual appetite.

But it wasn't to be. And the fallout had been bad for Mace's ambitions in the pack. Yet tensions with the Sparks pack had faded in the months since the incident. She couldn't see what was making Mace glower and worry.

"What do you think might mess it up?" she asked, tentatively.

"You." His glower turned his dark eyes into glittering coal.

She swallowed. "I'll do anything to help you make partner, Mace. Just tell me. I'll do it." And she meant every word of that.

He shook his head like he was disgusted. "Just give my father what he wants. If he wants you to have a degree and help in the business, then fine. I expect you to bust your ass and make that happen."

She was nodding vigorously. "I can do it, Mace. I can."

He grunted. "Good." Then he rolled up from

the bed and started pulling on the clothes that he'd hastily discarded once they'd reached the bedroom. "I'm going back to the office." After slipping on his pants, he pointed a finger at her. "You're not to leave the house. Just because you're a student now, doesn't mean you come and go whenever. I want you in class or studying here. And I want you done with studying by the time I get home. I may need some more stress relief after the board meeting this afternoon."

"Of course." She watched him slip on his tailored black silk shirt. "Maybe once I've taken some classes, I can help you with your work as well."

He snorted a laugh and shook his head. He didn't answer while he put on his socks and shoes. When he was done, he fixed her with a cold, dark stare. "That's not the kind of service I want from you, Arianna."

She pressed her lips together and nodded.

He sighed. "My father has some kind of plan for you, and whatever he wants, he'll get. Personally, I think the old goat just wants to see your sweet ass sashaying around the office. But beyond that, don't get any grand ideas. Eventually, the novelty of it will pass, and he'll want grandpups. Hopefully not anytime soon. But keep that in mind." He pointed his finger once more at her as he headed for the bedroom door. "No leaving the house."

"I know." She watched as he left, not moving until she heard the front door click shut.

As soon as he was gone, some of the fog in her mind lifted. She flopped back on the bed, still naked, and stared at the ceiling. But thoughts of Mace disappeared with his presence, and in their place rushed all kinds of grand plans for classes she could take, ways she could arrange the timing of them for maximum time spent on campus, and a fervent hope that tomorrow a certain dark-eyed, smiling shifter named Jak would be her bodyguard.

Chapter Three

THE STEADY THRUM OF CLUB MUSIC PULSED through Jak's head.

It was only Thursday night, but the place was packed. Hipsters from the dot-com crowd in their black t-shirts and jeans as well as newly minted millionaires in their silk shirts and tailored pants. The groupies were plentiful, too, college girls looking to score a rich geek… or just a hot screw for the night. There was plenty of flesh being pressed in the darkened corners of the cavernous warehouse-turned-trendy-bar. The lighting was intentionally weak with blue neon snaking along the walls and glowing from under the stage.

Arianna would never fit in here, with her wide-eyed innocence and world-weary smiles.

Jak shook his head. He hadn't stopped thinking about her since he took her to school the day before. Today he hadn't drawn guard duty, and he couldn't help thinking it was because he had somehow disappointed her, right there at the end. He wasn't sure how in spite of wracking his brain to figure it out. But something had been off, and he hadn't opened his mouth to figure out what. Because he was an idiot.

He slammed back his second scotch and set it on the bar behind Gage.

His alpha noticed his empty drink and signaled the barkeep for another. "Make any progress on that Silver Quick analysis?" Gage asked.

His alpha had brought half his pack out for drinks and carousing, celebrating the closing of another deal, but it was just like Gage to already have his mind on the next project. "Still buried in sifting through their reports," Jak said. "I'm not at all sure their data can be trusted. The test protocols are pretty sketchy, at least on paper. But I've made an appointment to visit their lab tomorrow at the University." Jak's thoughts drifted to Arianna, wondering if she would have classes tomorrow and if there was any possible way he could engineer to "accidentally" cross paths with her.

"Sounds like a solid plan." Gage nursed his drink and scanned a pair of leggy blondes as they passed. He had two mates at home, but an alpha like Gage didn't confine his sexual exploits to the Red pack estate. It was foreign to the way Jak was raised, but his family life as a kid was far from ideal, to say the least. He wasn't one to judge. And besides… the Crittendens were powerful men who made their own rules.

"I like the tech, though," Jak added. "If it's half of what they promise, there's real potential there."

Gage nodded then threw him a smirk. "Sounds like you might be at the University tomorrow anyway."

Jak frowned. "How's that?"

"Didn't you hear? Mace's mate has been asking for you."

Jak choked on his drink. "She's been what?"

Gage was an inch or two taller than Jak, but his eyes were now boring into his, judging his response. "I guess Alric's turn at guarding her today didn't go so well. She's expressed a preference for *you.*"

Jak's stomach tightened. "Well *of course* she expressed a preference for me. Alric smells like shoe leather and has a face that looks like it's been pounded together by a rock."

Gage chuckled. "Look, I don't want to turn you into a glorified babysitter. But I also wouldn't mind having you keep tabs on what Mace is up to. After the Sparks incident… I just want a heads up if he's going to drag us into another pack war. If his mate's asking for you, spend a little time with her. See what she knows."

Jak's pounding heart slowed a little. "Sure. I can do that. Like you said, I've got to be at the University tomorrow anyway."

Gage dipped his head. "Good. Shouldn't take too much of your time." He smirked. "And she's not exactly hard on the eyes."

Jak shrugged one shoulder, eyes on the crowd of writhing bodies moving with the low-thudding music. "Yeah, I guess. Not really my type." He steeled himself against a spasm of internal wincing. What the hell was he doing, letting that out of his mouth?

Gage laughed outright then held up a hand to signal Mason, one of the omegas from his pack that was hanging out at the periphery of the dance floor. "I know exactly your type, Jak." He lifted his chin. Mason was bringing over a doe-eyed brunette with a slim waist and ample chest.

"Yes, you do," Jak said with real appreciation.

His alpha knew him well, not least because he'd helped him screw his way through half the female human population of Seattle over the four years he'd been Gage's beta.

"She's a special I've ordered up, just for you."

Jak lifted one eyebrow. "What's the occasion?"

Gage clapped him on the shoulder and leaned over to whisper as Mason, and the girl approached. "Let's just say I want to keep you happy while you spy on my brother's mate."

Jak knocked back the rest of his third drink and got rid of the glass before the girl sauntered up to them. The liquid sloshed in his stomach. He told himself that was the source of his queasiness.

"Hi," she said, her deep brown eyes staring into Jak's.

Gage grinned and threw an arm around Mason, guiding him away and leaving Jak alone with the scantily-dressed girl. On any other night, he would be salivating over—or more accurately *on*—her within minutes. Her eyes were big and brown, nothing like Arianna's bright and lively blue ones. Her smile was sultry, not innocent. Hungry, not bursting with joy. She was everything Arianna was not… which was probably exactly what he needed tonight. Even if he had no stomach for it.

Besides, Gage would be watching him.

"You have a name?" he asked the girl.

She smirked. "Do I need one?"

"I'll just call you Mystery Girl, then."

She stepped closer, and her heavy vanilla perfume smothered his senses. His wolf whined, and Jak breathed through his mouth. Human girls always wore too much perfume. She probably had a perfectly lovely scent underneath the five different products she drenched her body and hair in to hide it.

"Your friend said you were feeling a little down."

"Did he?" Whatever Mason or Gage said, it likely involved *going down* not feeling down.

She leaned in close to whisper-shout over the music. "Thought maybe I could help bring you back *up.*" Her breasts brushed his chest, and her hand grazed his stomach, hot even through the thin silk of his shirt. His wolf was holding back, still recoiling from her perfume, but his cock had no problem responding to the feel of her pressed against him. Her hand drifted down, and if he didn't move this show out of the spotlight, she'd be stroking him right at the bar.

He ran a hand up to her face and held her an

inch or two away. "I think I want you with a slightly different background."

She grinned.

He took her hand and towed her away from the bar. Gage was a regular at this particular club, so Jak knew all the secluded spots, whether for just a quick make out or a full-blown sex-until-we-drop encounter. In fact, he knew the places better than he remembered the faces, and tonight he wanted a spot where he wouldn't have to look doe-eyes in the face while he made her come.

The buzz from the scotch was warming his body, and an image of what Arianna's face would look like in the throes of passion flashed across his mind. He shoved it away. He didn't want her here, in the overwhelming stink of a seedy human bar... not even in his thoughts.

Jak brought Mystery Girl around the side of the stage and down a hall that led to the bathrooms. He'd used those on more than one occasion, but only when desperate. The stench was nearly unspeakable. But tonight he cut left into a short corridor that led backstage. There was a tiny closet that served as a changing room for the band. It smelled perpetually of pot, but at least that masked all the other odors. And the music was deafening, a low thudding pounding that eliminated the need for talking.

Inside the room, there was barely space for the two of them, so he propped Mystery up on the small makeup table in front of the mirror. Her short skirt hiked up, and he wasted no time slipping his hand between her legs.

"You seem to have forgotten your panties," he whisper-shouted in her ear, but his words were lost in the music.

She didn't bother answering, just gasped at his sudden touch at her core. She was already wet, so he slipped a finger inside while he worked her nub. Soon, she was clutching at his shoulders and squirming on the rickety table. He kept his gaze in the mirror, watching her legs wrap around his back. He could have her coming in no time. Maybe he could just leave it at that. His cock was aching and hard, but he'd rather get off with his own hand, back at home, with sweet visions of Arianna in his head.

And maybe then, he could sort out what he had done wrong yesterday. If he was going to see her tomorrow, he wanted to figure out how to make it right.

Mystery Girl was moaning—he could feel the

vibrations through his grip on her, even if he couldn't hear her over the music—but even as he slipped in a second finger and pumped harder to get her finished, she started to claw at his clothes. She palmed his cock through the thin fabric of his dress pants then gripped it hard. He couldn't help groaning, and even his wolf was whining for release. Jak debated pulling her hands away and going down on her to finish the job, but less than a second later, in a series of expert moves that said she'd done this a million times before, she'd freed his cock from his clothes, and she was pumping it like a pro. She clearly expected him to do more with it than come in her hand, and he couldn't afford a disappointed groupie to get back to Gage.

Using both hands, Jak shoved the girl's short skirt up to her waist and plunged his cock into the slick wetness of her core. Her mouth fell open, and her head tipped back. Her lips moved—probably cursing or praying—but he couldn't hear anything over the throbbing music. He pounded into her, his thrusts racing the tempo of the beat reverberating off the walls, and he could feel her tighten around him. The squeeze of her climax brought him to the edge, and he came over a series of thrusts designed to draw out the last of her orgasm.

He hadn't used a condom, but it didn't matter —wolves didn't catch human diseases, even the sexual kind, something he knew from experience as well as pack lore. And she didn't scent in her fertile phase, something every young wolf learned how to detect early on in his exploits. She was probably on birth control if she was hooking up with random guys in bars anyway.

He tried not to pull out too quickly. Rushing the ending was worse than rushing the rest, but he itched to be gone, home, showering off the stink of the girl and the bar.

He leaned back and held the girl's cheeks for a moment, in what he hoped she would take as a tender touch. "You good?" he mouthed, peering into her eyes. They were half-lidded with the orgasm she was still coming down from.

She gave him a lazy smile.

He zipped his pants while she straightened her clothes. As long as she left with a smile on her face, he'd be free to go. Maybe he could offer to walk her to her car. That would give him a fine excuse to skip out of the club early. Gage would be more than willing to let him go if he thought Jak was getting laid.

If his alpha had any idea Jak was going home to

fantasize about his brother's mate, he'd haul him out to the alley in back and thrash some sense into him. And Gage would be more than justified. Wanting Arianna that way was stupid and dangerous, broke every pack law, and was contrary to the magic that bound the entire pack together… and none of that mattered.

Because Jak was going to see her again tomorrow.

Chapter Four

"WOOOOOOOO!" ARIANNA SCREAMED FOR ALL SHE was worth, and her inner beast howled like it was a full moon, but the wind just whipped away her words and sent them sailing down the highway behind her. She was standing on the passenger seat of Jak's car, half her body sticking out the open sunroof, arms raised to the glorious blue skies above. Yesterday had been miserable, rained all day, but today was gorgeous again. Beautiful days and Jak seemed to go together. It was another sign: this was how her life was supposed to be.

"Will you come down, *please?*" Jak said for the third time. His voice was barely audible above the wind whistling past her ears.

Arianna ducked her head back inside. "Why?"

She scanned the road ahead, but they hadn't reached the exit for the University yet.

Jak's eyes were wide. "I don't know. Maybe so we don't get pulled over by Seattle's finest?"

She scowled at him. "What's a sunroof for, if not to stick out your head?" She kind of hoped it was illegal. She didn't want to get Jak in trouble, but the idea of doing something—*anything*—that broke the rules tantalized her with a mouth-watering intensity.

Jak smirked. "I'm pretty sure it was designed to let the sun *in*, not the people *out.*"

His eyes were dancing, and she was sure he wouldn't object if she let out a few more whoops for good measure, but she dropped down the rest of the way into her seat anyway.

If they got pulled over, Mace would find out. He would be embarrassed, and that wouldn't be good for anyone. Besides, she didn't want anything to mess up today. She'd let Mace think bringing back Jak as bodyguard was really *his* idea: given that Jak was an alum, and things had gone fine the first day, whereas the second with Alric was one comedy of errors after another, starting with being late to class and ending with coming home late. The last one was what had set Mace off—he'd been waiting at the house for her. It was only logical that, since things had gone smoothly with Jak, he should resume bodyguard duties.

Jak's smile dropped away, replaced by an uncertain look. "If you really want to—" He was clearly still thinking about the sunroof.

She waved him off, pushing the button to close the roof then giving him a cheesy smile. "You can make it up by taking me out to lunch after class."

He smiled wide. "Actually, I was planning on asking if you minded grabbing lunch then heading over to one of the labs. I have a potential client I need to do a site visit for."

She frowned. "Oh." She figured Mace wouldn't begrudge them grabbing something to eat before coming back to the estate, but if she was gone much longer… "I don't think Mace would like that."

Jak's smile settled into a smirk. "Gage already cleared it with Mace. We're good for the most of the afternoon."

His eyes glittered, but that was nothing compared to the surge of joy running racetracks through her chest. She leaned over to impulsively hug him. It was awkward and gangly, and Jak looked shocked, but he didn't seem to mind. She retreated back to her seat and busied herself with buckling up. And trying not to blush too much.

This day was going to be *perfect.*

When she was settled, and the heat had mostly gone from her face, she said, "Tell me about this client! I want to know all about them before we get there."

"It's a bunch of tech stuff. You probably wouldn't be interested."

"Try me."

Jak raised an eyebrow. "Well, they're researching quantum computing. They think they might have a new way to access some of the quantum states with a complicated series of lasers and switches and a new crystalline material. They're looking to store data in the quantum state then access it again. It's been done before, but they're scaling up, trying to find ways to store lots of simultaneous data in the crystal then pull it out again very rapidly."

"Okay," she said with a grimace. She'd really only understood part of that. "So, they're trying to make a computer from crystals and flashing lights. Sounds very high tech. Not to mention New Age."

He chuckled. "Actually, that's exactly what it is. Pooky New Age physics that seems a bit iffy. Especially when I look at their testing protocols. I'm not sure they're actually measuring anything coherent. They could be influenced by power fluctuations from the laser for all I can tell, just looking at the reports."

"So that's why you're visiting the lab? To see if their setup is legit."

"Precisely." He looked askance at her, but his eyes were filled with mirth. "You sure you weren't a tech major at Bellevue?"

"Positive. Didn't even have a smartphone back then." She swallowed and looked forward again. "Not that I exactly have one now." Mace won't allow her to use the phone. Even though she was mated now, and her family knew there was no point in coming for her, he still didn't want her calling them. *Stirring things up* was what he called it. Her heart ached to talk to her mom again, but Mace was her alpha, so that was that.

She avoided Jak's concerned look and stared out the window at Seattle's downtown towers in the distance. Silence reigned as Jak took the exit and wound toward the University. His sedan was one of the pack cars, wide and roomy for transporting lots of hulking shifter men to wherever they went when they left the estate. It wasn't a luxury car, but the faux leather interior felt luxurious to Arianna.

Maybe it was the freedom that driving represented. Someday Mace might let her drive again. For now, she was happy to have a driver… as long as it was Jak.

"You okay?" he asked, looking at her sideways. He turned the car into the University grounds, and soon they were descending into the plaza's underground parking. She had Business Finance again today, and this was the nearest parking to Kane Hall.

"I'm great." She gave him a broad smile.

"On Wednesday, you seemed… not so happy at the end." He looked nervous again.

She frowned. She had liked everything about the first day of school… except when she faced the prospect of going home. "I was just sad to see it end. Didn't know if I'd have a chance to dunk you in the fountain like I was planning."

"Um… when exactly were you planning to do that?" He gave her a mock look of shock.

"Well, if I told you, it wouldn't be a surprise, now would it?" She grinned with all her teeth again, and it made him laugh. The sound of that lightened her heart even more.

Perfect day. She knew it.

They parked and took the elevator up to Red

Square. It was late Friday morning, and the plaza was practically empty of students: maybe they started the weekend early and decided to skip out on Friday morning classes. Arianna sighed, wondering how her life would be different if she could live on campus, stay in a dorm, have normal friends. *Boyfriends, all-night study sessions, and way too much alcohol.* That's what she had always assumed her life would be like during her college years. But there was no use in wishing for something that would never be.

They reached her classroom early, and there were only four students instead of the usual hundred or so.

"Light day," Jak said. "Get in there and sit in the front row. Your professor will remember you as one of the few who bothered to show up for the whole first week of class."

Arianna took her backpack, which Jak had been carrying. She bit her lip. "You know, you could go get a coffee or something. You don't have to stand in the hall for the whole hour of class."

He laughed. "Not a chance. You'll run off without me, and then I won't have a date for lunch." His smile did strange things to her stomach, and his dark eyes were sparkling again.

She ducked her head in acquiescence, but the heat was back in her cheeks. He was handsome and funny and… he was flirting with her. It ran a thrill straight through her heart, made of equal parts danger and desire for… *more.* More banter, more talking, more smiles. It was like he was feeding liquid friendship crack to her, and she couldn't get enough. But that innocent flirting was dangerous. She knew it. If Mace found out, he would rip out Jak's throat. And she didn't want to think about what Mace would do to *her.*

"I… better go in," she said, feeling suddenly awkward. She hiked her backpack up on her shoulder and turned to hurry inside the classroom.

She felt Jak's stare on her back all the way in.

JAK LURKED IN THE HALL, MESSING AROUND WITH his phone but making sure not to miss when the doors to Arianna's classroom opened this time. Right at the hour, students started filing out. His heart almost quit beating when the students stopped coming, and he still didn't see her. But then she hustled out, scribbling some final notes on her tablet before stuffing it in her backpack.

"How'd it go?" he asked.

She beamed. He was pretty sure his whole body lit up with it.

"Great!" she said. "This stuff is really easy. Nothing like your magic crystal computers. Can't wait to see what that's all about."

His smile was going to break his face if he didn't get it under control. "Well, our appointment's not for another hour. How about lunch at the HUB? They have sandwiches, soups, pizza… there's even a killer curry place I think is still there."

"Anything sounds awesome. Except for the curry. Not so sure about the curry."

He tamed the smile a little. "And now my life will not be complete until you try the Thai Green Curry."

She smirked. "Then I think your life will remain sadly incomplete."

They'd reached the outside of the building and strolled down the steps before Jak looked around enough to realize the plaza was empty. They turned to head toward the far end of Red Square, but he thought he might take her by the fountain again before they hit the food. He was tucking his phone back into his pocket but somehow managed to bobble it—the thing flew from his hands and skittered under the leaves still coating the red bricks.

He swore under his breath and bent to fish through the leaves to find it. Just as he did, Arianna tripped or something and fell.

"Hey!" he said, alarmed, and hustled back to her side. "Are you—" He stopped short.

She had shifted into her wolf form and was twitching and thrashing on the ground.

"What the—" Then he saw them: two figures in hoodies, coming at them from barely a dozen feet away, one with a giant, black sack held high, the other with a gun of some kind. Jak didn't speak or think, he simply dove to the side, shifting as he went, flinging off clothes, and coming up wolf.

Then he lunged for them, teeth first.

The one with the gun got a couple shots off, but they were silent whispers and bee stings that bounced off Jak's thick fur coat. He reached the man, fangs clamping on his gun hand, bones crushing under Jak's snapped-shut jaws. The man screamed. The gun tasted metallic then fell into a rustle of leaves and brick. Jak released the hand to go for his neck, but the second man pulled him off from behind. Jak whipped around and went for that one's throat. They both went down on the pavement, but Jak had a strong grip on his neck. He squeezed. The man flailed, hands trying to pull Jak's jaws away, but Jak just clamped harder. The flailing grew weaker but more frantic. Jak flicked his gaze around, searching for the first one, judging his next move.

What the hell was happening here? The men were both mid-twenties, gray hoodies and combat boots. The first one was desperately searching through the leaves for his gun. A gun that shot darts not bullets. The second one's bag was lying on the ground where he dropped it.

A dart gun.

A bag.

They weren't muggers—they were bounty hunters. Out to bag a wolf for some unholy witch magic or to sell their parts to the highest bidder for the black market. Both of which would be a death sentence for said kidnapped wolf. But how the hell did they know he and Arianna were shifters?

That didn't matter now.

He would kill them both before they could get their hands on her.

Jak growled a warning, but the first bounty hunter didn't seem to hear it. Then a second growl caused Jak to whip his head to the side, wrenching fresh cries of pain out of the hapless bounty hunter trapped in his jaws.

Arianna. She was limping towards the first bounty hunter, her gorgeous brown fur bristled out as she dipped her head down and growled again.

This time the bounty hunter froze in his search for the gun and stared at her. Arianna bared her teeth, making it clear she intended to go for his throat.

Arianna, no! Now that they were both in wolf form, he had access to her thoughts. And they were terrified. Angry. Confused. *Back away,* Jak thought. *I will take care of these assholes.*

I am not going to let him shoot you, Jak. But he could see her back legs quivering. One of the darts must have already found her. Or maybe it was just starting to work. He didn't know, but he didn't have time to think about it. Jak released the man in his mouth and shifted. As soon as he was in human form, he punched the man whose throat he had just held. The man reeled to the side, still conscious but stunned. Jak stood naked over him and faced the first bounty hunter.

"Take him and leave. Now. Or I'll kill you both." He hoped the man would choose the smart path—dead bodies caused all kinds of problems.

Arianna backed him up with a growl. It sounded a little stronger, but the last thing Jak wanted was to have her involved in this at all.

The bounty hunter was hesitating.

Jak lowered his voice to a growl. "You'll only get that offer once."

That shocked the man out of his crouched stance. He bolted upright and shuffled over to where his partner still laid reeling on the pavers. The second one scrambled to his feet, with no small amount of help from his partner, and the two of them stumbled off in the direction of the fountain. Jak didn't know where they thought they were going, but there was no one else on the plaza to see everything that had gone down. He kept an eye on them while he shuffled over to Arianna. She was still in wolf form, only now she was lying on her side.

"Arianna." His heart clenched. "Are you okay? Can you shift?" Her eyes were open, and she gave a few whines, but she didn't move. He stroked the soft fur of her head. "It's okay. I'm going to take care of you."

God, he hoped she was just tranq'd by the dart—if it was something worse, he would need to find a healer fast. Her natural shifter magic should be able to ward off almost anything… but who knew what was in that dart.

He kept an eye on the two bounty hunters until they were out of sight then quickly scooped up both his and Arianna's clothes, the bag and her backpack, and even found the gun. He didn't bother dressing, just stuffed everything in the bag and picked up Arianna, cradling her limp body and soft fur against his bare chest. He needed to get her inside, away from the scene, in case the bounty hunters changed their minds and came back. The classroom was closest, but they might be discovered there, and until she could shift back, her identity as a shifter was in danger. And if her professors or classmates even suspected… her days at the University would be over. The human world knew about shifters, even tolerated them in some capacities, but discrimination was rampant. And shifters in wolf form had no rights whatsoever. She could be killed, and no one would even be charged with a crime.

The car, then.

He hurried across the plaza, chest heaving, with his precious cargo in his arms.

Chapter Five

CARRYING ARIANNA IN HER WOLF FORM, AS WELL AS the bulky bag with all their stuff, was no small trick. But they had to get away from the scene of the attack as quickly as possible.

The icy weather worked its way past the heated panic of the moment and chilled his naked body. The parking garage was slightly warmer or at least sheltered from the wind. Fortunately, it was still relatively empty, so there were no witnesses to the naked man carrying a brown wolf off to a black sedan in the middle of the concrete underground structure. Arianna started to move in his arms, whimpering and struggling against his bare skin. He didn't know if she was in shock or if the dart had injected some kind of tranquilizer in her that was wearing off. He prayed it was only that and not something worse. There should be no reason to poison a wolf with a dart, but that didn't mean it couldn't happen. If she didn't recover quickly, he would have to get help.

"Just hold on," he said as she stirred, making it harder for him to carry her. "Let me get you to the car." She stopped fighting him. When he reached their car, he gently laid her in the back seat, and she immediately struggled up on two legs and dragged her limp hind legs behind her to the far side of the seat, giving him room to climb in, dragging along the bag of all their stuff. That she was moving again was a really good sign. When they both were safely locked in the car, he scooted closer, stroking her fur and trying to reassure her. He could feel her shaking.

"Arianna, honey," he said in his most soothing voice, even though it was still ravaged from the fight. "It's okay. You're safe now. Can you shift for me?" He couldn't tell what was wrong with all the fur and without the ability to speak. If she couldn't shift, he might have to shift back to wolf, just so they could communicate.

She closed her eyes, and it took a moment, but then she shifted human. Which meant she was suddenly naked in his arms, even more beautiful in all her bared glory than she had been in his fantasies. His cock twitched in response, but he already had a full-blown erection left over from the fight. It was always that way: the adrenaline, the testosterone, and especially with a female to protect and a shift to wolf and back. His raging hard-on wasn't quitting anytime soon, and now with them both naked… Arianna's shaking was even more visible once there was no fur to hide it. Jak cursed himself for his rampantly sexual thoughts and quickly dug his jacket out of the bag. The car was relatively warm, but he was sure she was in shock. He wrapped the jacket around her and rubbed her arms and back to heat them up.

"Are you all right?" he asked softly. "Tell me what happened."

"J… Jak," she said, her teeth chattering.

He stepped up his rubbing of her arms and pulled her into his lap. He tried to ignore what that did to his aching cock, while he focused on holding her, warming her, reassuring her.

"It's okay, just take it slow. Tell me what happened so I can see if we need to get a healer."

"No." She shook her head vigorously. "No healer."

He frowned, but he took that as a good sign. If she were really hurt, she'd be crying or wincing in pain. The fact that she was able to shift at all was a good thing. She took several deep breaths, obviously trying to calm down, so he waited until she was ready to speak again.

"I think…" She stopped to swallow. "I think one of them shot me with something."

"He had a dart gun. I brought it with us, in case it has some kind of poison—" He stopped at the worried, wide-eyed look on her face. "I'm sure it's *not* poison. Probably just a tranquilizer." He brushed back the hair that had fallen across her face. "I think you must be some kind of super shifter if they hit you with a tranq dart, and you just kept going."

"I felt something pinch," she said, her voice calmer now, "but it was on my shoulder. Through my jacket. I don't think it went all the way through. Plus, I pulled it out."

Jak smiled. "You pulled it out?"

"Well, with my teeth." She gave a small smile in return.

"With your *teeth?*"

"I shifted as soon as I felt it and yanked the dart out with my teeth. I don't know… it was just instinct. I probably shouldn't have."

"No, no…" Jak said with amazement. "I think that might have been the only thing that kept you conscious. Shifting probably helped dislodge the dart. Or maybe stopped the tranq from working the way it should have with your wolf biochemistry."

She shuddered. "It still felt… strange. For a while, I couldn't seem to move. Or shift. I was… I was so scared, Jak." Her voice hiked up.

"Hey." He brushed her hair back again, and this time let his hand stay on her cheek. "It's over now. And you were incredibly brave. Just next time… let me handle the bounty hunters, okay? That's my job, remember?"

She nodded, and it wasn't quite so shaky. His hand was still on her cheek. And the air was becoming warm around them: their breath and their bodies were heating the car. She was still mostly naked on his lap, her bare skin touching his. His thoughts were veering in dangerous directions. He should be helping her get dressed, get the situation normalized, recover from the shock of the attack, and figure out what to do next. Instead, he just kept holding her face and peering into her brilliant blue eyes. Which weren't looking at his but rather drifting down to his lips.

He licked them, frozen in indecision, unwilling

to move a centimeter away, unable to move any closer without crossing an invisible boundary…

"Jak," she whispered.

"Yes." He could barely breathe without moving into her space.

She leaned into him and pressed her lips to his. It almost wasn't a kiss, just a touch, and then she pulled back, but only a few inches. Her eyes were wide as if shocked by her own actions. Jak's hand had slipped into her hair with her movement. It was silky soft on his fingertips. Her naked body was still pressed against his, her thigh against his cock, her breasts peeking from the jacket draped over her shoulders.

"I… I shouldn't have…" Her breath was coming faster, and he was suddenly aware of her scent: her blackberry-and-lavender soap was overwhelmed by the earthy musk of her arousal.

It was more than he could resist.

His fingers curled in her hair and brought her back for another kiss. A proper one. His lips devoured hers, his tongue plundering her mouth and tasting all the sweetness there. His heart raced as her slender hands found his chest, and she kissed him back. Her kiss was eager, and she arched up in his lap, pushing his head back with her need. The ache deep inside him surged up and found expression in his hands: in her hair, sliding down her back and then up again, seeking the bare skin under her jacket. Their tongues fought for dominance, their hands roaming each other's bare heated skin: hers were on his shoulders, in his hair, then back to his chest; his hands switched places, the one on her back sliding into her hair to hold her fixed in his kiss, freeing his other to skim down the silky skin of her chest and cup her breast. It was heavy and hot, and her nipple was taut against his palm. She sucked in a breath, pulling it straight from him, and he moaned into her mouth.

Mine, his wolf growled.

But she wasn't. Not even close.

Jak stopped the kiss.

Arianna was breathing hard, eyes still wide, staring at him. Questioning. Quivering. Pinking up in the cheeks and gloriously naked on his lap.

God, she's beautiful.

"Tell me to stop, Arianna," he begged. "Tell me to get my hands off you and put my clothes back on, because I swear to God, if you don't, it's not going to happen."

One of her slender hands left his chest and held his cheek. Gentle. Exploring. Then her fingertips brushed across his lips, and he honestly thought he might die if she told him to stop. He had to have her. Right now.

"I've never felt this way…" she said, breathlessly.

"Arianna…" If she didn't stop trailing her fingers across his skin, he was going to take her right this second.

"I don't…" she breathed, her hand drifting down his chest. "I don't want to stop." Her thin fingers found his cock and wrapped around it.

Oh god.

His hand in her hair gripped harder and brought her back for a savage kiss: one that wasn't holding back. One that was just the start of wrenching every pleasure from her body that he could. While his mouth claimed hers, her hand started to stroke him, whipping his frenzy even higher. He spread her legs on his lap and slipped his hand between them. She gasped into his mouth when he found her sex and started circling the tight nub there. She squirmed as he teased her entrance with his fingers, and when he plunged inside, she let out a whimper.

"Jak." Her breaths were speeding up.

He slowly pumped one finger into her. "Yes," he said in between nips on her neck.

"Oh my god, Jak, what are you… keep doing that."

He chuckled. "Oh, I have no intention of stopping now."

She nearly jolted out of his lap when he lightly circled her nub again. Then he slipped a second finger in, and she started writhing in his hand. "Jak… what are you… oh god…"

Her lips parted, eyes drifted closed, and her head tipped back. She bucked against his hand, so he gave her more of what she wanted, thrusting a third finger inside and picking up the pace. Her hands were clawing and beating at his chest, and his cock ached with every strike, but he was definitely getting her there first. There would be time for seconds later. Maybe thirds, if he could hold out that long.

She cried out and convulsed and came all over his hand. He could feel every pulse of pleasure inside her, and she had a whimper-cry to go with each one. She was breathing so hard, he thought she might be hyperventilating. But as she started to come down, her body suddenly went rigid. She whipped up her head and popped open her eyes.

"Oh my god," she panted, looking amazed.

He grinned. "I take it you liked that."

Her eyes were wide like he had just spoken in tongues. "Is *that* how it's supposed to feel? Every time?"

His smile faltered. "You mean you've never..." He was stunned. Was it possible that was her first orgasm? The idea put him in awe... and flushed him with pleasure. Mace may have claimed her... he may have had her first... but *Jak* had pleasured her like she'd never been pleasured before.

And he was just getting started.

He withdrew his hand from her still pulsing body and slipped her off his lap, quickly laying her on her back and positioning himself between her legs. There was barely enough room on the seat for this, but he was going to work every inch of it.

"Yes, that's exactly how it's supposed to feel," he said, grinning into her shocked expression. She was surprised but definitely pleased. And, if he had his way, he was about to pleasure her a whole lot more. "In fact, my sweet little Arianna, I am just getting started with you."

Then she bit her lip, and he'll be damned if she didn't blush. He couldn't wait to bury his cock inside her any longer, so he didn't. Holding her shoulder tight to keep her from banging her head against the side door, he angled her hips and thrust deep inside. She gasped and arched up, hot and wet and oh so tight. He groaned and stilled for a moment, lost in the sheer pleasure of being in her.

"Oh my god, Jak," she breathed. "You're so big."

Pleasure flushed him head to toe again. *Take that, Mace, you asshole.* But then he banished thoughts of Mace from his head—this was all about Arianna. Pleasuring her, making love to her. In that moment, he wanted to give her everything she never had, no matter what those things were, no matter how impossible they were to obtain. He would do literally anything for her. Anything.

He slowly withdrew almost all the way from her deliciously hot body then thrust hard again. Her whimper of pleasure was like a drug to him. He thrust again and again, quickly finding the rhythm that bumped her cries higher each time, spiraling tighter, building tension low in his belly with each stroke. She was grabbing at his shoulders and the cushions and wrapping her legs tight around his back. He kept going, holding back his own climax, which was rushing at him like a freight train.

"Come for me, Arianna," he panted.

She moaned and arched… so close, but not quite there. His mouth watered, and he could feel his fangs come out. His wolf whined and growled and stomped, demanding that he claim her not just with his cock but with his bite. Jak clamped his mouth shut, knowing that would never be an option for him. Arianna had already been claimed… if Jak bit her, the magic in his saliva would wage war in her blood with the magic from all of Mace's previous bites. It would kill her, slowly and painfully. No… that was one part of Arianna that would always belong to Mace. He had claimed her first, and that was a magic only death could sever.

Arianna's moans were turning to shrieks, but she still hadn't come. Drawing it out would make it even better for her, and he wanted that: he wanted to bring her to heights she would never have with anyone else. But he was almost at the brink himself... he changed his angle, and that must have hit the spot because she screamed and bucked, and two thrusts later, he could feel her climax milking his cock. He groaned and couldn't hold back any longer. He kept thrusting as he came, but his head was so light, so flushed with the high of being with her, of pleasuring her, of being her first, her *true* first, that he felt like he might pass out. He kept going until her small cries of pleasure stopped wrenching free with every motion. Even then, he took his time easing them to a stop. He didn't want it to end. He didn't want to return to the world where he knew she belonged to another wolf. Where he had just broken every pack law that ever existed.

He pushed all of that aside, propping himself up by the elbows and looking down at her flushed face. Her lips were parted, her chest still heaving. Small tremors of pleasure were still racing through her, by the way shudders kept running up and down her body, leaving goose bumps and hardened nipples behind. Which reminded him that he hadn't lavished anywhere near enough attention on her gorgeous breasts. He slid his cock out and then trailed his kisses down her chest, giving each breast a few nips. He decided he would have to start there next time.

It amazed him that he thought there might *be* a next time.

He slid back up to look her in the face. The glow was still strong, but she had opened her eyes, and they peered back at him, crinkling at the edges. Worried.

"Are you okay?" he asked, frowning. He should

have made sure she had recovered completely from the dart before tossing her into the throes of her first orgasm… or two.

Her smile settled his heart. She reached up to touch his face, like she did before, with just her fingertips. "I feel like I'm floating. Like I'm actually on a cloud made of pleasure on some distant planet." She shook her head, her gaze roaming his face and then falling to look at their bodies where they touched, chest to chest. "I had no idea it could be like this, Jak. That I could feel like this." She looked back at his face. "Be honest with me. Is it like this every time? Is this what you feel with every girl?"

"With every girl?" he asked, eyes widening a little.

A shy smile crept onto her face. "Word gets around, Jak. I know what the Red pack wolves do when they go out. Mace comes home with another girl's scent on him all the time."

Mace's name on her lips made his stomach clench.

Her hands were on his face again. "I know I'm not your first. Or your last. I just… I just want to know if—"

"It's not the same," he said hastily, cutting her off with more force than he meant to. Here he was, lying on top of her, having just made love to her—and that's what it was, lovemaking, not having sex or a one-time screw—yet he had no idea what he was doing or how to put his feelings into words. "It's different with you, Arianna. You don't know how often I've… I've *thought* about you."

Her shy smile grew stronger. "Did you think of me like this?" She trailed her fingers along his back, just short of being ticklish, just strong enough to send heat to his groin.

He bent to kiss her, lightly, on the lips. "I *definitely* thought of you like this. Again and again." He lowered his voice to a whisper. "And in other ways, too."

She bit her lip. "This is the first time I've…" Her eyes grew wide as she looked up into his. "I don't think I've ever felt this way before."

He grinned. "Arianna Stefan, I promise you'll feel this way each and every time with me. I'll make you come any time you like. All you have to do is ask."

She laughed, lightly, and it warmed his heart. Then she reached up and pulled him down for a kiss, which he didn't object to in the slightest.

But when they parted, her voice was hushed. "I didn't mean *that.* Although that was amazing. I mean… I've never felt this way about anyone else before. I feel… *different* when I'm with you. Alive. Like the world has possibility again."

His heart both swelled and felt like it might burst with her words. He bent to kiss her again, then whispered, "Me too."

Her shy smile made his heart break. Because while his feelings were real, he knew what the difference was for her: she was away from Mace. As soon as she returned to the house, his domain, anywhere near his presence, the magic of the submission and mating bonds would amplify, and any feelings she had for Jak would vaporize like so much morning mist. Whatever tender, professed whispers or shrieks of passion she had with him, they could only exist here, far away from her alpha, and only for a few stolen moments.

When she returned to Mace, she would once again belong only to him—body, mind, and soul.

Jak gritted his teeth and eased back, helping Arianna up from where she lay on the cushion. Her hair was mussed, and her entire body was flushed from their lovemaking. Sitting next to him, her hand in his, naked and smiling… he'd never seen anything so beautiful in his life.

But she didn't belong to him. And she never

would.

"We should get dressed," he said quietly.

She nodded and solemnly took the articles of clothing, one by one, as he fished them out of the bag and handed them to her. He would have to tell the pack about the bounty hunters and their attempt to snatch Arianna. Somehow, someone had figured out who and what she was… and that mystery had to be solved before they came back for another attempt. Not only did Jak want to keep her safe, he knew Mace would never allow her to attend school, or even leave the house for that matter if he thought there was any chance of losing her.

In fact, there was a good chance, the moment she and Jak returned, that Mace would lock her away inside his house… forever.

Jak's wolf howled and snorted his objection to that thought. And Jak had to agree.

Completely unacceptable.

First, Jak would track down the bounty hunters and find out who had set them hunting for Arianna. And then… Jak had no idea how, or if it was even possible, but somehow, he would find a way to break an unbreakable magic bond and free Arianna from Mace.

Forever.

Chapter Six

Jak had scrubbed every last bit of Arianna's scent from his body, but he couldn't erase what happened between them from his mind.

Nor did he want to.

They had returned early from the University when the bounty hunters' attack cut short their plans on campus. Even with the brief delay due to their frantic lovemaking in the back seat, Jak and Arianna were still the only ones at the Red pack estate when he dropped her off at Mace's house. Which was fortunate: she had to eliminate Jak's scent before Mace returned, or they would both be dead. Or worse.

The idea of dying didn't bother Jak as much as

the knowledge that Mace wouldn't kill Arianna… he would only make her suffer. And for a wolf, there was a lot of suffering that could happen before the mercy of death arrived. The mere thought of that chastened and enraged him all at once: his wolf was on a constant low growl that filled his ears and rushed his veins.

If Mace hurt Arianna in any way… Jak wasn't sure if he could stop himself from killing her alpha. Or at least attempting to. The only thing that could possibly stop him would be the magic in Jak's own blood: he was bound to Gage, Mace's brother, and no matter what, Gage wouldn't allow his beta to kill his brother. And Jak couldn't disobey his alpha—his submission bond wasn't as strong as Arianna's mating bond, but it was still powerful magic. It would at least slow him down, make him weak… and doom him in a fight with Mace.

Which was seriously unfortunate: a dead Mace would solve more than one problem.

Jak climbed into fresh clothes after his shower. The soap and new clothes should safely hide his tryst with Arianna, although her scent was still strong in his mind… along with the way she moaned and flushed while she writhed underneath him. Just thinking about it was going to give him a hard-on, so he shoved that memory aside. Besides… finding the bounty hunters who attacked them was now his number one priority.

Jak sent a vague message to his alpha about urgent pack business back at the estate then logged onto the pack's WiFi—but there wasn't much to be found online. Of course, shifter hunters didn't hang a shingle out on bountyhunterforhire.com. But even the darknet sites that shifters used to communicate away from the prying eyes of the Feds didn't have any chatter about recent bounties or the hunters who answered them. Jak posted a description of the two men—mid-twenties, brown hair, gray hoodies, dart gun model—on a thread titled *Hunters, Witches, and Other Black Arts.*

Their attackers were pros, and even if they bumbled today's attempt at bagging a wolf, this wasn't their first time. Someone else on the net might recognize them. If Jak was very lucky, he'd score a lead on their base of operations, although that was information hunters kept very down low, for obvious reasons. Jak left off any identifying details about the place and time of the attack, just in case the hunters were lurking. He scouted around the other threads for possible leads on similar hits but came up dry.

Jak shoved away from the computer desk and paced the house's main gathering room, checking his phone for thread updates and scouring his mind for ideas about how to track the hunters. A crunching of tires from out front signaled several cars pulling into the estate. It was still early, and Jak prayed Arianna had already showered. He sprinted to the front door—maybe he could occupy Mace a little longer and buy her a few more minutes.

The three pack cars held a dozen wolves, including Gage and Mace, who were out of their respective cars and stalking across the red pavers of the drive almost before the vehicles stopped moving.

"What's the status, Jak?" Gage demanded in his usual no-nonsense approach.

"We had a run-in at the University," Jak filled his alpha in quickly.

Mace's face went from glower to livid in half a second. "What the hell!"

Jak threw his hands up. "Arianna is fine," he said, all while noting that Mace hadn't actually asked about her. Jak turned to Gage. "We were attacked by bounty hunters. Arianna was hit by a tranq dart of some kind, but she's all right now."

Mace seemed ready to choke on his own spit. "Some beta you have," he growled to Gage.

"*My* beta kept your mate safe," Gage spit back. "Care to wager where your mate would be now if Alric was in charge?"

Jak lifted his chin, daring Mace to question him, but his stomach was chewing itself to pieces.

Mace growled at them both but didn't argue. "I don't care what father says, she should never have gone back." It was more a pathetic grumble than an actual threat. At least Jak hoped. He knew school was the only thing that shone any light in Arianna's life—although he couldn't help hoping that maybe *he* was part of that light now, especially since he'd brought her alive in a whole new-to-her, steamy-hot kind of way. Regardless, Jak had to quickly find a way to put the attack behind them so she could keep going to class.

"It wasn't going to school that was the problem," Jak threw into Mace's face. He looked to his alpha for backup.

Gage's face darkened. "Jak's right. Being outside the compound just gave the hunters opportunity.

But they shouldn't have known Jak and Arianna were shifters in the first place."

"Exactly," Jak said. "*Someone* told them what we were and where we would be."

Mace pulled back, his face darkening. "No one in *my* pack. Obviously."

"Don't be an idiot, Mace," Gage said. Jak smirked. "It's not anyone from Red pack. It has to be someone we've worked with: associates, other packs, the shifter community. We have more than a few enemies in the shifter world, and many know about your new mate. But regardless… someone sold out the pack, and I want to know *who.*"

Several of Gage's pack members were gathered around their tight discussion, along with Mace's two betas Alric and Beck. A growl of agreement went around the group, Jak along with them.

"It could be anyone," Jak said. "Hell, maybe they were trying to stop my lab visit to Silver Quick. We don't even know if Arianna was really the target—they may not have even known she was a wolf."

Gage frowned. "What makes you say that?"

"She shifted during the attack—it seemed to catch them off guard." Jak wasn't sure that was entirely true. He had replayed the scene a dozen times in his head, and he suspected that when he dropped his phone he managed to avoid their first shot. They were aiming for Arianna as well, but they *did* seem unprepared for Arianna to ward off their dart, shift, and come after them.

"Of course she was the target," Mace said with scorn. He gave Jak a look like he was pond scum, a revulsion Jak had no problem returning. "She's a mated female."

There was no question that mated females carried powerful magic in their blood, and especially in their hearts. But that wouldn't mean anything if the hunters didn't know she was a shifter to begin with.

"Sure, witches *could* be after her… if they knew *what she was,"* Jak said. "She hasn't been outside the compound in six months. Hardly anyone knows she's here." Jak turned back to Gage again. Mace was too much of a hot head; Gage was the only one with a chance of sorting this out. "It could be the Sparks pack. Maybe they're out for revenge?"

Gage shook his head. "I doubt it. Things have been quiet too long on that front. Besides, their alphas aren't the kind who initiate trouble." He gave a pointed look to Mace.

He snarled in return. "They don't have the balls

to do what it takes. Not unlike some alphas in the Red pack."

"Really?" Jak lurched forward to get in Mace's face. "You want to be a little more specific about that?" *Mace just insulted his alpha.* Jak would be more than justified in tearing him into bloody strips… his mouth watered at the mere possibility.

"Your beta's big on words," Mace sneered to Gage. "Come on, beta. For once, I'd love to see your blood run instead of your mouth."

Jak's claws came out, and he was about to take a piece out of Mace when Gage yanked him back. Jak growled but obeyed his alpha and stayed back.

Gage jutted his chin at Mace. "Jak's the only reason your mate is home safe right now. Show some respect, or I might have to teach you some… *little brother.*"

Jak snickered along with the rest of Gage's pack. Their alpha had several inches and fifty pounds on his brother, and if it turned into a pack-on-pack brawl, Gage's pack outnumbered Mace's three to one. Those were only two of the many reasons why Gage was the dominant son in the hierarchy. That, and Mace was an asshole no one respected. Everyone knew it, even his own betas.

"So Arianna's home safe now—is that right?" The gleam in Mace's eye made Jak's blood run cold.

"That was my job, and I did it." Jak clenched his fists. The last thing he wanted was an enraged and frustrated Mace going home to Arianna and taking his impotent frustrations out on her. But Jak couldn't object without bringing suspicion. He was already walking a fine line, trying not to let his ever-intensifying feelings for her show. Jak growled his own frustration. "Why don't you run along home to your female, Mace? Let the big boys figure out who's threatening her."

Mace lunged for him, claws unsheathed and coming straight for his face. Jak bared his fangs, ducked, and came back up from underneath, pounding a fist into Mace's stomach. He doubled over, and Jak grinned, a flush of triumph thrilling his body. Gage outmatched his brother, but Jak and Mace were similar in size and speed: only Jak was smarter, and his hatred for Mace knew no brotherly bounds.

"That all you got?" he taunted Mace. The others were holding back.

Mace pretended to straighten but whipped a slice of claws at Jak's face instead. He caught one on the cheek even as Jak whipped his head back.

His blood ran warm, but Jak quickly swung back, catching Mace in the throat. The two men went down, grappling hands-to-throat, choking each other. The others cleared a circle for them, scuffling on the pavers to get out of the way. Jak couldn't breathe through Mace's hold, and Mace's claws were starting to dig into his neck… but Mace's face was turning purple with Jak's hold as well. It was a race to see who would pass out first—one Jak had no intention of losing. He lifted Mace's head and slammed it against the pavers, stunning him enough to loosen his hold.

"Enough!" Gage's roar sprung the others into action. Jak was lifted off Mace in an instant. Once his feet found the ground again, he stumbled backward, regaining his footing as Mace's betas helped him to his feet. Mace pushed them away and looked like he was going to lunge for Jak while he was being held defenseless by his own pack. That would start a rumble like nothing else.

Gage stepped between them. "I said *enough.*" The deep timber command of his voice stilled everyone. Jak felt it resonate through his body. Even if he wanted to rip Mace's head off—and he *very much* wanted to—his body wouldn't obey. Not in such a direct counter to his alpha's orders.

"These hunters aren't just a threat to Arianna," Gage said, his voice cooling a little. "They're a threat to the entire pack. If Jak and Arianna are on their radar, they've probably connected the dots and figured out the whole Red Wolf company is a pack. Which means all of us are at risk. And our father isn't going to like that very much. *Mace.*"

"No shit. *Gage.*" Mace's voice was laced with bitterness. "The question is why your beta didn't kill the hunters when he had the chance."

"Gee, sorry, Mace." Bile bit at the back of Jak's throat. "I was too busy making sure they didn't cut out Arianna's heart." He wiped away the blood that was still running down his face. The truth was he had let them go because keeping Arianna safe was more important than ripping out their throats—but that *did* complicate things now. And left a looming threat over her and everyone else.

Mace just growled and crossed his arms.

"We need to work together as a pack to take care of this." Gage sighed and shook his head. Jak didn't blame him—Mace was more a hindrance than anything else, even when his own mate was threatened. If she were Jak's mate, he'd be tearing out throats. Not to mention racing home to make sure his mate was actually all right. As it stood, Jak was the only one actually trying to take care of this mess… along with Gage, who would make sure the right thing happened, in spite of his brother.

Jak's phone pinged in his pocket. It was an alert from the message board.

"What's that?" Gage asked as Jak quickly scrolled through it.

"Darknet," he said, not taking his eyes from the screen. "I posted a description of the hunters. This is a private message response… but it's just an address."

"Sounds like a trap." Mace grinned a sickly smile. "I think your ace beta here should go check it out. That way, if there are any witches waiting, we'll just have a minor loss to the pack."

Jak narrowed his eyes but going alone was exactly what he wanted. "Works for me," he said to Gage. He didn't know what was going on, or who outed the pack, but Arianna depended on him. He could take care of business better without anyone else looking over his shoulder. *Especially Mace.*

"I don't like it," Gage said. "Take Mason and Johnson with you. Guns, stun weapons, the whole arsenal if you like. No reason to take unnecessary risks."

That wasn't going to work for keeping this a

solo operation. "Strangely, and believe me, I didn't think I would ever say this, but Mace is right."

Gage arched his eyebrows. Mace just sneered, throwing a smirk to Alric behind him.

"If it's a trap," Jak said, "We don't want to risk any more of the pack than necessary. I'll go in armed to the teeth and just do reconnaissance first. Once I know it's clear, I'll call for backup." He fully intended to pummel the answers out of the hunters personally. "Besides, there's an outside chance the hunters are working for law enforcement. Still doesn't explain *how* they knew we were shifters, but if they're working for the cops… it's better for them to think I'm working alone and not part of a pack."

Gage sighed, but Jak knew his logic was sound. Shifters kept their identity secret precisely because when they shifted into wolf form, they were *all wolf:* no identifying DNA to finger them in whatever crime they might be involved in. And while Red Wolf stayed mostly on the legal side of things, there were a few very *not* legal things that happened in both the company and the pack. If the whole pack was identified and hauled in as a group for DNA testing, forced to shift to match wolf-to-human DNA for the federal records… well, that would not play well with Red Wolf's business plan. Which included, among other things, gaining the trust of up-and-coming dot-com startups. It was a reputation business, and being outed as shifters and potential criminals would shoot it all to hell.

"All right," Gage said, reluctantly. "But I still don't like it. I want you to play it safe, you hear me? Go there, check it out, monitor the situation, and get the hell out. Understood?"

"Got it, boss." Jak had every intention of wrenching the truth from the hunters, by very *not* legal means if necessary, but his alpha didn't need to know that right now. After the fact, Jak would be forgiven, even if he bent the command his alpha just gave him once he was out of his presence. Besides, if Gage really didn't want him to bend the rules, he would come along. Jak had been his beta long enough to know that much.

Gage nodded, and the pack dispersed, heading inside for food or whatever the beginning of their weekend would look like, now that the fighting was over and a plan formed.

Mace stalked off, his betas lingering behind, following the rest of the unmated wolves into the main house. It twisted Jak's stomach in knots to think of Mace walking into his house and finding Arianna waiting. It took everything he had not to follow after and make sure she was all right. But that would tip his hand far too much. He had to trust in the fact that Mace was a lot calmer now than when he arrived… and that Arianna was smart enough to take care of things on her end.

Meanwhile, he had some wolf hunters to catch.

Chapter Seven

ARIANNA SLIPPED ON THE LITTLE BLACK DRESS SHE knew Mace liked best.

She had seen the pack cars winding down the long drive through the forest that surrounded the Red pack estate, but Mace hadn't yet arrived home. Whatever was keeping him at the main house, she knew he would be ready to kill something when he got home.

She didn't want it to be her.

The shower had washed away all traces of Jak, but his scent would be forever etched in her mind. The way his fingers had touched her, the way he had filled her… he had brought her a pleasure like nothing she had ever felt. She had used her own hands before, of course, especially after a vigorous session with Mace, but that had been more like… *relief* than anything else. With Jak, it was entirely different. He had awakened something inside her, something deep and primal and… *hot.* Dampness pooled between her legs…

Stop thinking about Jak! She smacked herself on the face and stabbed an accusing finger at her reflection in the bedroom mirror, trying to rein in her treacherous thoughts. The soap and the fresh clothes wouldn't help if she kept getting aroused—Mace would scent that in an instant, and there would be no way to explain it without giving herself away.

Without giving Jak away.

If Mace found out, she knew what he would do, and it ran pangs of guilt through her. What had she been thinking, kissing Jak? And then boldly grabbing him, urging him on? He had been nothing but kind to her, and now her lack of restraint, her inability to control herself around him had put him in terrible danger. The guilt sliced twice as hot, now that she was back in Mace's house, his presence clamping down on her even while he was still in the main house…

She had betrayed her alpha.

Her wolf was cowering, tail tucked between her

legs, whining in terror of the impending return of her alpha. But in spite of knowing in her mind that making love to Jak went against everything she knew—breaking pack law, going against her alpha's wishes—a glowing spark inside her heart refused to believe it was actually *wrong.* How could something so beautiful, that felt so amazing, be bad? How could the sweet way Jak looked into her eyes while he confessed to thinking about her be *wrong?* Her heart knew those things were filled with goodness. Even under the heavy weight of her mating bond to Mace, her brain still worked… and it *knew* what she and Jak shared was precious and rare and good. Her whole body ached to have his hands on her again. She craved all of it: the mind-blowing pleasure, the tenderness of his touch, the grin on his face as he watched her squirm…

Her face in the mirror was pinking up, and the heat between her legs was growing… Arianna smacked her face again then dashed down the stairwell to the first floor. When she reached the kitchen, she splashed her face again and again with cold water from the tap. She *had* to stop thinking about Jak… or she would get him killed.

Just as she was drying off, the front door swung open hard and banged against the wall. Mace stalked in and slammed the door closed again. Arianna's heart thudded in her chest. Her best chance was to go on the offensive.

"Mace!" She hurried up to him, stopping just short of throwing her arms around him. He wouldn't like that. "I'm so glad you're back!" She tried to sound desperate and panicked and all the things she should be after just having survived an attack by bounty hunters.

His face twisted up, the skulking glower transforming into a look that said he thought she was crazy. "You appear to have lived."

"I was so scared." It was hard to conjure that sound of fear into her voice, even though she'd been scared to death when the attack had actually happened. Jak's tender concern and passionate touch had erased all of it from her mind.

Don't think about him!

Mace's skeptical look had turned into a frown. He raked his gaze over her skimpy black dress. "Is this what you wear to school now?" There was a dangerous, leaden note under his words.

"No, no." She held up her hands, trying to look innocent. "I just couldn't stand to have those clothes on me anymore… they reminded me of the attack. I put this on because I thought you would like it."

The tension eased from his shoulders. He gave a short nod and stalked toward the white leather couches in the center of the living room. "I need a drink."

Arianna scurried over to the wet bar at the far side of the room. "Vodka, neat?" It was his favorite, but she always asked, just to make sure.

He snorted in acknowledgment and eased into the couch. She hurried back with the drink. As he gulped the entire thing down, she noticed blotchy red marks on his neck. They seemed to be the shape of fingers… her heart rate picked up again. Had he been in a fight? With who? What had happened? She shoved those thoughts aside before they could conjure a painful worry for Jak.

Mace wiped his mouth and stared at the fireplace across from the couch. "Jak is a real asshole."

Arianna's body jolted in place.

Mace narrowed his eyes. "He's also fucking incompetent. Some guard! Letting hunters get within a hundred yards of my mate…" He set the glass down on the low table in front of them.

Arianna couldn't help it. She had to say something. "It wasn't Jak's fault. They snuck up behind us, and—"

"Are you *defending* him?" Mace's eyes turned to glittering coal.

Her heart seized. "I'm just saying, there's no way he could have—"

She was cut off by Mace's hand on her throat. He shoved her back onto the couch, his enraged face in hers… before she could think or respond… *she shifted.*

Her claws were out, but she was trapped in her clothes and under the weight of Mace's body. Her wolf took over, squirming and pushing her way out from underneath him. She rolled off the couch, knocked over the table, scrambled to her paws, and stood, fur all bristled out, facing him.

The growl was out before she could stop it.

Mace's eyes were wide. But the dumbfounded look on his face vanished as he shifted, fast as lightning, and pounced on her. Before she could blink, he had her pinned to the floor, her throat in his jaws. The weight of his body was nothing like the oppressive heaviness of his thoughts pressing on hers. His *alphaness* overwhelmed her, and her wolf instantly cowered, tucking her tail up and pulling her legs in.

You haven't fought me in a long time, Arianna. In

between the fangs clamped on her neck, his thick tongue lapped at her fur, tasting her.

Mace was in her thoughts—she realized with horror that she had far too many secrets to allow that for even a second.

I'm not fighting you, Mace, I promise, I promise. She focused her thoughts hard on that while pushing against him with her paws. Her own body was betraying her intentions, but she had to shift. *Now.* Before any stray thoughts could betray her. Even if that meant Mace's razor-sharp fangs would slice open her throat in the process.

She barely managed to loosen his hold before the shift turned her human. The delicate human skin of her throat tore, sending a gasp of pain out of her gaping mouth. She was still in his grasp, blood surging out of the gash. It ran hot down her neck, no doubt soaking the white carpet below her. She might bleed out, but at least now her thoughts and secrets were safely locked inside her head.

Mace released his hold on her then shifted back to human. Her hands flew to her neck, trying to staunch the flow of blood. Her skin was slick with it, as was Mace's face. He wiped it away but remained lying on top of her. They were both naked now, and his weight made it even more difficult to breathe.

She coughed and gagged, his body holding her down as she convulsed. His hand closed around hers, holding her throat like he was also trying to keep the blood from flowing, but she knew it was more than that: it was a reminder that he still held her life in his hands.

"Is that what you call *not* trying to fight me?" Mace trailed his other hand along her cheek. "I can't wait to see what you do when you *try.*"

He leaned forward and licked the side of her face, running the tip of his tongue along her jawline and up to her ear. She shuddered under his touch.

"I… I'm not fighting you, Mace, I promise." She could barely get the words out with his hand on her throat. "It was just a reaction. A left over from the attack."

He ignored her, still nuzzling her ear. "It's been so long since you've fought me, Arianna," he whispered. "I'd forgotten how much I enjoyed it."

Her heart thudded even harder. She realized with a sickening drop in her stomach that his erection was throbbing against her thigh. Over the iron scent of her own blood, she could smell his arousal thick in the air. She almost gagged against it, but the mating bond fog was descending on her mind.

"A little time at school…" he whispered, his

voice husky, "… a little excitement with some hunters… and you're back to that feisty wolf I broke when you first arrived."

Arianna's stomach churned. *Her alpha wants to play rough.* So that's what she would have to do. It wouldn't be hard to fake a struggle against him… a panicky feeling in her chest fought against the haze clouding her mind. *Get away,* the flutter said, but her mind screamed, *Lie still.*

She bucked against him.

He grinned a sickly smile and dragged her free hand up over her head, holding it hard against the carpet. "That's right." His voice was heavy with lust. "Fight me."

She struggled against him again, but he pushed her legs apart with his knees and slid into her. Her mind floated away as he thrust and grunted and took her body. Even with the mating bond hazing her mind, even with the complete submission of her wolf and her body to him, her thoughts were still free to fly somewhere else, somewhere distant… and to see Mace's rough claiming of her body for what it was. This wasn't lovemaking. Making love was what she and Jak had done in the back seat of his car. She clung to that idea, the pureness of it, like a light beam lifting her up and out of her body, leaving behind Mace's grunts and hot breath on her face. What Mace was doing… her alpha was supposed to protect her from this, not force it upon her. Never in a million years would Jak do this, to her or any female.

Her alpha was… *hurting her.*

She hoped someday Mace would die for it.

Chapter Eight

Jak had been camped out for so long his back was getting stiff.

The address from the darknet thread was a seedy walk-up apartment in one of Seattle's rougher neighborhoods. One drive past the crumbling brick building, and he knew there was no way he could just hang out in his car until the bounty hunters decided to make a showing. He'd taken a risk his car would get jacked just parking for a few minutes while he banged on the door and peeked in the one front window. There was no one inside… or at least no one answered the door. Either they were stoned out of their minds, or they were gone. And hunters weren't known for being into drugs—they worked with too many shady characters to take the risk of not being sharp.

Jak was doing his best homeless person impression, including ragged clothes and a long trenchcoat to hide his weapons, huddling under a couple layers of cardboard in an alley across from the walkup. His vantage point was excellent, and absolutely no one looked at him, no on purpose at least. But it was quickly getting cold and dark, and his ass was numb from cuddling up to the pavement in the stench-filled alley.

All of it paid off right at sunset. As the sky flamed overhead, the two hunters, still sporting their gray hoodies, skulked down the sidewalk and up the four steps to the front door. One had a bandaged hand: the one Jak had crunched in his jaws when he disarmed the hunter earlier in the day. As they keyed themselves in, Jak sprang into action, crossing the street before they could make it past the threshold. He barreled into them, shoving them inside. If he was forced to shift, he wanted to do it off the street.

The hunter with the bandaged hand fell face first into the tiny living room while the other one rolled on his shoulder going down. Jak slammed the door behind him and tried to draw his guns, one in each hand, but the bandaged hunter swung up from the floor and charged him. Jak almost shifted, but then he would lose the guns. The hunter grappled with Jak, gaining a hand on the pistol and punching at Jak's face with his wrapped hand. Jak's shifter strength worked in his favor, but he didn't understand why the hunter was tackling him. He had to know Jak could shift and rip out his throat. It made no sense to go hand-to-hand with a shifter, unless… *it was a distraction.*

Jak dropped his pistol, yanked the hunter close with his free hand, and pivoted to use him as a shield. Three soft pops sounded, and darts intended for Jak sunk into the hunter's chest. The dart-gun-wielding hunter's eyes went wide. He dropped to the floor, scrambling after Jak's pistol, which had clunked across the dusty carpet. Jak's human shield crumpled to his feet, and Jak lurched after his pistol as well, but the second hunter beat him to it.

A shot rang out, and hot metal tore through Jak's arm.

He roared and shifted. His fangs ripped the gun from the man's hand, along with a good chunk of his flesh. When Jak shifted back, he still had the gun in his mouth: he dropped it into his hand. His clothes lay in a heap next to the man, who was clutching his bloody hand to his chest while he cowered on the moldy oriental rug. Jak wiped a smear of the hunter's blood from his face and glanced at the mess that was his shoulder: it was a clean shot through-and-through, and it seemed to have missed the bone. It would heal soon enough.

"You know, what?" he said to the man on the floor. "That really fucking hurts."

The hunter just shook, clutching his hand closer.

"But I'll get over it." Jak raised the pistol to point at the man's head. "You, on the other hand…"

"No, wait!" The hunter's hands flew up like he could ward off the bullet that way. "Come on, man, just tell me what you want." He was shaking pretty good, and now that Jak had a look at him, he was about Jak's age—twenty-four, give or take a year. Jak took two steps forward, the gun barrel drilling a line of sight into the hunter's skull. He edged back, still on the floor, hands up.

"I want to know who hired you to bag a couple wolves at UDub this morning."

The hunter swallowed and looked at his fallen partner. "Dude, she'll kill me. You know how crazy witches are. She was just out for some blood, that's all. Just bag and drain and…" He stalled out. "We would've let you go after that."

"Sure you would." These assholes would have let the witch carve up Arianna, and that made him want to pull the trigger right then. But he needed answers more than he needed to vent his anger. Jak stalked forward and pressed the tip of the gun against the man's head. He shrunk back and trembled. "Now how about you stop shitting me and tell me the truth? Because I'd be happy to put a bullet in you. Or maybe shift and tear you apart one small piece at a time, if you really piss me off."

"Hey, man, come on, be cool… I'm telling you the truth. I mean…" He swallowed. "Okay, okay, we weren't just after your blood, we were going to bring you in. The witch was looking for parts. The girl's heart in particular. It wasn't personal, dude, I swear, it's just… that's what the lady wanted, and I'm not going to mess with a witch, you know?"

Jak understood that much. He didn't know half of what witches could do, but what little he'd seen was brutal and painful, at least for the wolves involved. Witch magic was powerful and mysterious… and all that power tended to make them a little crazy in the head. Like cats playing with mice, witches had their own reasons for tearing people apart. And they didn't need a good one, either. They did that shit for fun.

But who was this witch? And how did she know about Arianna? Or Jak, for that matter…

"You know," Jak said, "maybe I'll just get on the darknet sites, post your address, and mention that you've screwed a witch out of her wolf score." Someone already outed the hunter online, which meant he'd been in the business a while. If word got out he'd double-crossed a witch, maybe trying to sell his booty on the black market… well, Jak wouldn't want to be him. "I don't think it will take long for your witchy friend to find you. I'll just sit back, watch while she fries you like an egg, then get what I want from her."

"No! Wait… come on, man!" The hunter looked like he was about to piss his pants.

Jak eased back and shrugged. "Doesn't matter to me. I get the witch either way."

"Okay, okay…" His hands were up again, imploring. "I can tell you her name. But you gotta give us time to clear out, okay? I mean, go ahead and go after her, I got no problem with that." He pressed his hands to his chest. "Better for me if you take her out, right? Otherwise, it gets back to me, and I'm sunk. Just… give me and my partner time to clear out of Seattle. The witch community here… they talk, man."

"Oh, I know they do." Jak gestured to him with the gun. "Tell me her name, and I'll take your proposal under consideration."

The hunter grimaced. "She's a really powerful witch, man. I'm just saying… you probably don't want to mess with her…"

"Name."

He swallowed then seemed to force the words out. "She calls herself Hecca. That's all I know." He was shaking his head, sadly, like he thought he had just signed his death warrant.

And it was quite possible he had.

Because Jak knew Hecca—she was one of the witches Red Wolf kept on retainer for their "special projects." If she had betrayed the pack, there was going to be serious hell to pay for that. Possibly a full out witch-wolf war.

"Thanks," Jak said. "You've been very helpful." He stepped back, scooped up his fallen dart gun, and pumped the hunter full of darts, just like his partner.

The thing was… Jak believed him. Hecca was too powerful a witch for the hunter to call out for no reason. But it didn't make sense for Hecca to sell out the pack, much less Arianna. Female wolf hearts were valuable, but nothing like the business Hecca did with Red Wolf on a regular basis. There was something deeper going on here, and Jak had to figure it out… before he tipped off all-out war.

If the hunter was lying about Hecca being the source of the hit, Jak would be back to claim another chunk of flesh in search of answers. The darts wouldn't hold them long, but they would at least stay put for a while.

Long enough for him to call on a certain witch.

Jak pulled on his clothes and strolled out of the apartment, leaving the bounty hunters unconscious on the floor like the trash they were.

Jak strode out of the elevator onto the thirty-fifth floor: *Morgan Media and Art* took up the entire wing with a glass barricade and an imposing reception desk between the public entrance and the company inside. Morgan Media was a successful social media management group, well-known in Seattle for performing near-magical feats of social awareness ad campaigns for their clients. Only a few people knew that Morgan was actually a coven of witches, and their combined magical strength was no small part of Morgan Media's success. Social media was only one part of their empire—they trafficked in all kinds of dark arts, playing the field far and wide, everything from helping law enforcement identify shifters to helping shifters evade exactly that kind of detection. They were amoral, powerful… and it was precisely Jak's need for a very dark art that had him venturing deep into the heart of Hecca's world.

The rail-thin blonde at the receptionist desk was so beautiful, Jak had a hard time tearing his eyes away. He had only seen Hecca a couple of times, but she was supermodel gorgeous as well—it was rumored that all witches used dark arts to enhance their beauty, and the receptionist was no doubt part of the coven. If she had been human, Jak might have tried to charm his way in to meet with Hecca. Instead, he kept his distance, stopping a good half dozen feet away from the desk. The spells she could cast were dangerous enough, but a witch's touch accessed the very deepest of shifter magic… something that precluded a friendly handshake, in any event.

"I'm here to see Hecca," Jak said without preamble. He hadn't called or messaged ahead—

the pack's usual method when contacting the witch for her services—but then he wasn't exactly here on pack business. If the hunters were telling the truth, and Hecca had been behind the hit, then Jak suddenly had unique leverage against a very powerful witch… leverage he planned to use to find a way to break an unbreakable magic bond.

If the hunters were lying, Jak was taking a huge risk… but Hecca could scarcely afford to kill him in her office, not while his pack was expecting his return from the bounty hunters. If he went missing, his pack would come for him… and find Hecca in the process. Jak just hoped his scheme wouldn't inadvertently set off a war between his pack and Hecca's coven.

"Ms. Morgan's not available," the receptionist said. She lifted her pointed nose and gave him a disgusted look. "She only meets with shifters by appointment."

He didn't know what magic she had used to detect him—normally even witches couldn't detect a shifter without a spell—but maybe he had given himself away by barging in. And by using Hecca's witch name, instead of her human façade: Ms. Elizabeth Morgan, social media princess.

Jak glowered at the receptionist but didn't

venture any closer. "She's available for Red Wolf. That's the definition of a retainer. Or perhaps you'd like to explain that you turned away one of her best clients?"

The woman pursed her glossy-red lips and slowly rose from her seat. She was tall—he'd heard that all the witches were—and her six-inch heels made her even taller than Jak.

"Please wait here." She gave him a cat-eating-mouse smile then sauntered to the frosted glass door leading to the interior of Morgan Media, taking the jasmine scent of her perfume with her. Jak was tempted to stalk after her, but he didn't want to give the impression he was here to cause trouble: Red Wolf and Morgan were business partners, and this was just a business call. At least, that's what he needed the office to think—he was already walking a tightrope, he didn't need to put the whole coven on alert.

Not if he'd like to come out of this alive.

The receptionist returned with a dark-haired witch Jak didn't recognize. She was curvy—hips swaying under the clingy red silk of her dress and an ample chest bouncing under fabric that barely restrained it—but that was where the softness ended. Her face was carved from porcelain, all angled lines, high cheeks, and perfectly-pale skin.

She strode up to him, confident in her power-red heels. He almost objected to being handed off to some low-ranking witch, but the way her glittering blue eyes were raking over him gave him pause. They were alive and intelligent and had a small glimmer of… something. Curiosity? Attraction?

He swallowed. He couldn't afford to have a witch—any witch, even a low-ranking one—be overly interested in him. Not in that way. Usually, witches and wolves mixed like gasoline and campfires, but he'd heard of witches who had a taste for shifters and kept them as pets. The shifters—usually males—were kept imprisoned under some kind of love spell. The witches used them for sex toys, and when their captors tired of them, they slowly bled the shifters of their magic-filled blood.

It was a particularly pathetic and disgusting way to die.

"I'm Circe, Hecca's sister," the witch said, her gaze still lingering uncomfortably long on Jak's body.

Sister? Why was Hecca sending her sister out as

an advanced scout? Jak didn't know Hecca even had a sister, although witch families were often primarily female. Male witches were as rare and sought-after as female shifters. Circe had the same waist-length sheet of flowing black hair as Hecca, only with a red streak of tint down one side, instead of Hecca's purple.

"You're one of the Red Wolf pack, aren't you?" she asked, curiosity enlivening her face. "Please… tell me what Morgan Media can do for you today."

Jak frowned. Circe's overly friendly tone was completely the opposite of Hecca's normal arrogance… and it was sending warning signals crawling up his back. But he needed to get through the advanced guard as quickly as possible.

"Can we speak in private?" Jak asked, throwing a frown at the openly curious face of the receptionist watching them.

Circe fluttered her fingers, and the receptionist witch practically levitated out of her chair and scurried from the room in a blur of heels and whispered silk.

"Now that we're quite alone," Circe purred, "what can I do for a handsome wolf like yourself?" Her gaze kept dropping to his tailored pants.

Jak swallowed again and hoped he hadn't made a terrible mistake in coming alone. And without actually telling his pack. "Look, I really need to talk to Hecca—it's a matter that concerns her. And her alone."

"Hecca is out of town at the moment." Circe stepped closer, wafting her spiced clove and sage scent past his nose. "But my sister isn't the only powerful witch at Morgan. I'm certain I can give you whatever you desire, wolf."

She reached out with just a single red-nail-tipped finger. Before she could touch his face, he stumbled backward, out of reach. That finger was more dangerous than a loaded gun: a bullet he could recover from.

The witch chuckled. It was a dark sound, and it filled Jak with chills that sent his wolf whining. Something wasn't adding up here. If Hecca put the hit on him, why wasn't she in town to take possession of the goods—he and Arianna? Maybe her sister was in on it… although she certainly wasn't acting like she had expected bounty hunters to show up this morning with his body.

"I have some personal business with Hecca," Jak said, regaining his composure but keeping out of arms' reach. "When will she return?"

Circe sauntered closer, forcing Jak to edge backward until he bumped up against the receptionist desk. Her red-lipsticked smile grew more lecherous. "Hecca will return tomorrow. But what is the nature of your personal business? I have to say, you've *aroused* my curiosity, wolf. And my sister isn't quite as fond of shifters as I am… I'm sure whatever you want, I'll be much more inclined to strike a deal with you. You might even enjoy it."

"I'm not interested in that kind of deal."

Circe gave an elaborate pout. "You wolves really aren't any fun outside of bed."

Jak fought off the chills that were racing up his arms. "I have a message for Hecca: I know about her extra-curricular activities, but I'm willing to strike a deal to keep that knowledge under wraps. If she wants that to happen, she should call me as soon as she returns. Do you think you can deliver that?"

Circe arched her pencil-thin eyebrows. "You're threatening my sister? You *are* a bold one. I like that." She licked her lips, sending more shivers down Jak's back.

"It's not a threat," Jak said carefully. "It's an opportunity to avoid some… *complications* that I doubt Hecca, or Morgan Media, would like to deal with."

Circe's leering stopped for a moment, and she

frowned. But Jak wasn't saying any more until he could deal with Hecca directly. Before Circe could corner him or grill him any further, he turned and hurried out of the witch's lair as fast as his legs would take him. She hoped someday Mace would die for it.

Chapter Nine

THE WAITING WAS KILLING HIM. JAK KNEW THERE was no point in pacing, but his legs carried all his agitation, and he couldn't keep them still. He was wearing a path through his room, from the door, to the window, and back to the bed. In each pass, he scoured Mace's house with his gaze, looking for a shadow passing by the lit-up windows, but the shades were drawn, and he couldn't see anything. His wolf snorted and pawed the ground, insisting that Jak go and check on Arianna, but there was no plausible excuse for it. She was back inside Mace's domain… and Jak didn't know if Mace would ever let her leave. Add in that Hecca wouldn't return until morning, giving him no way to explore alternative options for freeing Arianna, and Jak's wolf was clawing at him from the inside, wanting him to relieve the tension by doing *something.*

A pounding at Jak's door almost made him shift with the sudden jolt it sent through him.

He strode over to answer it, heart hammering, but it was only his alpha.

"The boys and I are going out to the club," Gage said. "Come on, Jak, you could use some blowing-off time. It's been a helluva day."

"You are not kidding." Jak sighed out some of his frustration. But the last thing he could stomach at this point was an anonymous hookup with some random brunette… and his alpha would almost certainly find someone for him. And insist he take a bite. "Look, those hunters are still on my mind. I think I'm going to take another swing by their place, camp out for a while." Jak had already lied to his alpha once today, telling him the hunters had never showed, but a second lie, face-to-face, still twisted his gut. He would tell Gage the truth eventually… just not until Jak had sorted everything out. And used his temporary leverage with the witches to figure out a plan for getting Arianna away from Mace.

Gage nodded and gave him a small smirk. "All right. I figured you hadn't given up on that yet." He pointed a finger at Jak that felt like it speared him with guilt. "Just be careful and call us when you see something. Don't tackle it alone."

Jak swallowed. "Got it." That was pretty clearly a direct order… and Jak was already violating it. It made his stomach turn even harder.

Gage called out to the rest of the wolves on the floor while Jak retreated back inside his room. He hung out by the window, watching for Arianna and listening as the main house emptied out. Then two dark figures approached Mace's house, and a third emerged from it. *Mace and his betas.* Jak's body went on full alert. Apparently, Gage's pack wasn't the only one going out on a Friday night.

Jak watched as Mace and his betas slipped around the side of the main house, heading toward the pack garage and the fleet of vehicles kept there. Back at Mace's house, the lights were still on… and Arianna was almost certainly still there.

An idea sprung into his head.

A foolish, stupid, reckless idea.

But he was going to do it anyway.

His wolf yipped and pranced and pawed his anticipation, but Jak forced himself to stay put in his room while the dancing headlights of the pack cars bounced along the long drive that wound through the forest and out of the estate. When he was absolutely certain both Mace and Gage and their respective packs were long gone, Jak jogged down the stairs to the main security office. Mason was on duty.

Perfect.

"Hey man," Jak said, hanging onto the edge of the door.

Mason was playing his favorite first-person-shooter game on his tablet, barely even watching the bank of cameras and security panels in front of him. Not that he really needed to… it was all automated with infrared and visible spectrum motion detectors, as well as an electrified fence that surrounded the vast Red Wolf compound. Jak knew the security inside and out: he had personally approved the software design when it was installed.

Mason finally looked up. "Hey, Jak. What's up?"

"I'm going to head out for a little while. Take another run at those hunters."

Mason looked disappointed. "Man, *everyone* is having more fun than me tonight."

"I know, guard duty sucks." Jak nodded in sympathy. "Hey, I'll call you first if the bounty hunters show, okay?"

"Cool."

"Listen, why don't you grab some dinner from the kitchen before I go? I'll keep an eye on the panel until you get back, then I'll head out."

Mason set down his game. "You're the man, Jak." He clapped Jak on the shoulder on his way out.

Jak waited until he was out of sight then quickly worked the control panel to disable one section of electric fence and turn off the cameras at the perimeter. If Mason noticed anything when he returned—which was highly unlikely—Jak had disabled the same section that the Sparks pack had tampered with over the summer. It was at least plausible that it could have shorted out on its own. And it would give him just the hole he needed to slip back into the estate unnoticed while ostensibly out catching wolf hunters. It would be easy to come around the back side of Mace's house without being seen.

By the time Mason returned, Jak was sitting in his chair and playing his game. He handed the tablet over and hurried out the front door. Jak didn't know how long Mace intended to stay out, but he was taking advantage of every minute.

The relief when Mace left the house was like coming up for air after almost drowning. Arianna stood in the middle of the living room, arms wide, head tipped back, just… *breathing.* She had already showered off the feel of him, but with Mace stomping around the house and ordering her about, his presence had been seeping into her pores all evening. It wasn't until Mace left the house that she finally felt the *awfulness* of the day start to dim.

While Mace was in the house, it had been just too dangerous to allow thoughts of Jak into her mind… but now she practically skipped back to those stolen moments in his car. Arianna closed her eyes and imagined Jak holding her. It wasn't the memory of the mind-blowing lovemaking that grabbed her first—it was the tender way he held her and told her how brave she had been.

A tapping sound jerked her out of her memories and almost gave her a heart attack.

Had Mace returned already?

But the sound was coming from the kitchen… a place Mace never ventured. Frowning, Arianna crept across the plush white carpet of the living room and peeked inside.

Then her mouth fell open.

At the back door stood *Jak.*

He was tapping furiously but quietly on the glass window of the door. Her heart leaped into her throat, and she sprinted across the tile floor. What was he doing here? What if Mace came back? Jak couldn't come in… Mace would scent him for sure. As Arianna arrived at the door, she hesitated to even open it. Uncertainty fisted tight around her heart: what would Mace do if he found out she let Jak in?

As she waffled, one hand on the door handle, she forced herself to look up, through the glass, at Jak's face on the other side. His chest was heaving, but his gaze was locked on her face. He blinked then pressed his hand against the window, fingers splayed. She placed her hand over his, the cool glass a reminder of the harsh reality that kept them apart. It pricked her eyes to think Jak had risked coming for her, and yet fear and a quarter inch of glass was keeping her from touching him.

You were incredibly brave, Jak's voice came back to her. On the other side of the glass, his face pinched in, and it tore through her heart. He was being brave and reckless and crazy in showing up at her back door… the least she could do was open it if only to tell him he had to leave.

She twisted the knob and pulled the door open.

A smile lit Jak's face. He braced his hands against the door frame on either side but didn't come in. "Arianna."

God, just hearing her name on his lips made her wolf sit up and hum with pleasure.

"I can't… I can't let you in." Her voice was whispery and apologetic, but already the cool night air was wafting in his scent: woodsy and earthen with a hint of mouth-watering musk. He had been running, so there was a sweet-sour undernote of sweat that made her bite her lip.

Jak's smile only got brighter. "No, of course not. Which is why you need to come outside with me."

"I… what?" The haze on her mind, the one that had been clouding it all day since she had returned home, grew thicker. She almost couldn't understand the words he was saying.

Jak stepped back from the door, giving her room. "You can do it, Arianna."

"But I can't leave. Mace doesn't want me to leave." She shook her head quickly. He was asking her to do the impossible.

"Mace isn't here." Jak's dark eyes bored into hers.

"But he wouldn't want me to." Her wolf whined in her ears, tail tucked and afraid. If Mace found out if he even knew she *thought* about leaving…

Jak lunged forward and grabbed her hands, which were clasped together. Before she realized what he was doing, he had yanked her across the threshold. She stumbled and almost lost her balance, but Jak caught her and held her upright.

She was in his arms.

His eyes were wide, waiting for her to speak. She looked back at the door, only a couple feet away, but it suddenly seemed like a distant planet. The haze had lifted almost instantly from her mind as soon as she was out in the night air.

Jak's hands went to her shoulders, holding her gently. "Are you all right?"

Arianna smiled. "Yes." But then her smile dimmed… she didn't know what Jak had planned, but even if he'd managed to wrench her free of Mace's domain, this was still crazy. She couldn't be out here with him. What if someone saw them together?

"Come with me." He grabbed her hand and towed her toward the forest. The lights from the main house spilled out onto the lawn, but from this angle, at the back of the house, no one could see them. They ran in a straight shot between the back door and the darkened forest that surrounded the estate.

She still couldn't help questioning the sanity of this. "What are we doing?"

He threw a playful grin back to her. "Having some fun."

They were running across the open lawn now, halfway to the beckoning dark of the trees. "We're having fun in the forest?"

"Oh yes." His grin was decidedly wicked now, but she let him keep tugging her along with their clasped hands.

She glanced back at the estate, still convinced that someone must be able to see them, but there wasn't a soul in sight. "What if we're caught? What if Mace finds out?"

Jak didn't answer, just picked up the pace until they broke the edge of the forest and plunged into the darkness within. He kept going until even the lights of Mace's house were obscured by the thick tree trunks. Fall leaves crunched under their shoes, and spots of moonlight speared through the canopy where the trees still held their leaves, providing islands of white light in the darkness. Jak pulled her into one of them then spun to take her into his arms.

His lips were on hers before she could speak… and then there was no need for words. His hands pulled her close while his mouth claimed hers. She melted into him, not wanting even the moonlight between them. Her own hands clutched at his shoulders, wanting him closer and closer still. When Jak broke the kiss, pulling back to look her over, she was momentarily stunned—she had been so lost in their kiss, she had forgotten that what they were doing was pure insanity.

But she wasn't the only one slightly breathless… which edged a smile onto her face.

Jak leaned back to look over her jeans and t-shirt, her third change of clothes since this wild day had begun. "Are you all right? I've been going out of my mind, worrying about you. Please tell me you're all right. That Mace didn't find out or hurt you or…" He stalled out, and the torment on his face wrenched Arianna's heart.

"Mace doesn't know." She couldn't bring herself to say that Mace had… forced himself on her. It wasn't like it hadn't happened before. Every day, whether she had realized it or not.

Jak's hands cupped her cheeks, and his dark eyes peered into hers. "What's wrong?"

"I just…" Arianna didn't know what she could

say. "I don't want to be there. I don't want… Mace's hands on me. Not anymore."

Jak slowly slid his hands away from her face, his expression turning to moon-glinted stone. She was afraid she had said something wrong, but then she saw his claws come out and curl around into his fists, biting into his own flesh.

"Did he hurt you?" The words were a half-growl.

Arianna covered his clenched fist-paw with her two hands. "No, I promise."

"You're not telling me the truth." His fist was still as hard as a rock under her hands.

She moved her hands to his face, touching his cheeks with her fingertips. His shoulders relaxed with her touch. "The truth is that Mace holds me captive every day. Today was no different… except that *you* were part of it. And, for the first time since I came here, I actually felt alive."

"Arianna." His voice was soft, almost broken. "I swear I'm going to free you from him."

She slid her fingers across his lips. "Shhh…" She still felt the ghost of his kiss branding her own lips. "There's nothing you can do about it, Jak. You have to just let it be. And…" She glanced around at the silver-frosted forest around them. "This is madness. If we're caught, he'll kill you."

"I don't care." His dark eyes were piercing hers. "I don't care about any of that. All I care about is you. I want you. I want to be with you. And not just once, in the back of my car. I want you free from Mace forever."

She shook her head. "You know that's impossible."

"Maybe," he said. "Maybe not."

She frowned. "What do you mean?"

"What if…" He licked his lips, and a glint of moonlight danced in his dark eyes. "What if there were a spell—a witch's spell—that could free you from Mace? That would break the mating bond. Would you do it?"

"What?" She drew back from him. "I've never heard of such a thing."

"Neither have I… but I've seen the witches and their magic. There's no telling what they might be able to do, given the right persuasion. And I think I just might have the right persuasion for the right witch."

Her heart was starting to pound. "You're talking about using dark arts."

"I am." Jak bit his lip then let it go. "Arianna,

I'm sure it won't be easy. It might even be painful. I won't know until I talk to the witch. But before I go in there and ask, I need to know: do you want to break your mating bond with Mace? I mean, if she *can* do it… will you come away with me?"

Arianna's eyes went wide. "You would leave your pack? For me?"

"Yes." He swallowed, visibly, and she could hardly believe what he was saying.

"Jak, I can't…" She was shaking her head. "I can't ask you to do something like that for me. I mean, you hardly know me—" He cut her off with a finger pressed gently across her lips.

"I know your smile brightens my day." Jak's eyes were shining again. "I know you like to run free, but you won't run from a fight. I know you flush pink when you're excited, and you're beautiful even when you're sad. I know, right here, right now, you're more worried about me than you are about yourself. And I know you were only beginning to live when Mace forced you to mate… and that's something so horribly wrong that I can't stand by and watch it any longer."

Tears welled in her eyes. "Jak… how can you feel all those things…" She didn't want to say that every single word pierced her heart in a way he couldn't possibly know.

"Arianna, I've been dreaming about running away with you ever since you arrived."

She threw her arms around him and pressed her face into his shoulder so he wouldn't see the tears crest and fall. "I had stopped dreaming of anything… until I met you."

He held her tight, nuzzling his face into her hair. The feeling of elation running through her was so intense that she thought she might actually be floating.

"It may take some time," he whispered into her hair. "Maybe days. Maybe weeks. But I swear to God, Arianna, I will get you free."

She pulled back enough to seek out his lips with hers, reaching up on her tip-toes to show him with her kiss what those words meant to her. Her hands threaded through his hair, bringing him down so she could revel in his mouth on hers, his tongue flicking across hers, his hands on her body. Her heart pounded, and blood rushed in her ears. She had that floating feeling again like she had been transported to another world, one filled with magic and moonlight and heart-stopping sex-drenched kisses.

But the truth was she and Jak could only have stolen moments. Until Jak could find a way to free her—and the mere possibility of that sent her soul flying—she would have to continue to live in Mace's world.

Arianna pulled back from their kiss before it got too hot. "We can't…" She was breathless with it. "…even with a kiss, your scent is on me. It's too risky. Mace will find out."

Jak pulled her close again, an adorable smirk lifting one side of his mouth. "You can wash away my scent when you get back to the house… but first I want to give you something worth the shower."

Then he kissed her again, but this time, his hands didn't stay confined to gripping her back and holding her close. This time they came around front and caressed her breasts. His fingertips sought out her nipples, and he groaned into her mouth when he found they were already hard, pushing against her thin t-shirt and bra.

Without a word, he lifted her t-shirt over her breasts, freeing them from her bra as well, and then dropped down on one knee before her. She gasped at the cool night air on her flesh and Jak's hot mouth nipping at it. He lavished attention on one breast, then the other, sucking in her rock-hard nipples and grazing them with his teeth. Wetness was already pooling in between her legs, but each near-nip on her sensitive flesh sent electric sparks of pleasure to her core. She fought for breath, hands in his hair, awash in the pleasure he was giving her.

"Oh, God, Arianna, I want you so badly." His words were whispers on her skin, while he unbuttoned her jeans and worked his hands under her panties. She gasped again when he touched that spot, the one she barely even knew she had before this morning, but that he had brought alive with the orgasms he had already given her. It was swollen, sensitive to him, and he seemed to know exactly how to touch her to make her want to squirm the rest of the way out of her pants.

Then he worked her panties down and seemed to freeze up. His gentle hands skimmed her hips as he peered at them. When she looked down, she could see the myriad scars left behind by Mace's claws by the many, many times he had marked her. Heat rushed her face, and she tried to cover the scars with her hands, but Jak just pulled her hands away and looked up at her.

"Did he do this?" There was a cold fire in his eyes.

She nodded, suddenly shaking in the cold and not sure what to say.

Jak turned his attention back to her hips, gently kissing right where the scars were. Relief flooded her body. When he looked up at her again, his eyes held that deep sadness she'd seen before.

"I will never hurt you, Arianna," he said, but she already knew that. Jak was better for her than Mace ever could be in a million years.

Jak returned to kissing her scars, gliding his fingers over her skin and slowly working his lips across her belly. Then he moved farther down until his tongue found that sensitive spot that was aching for his touch. She nearly shrieked as his tongue worked her, but she managed to clamp a hand over her own mouth, the other still on his head, keeping her upright as the tip of his tongue slowly turned her legs into jelly.

"Jak," she panted. "Oh god, Jak, what are you doing— " But then words were obliterated from her mind as his fingers slipped inside, pumping her while his tongue worked her electrified flesh. She bit down, hard, on her hand to keep her moans from filling the forest. Jak lifted her knee over his shoulder, and his one hand held her back, keeping her upright while the other brought an orgasm crashing out of her. She bucked into him, unable to control herself, and nearly crumpled to the ground as the waves of pleasure washed through her.

Just as her body crested the peak of those waves, Jak's hand and mouth left her, and he stood. He shucked off his jacket and tossed it on the leaves.

"I need to be in you." He quickly unbuckled his pants and kicked them off. His erection was thick and strong in the moonlight. She couldn't help reaching for it, but he held her wrists away. "None of that. I want you to ride me with that beautiful body of yours, not your delicious little hands."

His words made her body throb.

His hands left her wrists and trailed down her legs, tugging her pants off. Then he sat on his jacket and pulled her down facing him. She straddled him and took him inside her. He groaned and leaned back, giving her room to get settled. He was so deliciously big, filled her so completely, but she wasn't quite sure what to do next.

"I've never…" Her breath steamed the night air. "I've never been on top."

Jak half-laughed and grinned up at her. "You just hold still then, my love, and let me do the work." He held her hips in place, hovering over him with only about half his length inside her, then he quickly lifted his body to thrust up into her.

She gasped with how deep he went and how his body met hers in just the right spot, sending an electric pulse of pleasure through her. He groaned again. "God, Arianna, you're so tight… so good…" He thrust up into her again and again, faster and faster until she saw stars dance in front of her eyes, more than just the ones peeking through the canopy overhead. She bit her lip to keep her gasps and shrieks inside, but the pressure kept building until finally, that mind-blowing pleasure wracked her body again. She came and came, and it seemed like an endless time until Jak stopped thrusting, his own body stilling with his climax. Her body deflated, collapsing on top of him, all pleasure completely wrung out of her.

She had never been so completely and wonderfully close to someone in her entire life as she was at that moment, half-naked on the forest floor, joined together, panting into Jak's chest like she had just run a mile.

When her breathing settled a little, she sighed, long and contented. "I want this, Jak. I want it forever."

His hands were in her hair, touching her face,

running along her back. "I promise, Arianna. I promise."

And she had no doubt in her heart that Jak could make the impossible happen. Because he had already done it: he'd already found a way to rescue her when she hadn't even known she was drowning.

Chapter Ten

It was nearly Saturday night before Jak got the call.

The evening before, with Arianna in the forest, had sealed everything in his mind: he would find a way to free her, no matter the cost. That he would have to leave his pack was a given. It would mean moving away, getting a new job, and starting over... but it would be worth it. He might have to wait, though, at least a week, until the full moon, when the entire pack pledged their submission to Gage. If Jak didn't re-up his submission to his alpha then, he would be free to do anything he wished: including killing Mace.

But he was hoping the witches would have a better way—one that wouldn't involve him going to jail for murder. Not least because that would leave Arianna unprotected in a world where she was far too vulnerable.

But he needed to get Arianna free as soon as possible. Every day she was in Mace's house was another day he was putting his hands on her. Jak's claws came out and sliced into the leather grip of the steering wheel. He had a hard time keeping his wolf under control when he thought about Mace and Arianna together, so he pushed that image to the back of his mind and focused on the dangerous task at hand: bargaining with witches.

Hecca had messaged him using Morgan Media's account—it was nothing more than a time, but he knew exactly what it meant. Circe had delivered his cryptic threat, and Hecca had realized her plan to capture Arianna and him for her dark magic had been exposed. And that Morgan Media's relationship with Red Wolf was at risk. Hopefully, that meant she was ready to bargain… and not merely summoning him to his death.

Jak pulled his car into the parking garage and took the elevator to the 35th floor. He was right on time, and this time, the hot blonde witch in front didn't even ask, she just escorted him through the cubicle-and-art-table open area to Hecca's corner office in the back. The receptionist knocked and let him in, closing the door behind him, once he was inside.

Hecca stood at the window, gazing out over downtown Seattle with her back to him. The dying rays of the sun were turning the city's towers into purple obelisks and Hecca's office into a palace of gold and shadows.

Jak waited.

"Give me a reason, wolf," she said.

"A reason?" He didn't like how this was starting out.

"A reason not to turn you into ash where you stand." She finally spun to face him. Her long black hair flowed in a wavy flare, settling on her generous curves once she had turned. Her purple-tinted hair streak gave an artistic flair to business-sexy, curve-hugging lavender suit. But it was her eyes, alive with a dark fire, that told him they'd already skipped to the heart of the negotiations.

"You could kill me," he said as coolly as he could manage, thankful that witches didn't have a shifter's ability to scent. Otherwise, she would smell the tremor of fear clutching his gut. "If you want to lose Red Wolf's business and possibly start a war."

"A war?" She was smiling, but there was no

warmth in it. "A little dramatic for a wolf, don't you think?"

"Wolves tend to take the attempted murder of our females rather seriously."

Hecca's smirk faded. "What are you talking about, beta?"

"Yesterday, two bounty hunters nearly captured one of our mated females and her guard. But you already knew that."

Her dark eyes narrowed. "Bounty hunters."

"Armed with dart guns and a bag." Why was she pretending she didn't know anything about this?

"So someone came after your pack. It's hardly the first time." She flicked her purple-nail-tipped fingers at him as if this was some kind of pack business that was inconsequential to her. "Who says Morgan Media was involved in any of it?"

"The bounty hunters said so. After I beat the shit out of them."

She frowned. "These bounty hunters pointed you *here?*"

"They called you out by name, Hecca." Why was she dancing around this?

Her frown deepened, and she drummed her dagger-like nails on her desk. Then a phone appeared in her hand from somewhere in the folds of her purple dress. She spoke into it. "I need you in here." A pause. "I don't care. Drop it. I need you *now.*"

Jak was half-certain she was going to have him thrown out, and he wasn't sure what his play was going to be then, but after a strained moment of silence, Circe floated into the room.

Now that they were standing together, Jak could see the sisterly resemblance: same dark hair, same carved cheeks of ivory. Circe's red hair streak echoed Hecca's purple one, and she favored the same tight-fitting suits. But Circe's eyes were once again roaming Jak's body, whereas Hecca's had nothing but contempt for him.

"Please tell me," Hecca said to her sister in a voice filled with danger, "that you haven't been tramping around in my playground again, Circe."

Circe curled a lip at her sister. Apparently, there wasn't much sisterly love among witches. "I have no idea what you're talking about."

Jak decided he needed to lean into this conversation. "Well, *someone* sent bounty hunters after Arianna… and given that the hunters say it was Hecca, I'm thinking someone in this office is operating in your name."

Circe's eyebrows lifted, and she seemed

genuinely non-plussed. "Sister," she said to Hecca, "you may disagree with my preferences in many things, but surely you know I'm not idiot enough to do magic—or kidnappings—in your name."

Hecca looked grumpy but not the fire-spitting anger she had a moment ago. "No, that doesn't seem reasonable. Even for you. And even if you did, I doubt you would be caught by the likes of a beta wolf."

Circe tipped her head in acknowledgment.

"Wait a minute," Jak said, his frustration growing. "Are you actually saying none of you were involved in this? Is that really your story here?"

Hecca sauntered forward, and her sister watched on with amusement. "Little wolf, you should take care to come here making accusations when you have no proof."

"I guess I can haul in the bounty hunters." If they haven't already fled town. Jak winced at his misjudgment there: he should have brought the hunters back to the pack. But he was so bent on working a deal with the witches, he couldn't see past that.

Hecca arched an eyebrow. "Even if they squealed my name, that means nothing to me, wolf.

I don't know who was after your mate, but it wasn't anyone in this office."

"She's not my mate. I'm just the guard."

Hecca's eyes narrowed. "And yet you're on quite the quest here, storming in and making demands. Bargaining…" She looked Jak up and down and began to circle him, taking him in from all angles. Hecca threw a pointed look to Circe, who nodded. Jak didn't like this silent witch conversation. *At all.*

"Tell me, little wolf, what did you expect to gain, coming here?"

Jak gritted his teeth. His leverage was gone. He had no idea who was actually after Arianna… or possibly even himself. And now he was deep inside a coven that he had just, apparently, falsely accused of capital crimes.

"I just wanted to keep a wolf-witch war from breaking out unnecessarily," he said, backpedaling.

Circe floated across the room, the wisps of her red dress flitting around her legs as she moved. "He said he had *personal* business, Hecca dear."

"Yes, I can sense that," Hecca replied, still looking him over. "Your aura is giving you away, little wolf. You have *very* personal business here… about a woman who is not your mate… ahhh, yes. Now it's clear."

Jak didn't like the look of recognition on Hecca's face *at all.*

But she just twiddled her fingers again. "This is your domain, Circe," she said, turning her back on him and heading for the door. "Kill the beta or… whatever. Just clean up after yourself and keep us out of a pack war, yes?"

Jak's mouth dropped open as she whisked through the door and closed it behind her, leaving Jak alone with Circe.

"So, little beta. You want a female who doesn't belong to you," Circe said with a smile that made Jak's stomach clench tight. "And you're willing to walk into a witch's coven to protect her. Or is there more to it than that?"

Jak shut his mouth and swallowed. This had spiraled quickly out of control. What was he thinking, coming here without his pack? They didn't even know where he was: as far as they were concerned, he was still staking out the bounty hunters, who had probably fled the state. Which left him with precisely zero bargaining power. And a sinking probability of getting out of the building alive. Which, strangely enough, also left him with nothing left to lose.

Jak stood straighter and withstood Circe's

roaming gaze. "I have a need for a certain dark art. I can pay you well if you have the ability to do the magic I need."

"The *ability...*" Circe's blue eyes flashed. "I have bent the knees of witches more powerful than you've dreamed of in your small, wolfy dreams, beta. You have no idea what I'm capable of."

"Then you should have no problem breaking an unbreakable magic bond." He folded his arms and dared her with his eyes.

They narrowed at him. "The mating bond. The female is mated already, and you desire her."

There was far more to it, but... "Yes."

Circe's pointed look softened into boredom. "So simply kill her mate. That's what you wolves like to do anyway, isn't it? Brawl and thrash around with your claws and teeth, all *animal-like.*" Her lips were twitching into a barely repressed smile.

Jak had a strong feeling she had a taste for wolves and would very much enjoy his *animal nature.* That must be why he was still standing, still alive, and dealing with Circe, not Hecca, whose revulsion for wolves was much more typical of witches. But sex was a dangerous bargaining chip with a witch—one that before this very instant he wouldn't have even thought possible—but it was also one that would likely land him as her permanent, and eventually deceased, love slave.

"Can you break the bond or not?" he asked as if he might march out if the answer was *no.* He could only hope that option was still on the table.

She smirked and stepped closer, enveloping him in her spiced clove and sage scent. "What you seek can be done, little wolf. The question is: what would you be willing to give for it?"

"I can pay you handsomely." Jak had more than enough cash tucked away. He never spent anything anyway, and Gage had brought him in early on the bonus pool for the projects he had worked. Over four years, that added up.

She edged even closer. "Maybe I'm not interested in money."

Jak leaned back, regaining space. "Maybe money's all I'm interested in offering."

She moved in again, and he would have backed up, but he was already up against the door.

She smiled. "You might enjoy it more than you think, little wolf."

"I'm certain you would find I'm *not* a little wolf."

Circe bit her lip. And there was *definitely* a scent of arousal under the sage. He wasn't sure if this was smart—in fact, he was certain it wasn't—but he didn't have many options at the moment.

He leaned forward, meeting her halfway, close enough that his whispered words would brush her skin. "I would definitely take my pleasure from you —repeatedly, *little witch*—but you can be sure that the females in my bed will always get their pleasure first. And often."

She breathed a low sigh. "So you would bargain with me, wolf?"

He leaned back. "I would… except that spending time in your bed seems like a good way to lose all my blood."

She pouted. "Why would I drain someone who kept me so completely satisfied?"

His wolf snarled, and even Jak could see that wasn't exactly a denial. "You're forgetting one important thing, witch."

She was back to looking amused. "And what's that?"

"I happen to be in love with another man's mate. I'm willing to make a *one-time* payment to break that unbreakable bond. But that's it. And payment comes *after* the spell has worked."

She tipped her nose up to look down at him.

"The spell will work. You might not like the result, however."

He frowned. "What do you mean?"

"What makes a mated female's heart so powerful in magic?" she asked rhetorically, amusement returning.

"I have a feeling you're going to enlighten me." Jak knew mated females were highly sought after for the properties of their blood, and he figured the heart was especially drenched in it… but he hadn't really thought about *why*. Delving into what ghastly things witches did with wolf internal organs wasn't something he spent a lot of time ruminating upon.

Circe licked her lips, still eyeing him. "A mated female has twice the magic of an unmated female or a male in either case. That's because she has two forms of magic in her blood, intertwined—her own magic and the male's magic. The second one is what binds her to him. It's a living force inside her. The stronger the male, especially an alpha, the stronger the magic and the greater the bond. The reason you cannot mate with this female you desire isn't because the bond holds her to him—"

"It's because my magic in her blood will kill her," he cut her off impatiently. "Yes, I know this.

I'm not a *complete* idiot, in spite of the evidence of me standing here right now."

She smirked and ran an appreciate gaze over him again. "No, you're not stupid, little wolf. Foolhardy and brave in your love, perhaps, but I can see you are not dim."

"Gee, thanks." He glowered at her. "Now, how does this spell work?"

"Inside your beloved female's blood, there are essentially two wolves: hers and her mate's. To extract one while leaving the other is a delicate thing. A dark art, not unlike slicing out half of her soul while leaving the other half behind."

Jak felt his own blood drain from his face. "Will it hurt her?"

Circe's eyebrows arched up. "I imagine so. Although the pain is the least of your problems, little wolf."

"Just… *tell me.*" He was growing tired of this witch's games.

She scowled at him, but there wasn't much heat to it. "In order to entice the wolf that lives in her blood, we will need somewhere *else* for it to go—another host, you might say. If you have an unmated female available, transferring the bond from one to the other would be relatively straightforward. Not least because the essence of the male is drawn to the female."

Jak's heart rate picked up. He could see where this was going. "There is no other female available."

Circe nodded once, solemnly. "Then it will have to be a male. And the transfer will not be so simple."

Jak's face twisted up, disgust clawing at his throat. "You mean you have to transfer her mate's essence into a male's blood. But… what happens then? One male cannot be bound to another, not with a mating bond at least."

She lifted one eyebrow. "What do you think will happen when the essences of two males are trapped in the same blood, little wolf?"

"They will fight."

"To the death." Circe sniffed and held her head high. "It's not my fault that your species is so ridiculously violent."

Jak felt suddenly light-headed. "They would fight to the death," he repeated, the words bouncing around inside his head. With the witch's spell, he could draw Mace's essence out of Arianna, but only by bringing it inside his own body… where the war between their wolves would happen at the DNA level. And Jak would be the one dying because of it, slowly and painfully.

He could set Arianna free, but only by dying in her place.

Jak blinked and dragged his gaze up to meet Circe's steady one. "Is there no other way?"

"I'm afraid not, little wolf." Her voice was soft, and not entirely unkind, but her sympathy rang hollow in his ears. "Perhaps now you can understand why I would want my payment in advance." She pursed her lips into a tight line.

Jak didn't have to worry about the witch draining his blood after a night of wolf-on-witch sexual depravity… because the spell he was bartering for would kill him anyway.

He swallowed. "I'll have to get back to you on this."

Then he turned and stumbled out the door. As he fled the coven, he had just one thought: he had promised to free Arianna, and he was going to keep that promise. But if a wolf had to die to make it happen, it wasn't going to be Jak…

It was going to be Mace.

He would have to do this the old-fashioned way: by killing Arianna's mate.

Chapter Eleven

KILLING MACE WOULD BE THE EASY PART—IT WAS the idea of leaving Gage's pack that twisted Jak's stomach in a knot.

He had just left Circe and her coven a few hours ago. Normally on a Saturday night, Gage's pack would be out club-hopping, but tonight, he had brought them straight here, to the Olympic mountains, for some pack bonding time.

Jak kicked at the fall leaves with his boots while he leaned against the pack's van. Gage was instructing Mason and the others—Joe, Frank, Billy, and Sampson, the youngest and wildest of the bunch, and all the rest—about the rules. All fifteen were in attendance tonight—the hunt was mandatory for everyone, including Jak. It was a standard hunt, and he had developed the game, so he already knew what Gage had planned. The half-moon lit up the meadow well enough for Jak to see the rest of Gage's pack punching each other good-naturedly and laughing too loud in each other's faces.

It wasn't actually these jokers he would miss, although they were the closest thing he'd ever had to real brothers—his own were more sadists than siblings. As the youngest, Jak was always omega to their abundance of alphas. It was a regular sport for them to see how many pieces they could take out of him without requiring a healer to stitch him back together. Jak's father only encouraged them: he was the leader of their small, country pack, a real alpha's alpha, and he had a barely disguised disdain for his youngest son, the tech geek. Jak's mother had protected him from the savagery of his older brothers, but as Jak grew big enough to fight back, it got uglier.

And then his mom died.

Jak's wolf still howled a long mournful cry every time he thought about her. But Jak's human side had nothing but rage… and a single photo that he'd had on him when he left his pack and family for good.

His mom was as gentle as they came and beautiful besides. She always kept him close—he had already been the target of his brothers' twisted humor more than once when she wasn't watching. Her kitchen was the safest place for him in his family's sprawling ranch in the mountains northeast of Seattle. She was a captive mate, like Arianna, and dutifully bore pups for his father, but their mating was never a love match—Jak remembered with nauseating clarity the day he figured *that* out.

He was just a kid, maybe ten. His father came home drunk in the middle of the day, somehow missing that Jak was curled up under the kitchen table, putting together computer parts. He had scored a motherboard from one of his teachers—along with parts scavenged off the internet and his friends at school—and he was buried in building a computer of his own.

Jak hardly made a sound, and he had always wondered if things would have been different if he had. His father had always been rough and demanding—Jak loathed him more each day of his childhood. But that spring day, he watched, silently, as his father forced himself on his mother, right above Jak, on the kitchen table. His father never realized he was there.

His stomach still heaved every time he thought

of it: the shaking of the table, his father's grunts, his mother's quiet sobs afterward. It would forever be seared into his mind.

From then on, Jak tried to protect his mom, to keep her away from his father, even going so far as to take the beatings his father liked to mete out, as long as he didn't vent his frustrations, whatever they were, on her. But it was no use: Jak was still just a kid. Then one day he came home from school to find her dead.

It takes a lot to kill a wolf.

Jak's inner beast howled again, and Jak ground his boot into the rocky forest floor. He had no doubt his father had done it. You could hardly see the bruises on his mother's neck under her fur, but they blared out his father's guilt. Jak could only imagine how much she had to fight at the end, even shifting to do it... Jak never figured out why his father did it, but brutes like him didn't seem to need a reason. Maybe his mother had finally stood up to him. Maybe she had done something innocent that set him off. Maybe his father had just come home stupid drunk one day and didn't know what he was doing until it was too late.

But Jak knew his father would get away with it because she was *wolf* when she died. If Jak hadn't been a scrawny 14-year-old at the time, he would have killed his father right then. But he was weak. And outnumbered by his brothers.

The best he could do was to stay alive himself.

His mom would have wanted that.

Even so, he almost didn't make it out of adolescence alive. Wouldn't have, if Gage hadn't saved him from Jak's own kin. Right in this very meadow in the Olympic mountains, in fact, where he now stood waiting for his alpha to give the signal for their pack games to begin. Back then, the games Jak's brothers played nearly killed him. Gage was only a few years older than Jak, but he was a decent alpha, even then. Gage stood up to them, rescued Jak from being turned into hamburger, and from then on, Jak had been steadfast by his side.

He literally owed his life to Gage Crittenden.

And now he was going to not only leave his alpha's pack… but kill Gage's brother in the process.

This situation is so fucked up. Jak's logical side insisted there had to be another way around this, some way he could save Arianna from the same fate Jak's mom had endured without having to kill Mace… but he just couldn't see it. Mace would never let her go—he'd rather see her dead.

And Jak could all too easily picture her that way.

"Hey, you all right?" Gage's boots tramped through the leaves nearby.

His voice startled Jak out of his morbid thoughts. "Yeah, just… have a lot on my mind."

Gage gripped his shoulder for an instant in a manly sort of way then let his hand drop. "Don't let this thing with the bounty hunters rattle you. They're nothing but cowards and assholes."

"Cowards with guns," Jak grumped. He had ended up telling Gage most of the truth: that Jak had found the bounty hunters, beat the shit out of them, and that they'd fled the area… but that he hadn't gotten much out of them in the process. Jak had verified that they'd left by checking on their dive of a hideout on his way back from the witch's coven.

He folded his arms and gazed out at the pack. They'd shifted to wolf form and were wrestling through the leaves, nipping at each other's tails. It was like watching overgrown children play—the innocent kind, not the kind who tried to kill the weak among them.

"Just wish I knew what the hunters were after." Jak's wolf growled his unhappiness.

"Probably just freelancers," Gage said, leaning against the van next to him. "Got wind of who you were, or maybe Arianna, through someone… then kept that tidbit to themselves until they could profit from it. If they were affiliated with someone we know—someone with a grudge—they wouldn't have given up so easily. And they would have offered up a name under your *gentle* persuasion."

Jak snorted a laugh and nodded.

"Honestly?" Gage said, drawing Jak's gaze back to him. "I was mostly concerned it was your family looking for you. I know it's been a long time, but blood runs thick."

Jak shook his head fiercely. "*This* is my family now." And he meant those words, but it only clamped the knot in his stomach tighter.

Gage gave him a half smile. "You know you're more family to me than my own blood, right?"

Jak's throat grew tight. "That's only because you got screwed in having Mace for a brother." If only he could confide in Gage, gain his help in this… but as much as his alpha hated Mace, Gage would never approve of actually ripping out his throat.

"At least I only have *one* asshole brother," Gage said with a smile.

Jak coughed through the thickness in his throat.

Gage looked over the wrestling wolves of his pack. "It was here, wasn't it?"

"Eight years, three months ago," Jak said with a small smile. "Not that I'm keeping track."

"It was a lucky day for both of us." Gage gave him a nod, and Jak thought he might choke on it. How was he going to betray the only wolf who had ever had his back in all things?

Jak swallowed and lifted his chin to the meadow. "Are we doing the ceremony here next week?" The full moon was next Saturday—time for Jak and the rest of Gage's pack to officially renew their submission to their alpha. It was what made them a pack, strengthened them, and bolstered the magic in all their blood, Gage most of all. The submission ceremony made their alpha strong. And it would be the day Jak betrayed the man who was even more than alpha to him.

"No," Gage said. "I think we'll stay close to home this time. I'm fairly certain those bounty hunters are history, but no need to tempt them. Besides, I doubt Mace will let Arianna go off property."

"Yeah." Another problem he had to face: how to tell Arianna that his plan with the witches won't work, and he has to kill Mace instead... not to mention the details of their grand deception scheduled for next Saturday.

"That's why I wanted to come here today. We won't get to run as a pack after the ceremony like we normally do. And we need that time together. I don't know who's out there targeting us, but if those hunters can find out who we are, anyone can. We need to stay on our toes, work together to keep things tight. I don't want this rattling them…" He lifted his chin to the rest of the pack. "…any more than I want it to rattle you. We're in this together. Got it?"

"Got it, boss." But his stomach just churned more. What would it do to Gage's position in the Red pack if his own beta betrayed him? How would it shake the confidence of the others? Not to mention that the wolves who were his brothers today would, by this time next week, want a piece of him for betraying their alpha—a very bloody piece.

He and Arianna would need to get far, far away from Seattle.

"All right, time to get these guys started." Gage shifted, leaving his clothes next to the van, and loped over to where his pack was still wrestling in wolf form.

Jak took a moment to banish all thoughts of Arianna, Mace, and the coming deception from his mind: once he was in wolf form, Gage and the others would be able to hear his thoughts. He could control them a little, but you never know when a stray thought will slip through: there are no true secrets in the pack, not for long anyway.

With that thought, a chill settled deep in his stomach: he would never be able to keep his feelings for Arianna secret forever. Eventually, it would come out. Jak needed to be gone before his entire pack realized he had already broken pack law. As much as he hated the idea of leaving, staying wasn't really optional anymore.

Jak took a deep breath and shifted. His clothes fell to the ground, and the cool fall air was even crisper with his shifter senses. It was filled with earthy scents that spoke to his wolf form. He yipped and trotted over to join his pack. Already he could hear their jumble of thoughts, excited for the hunt.

Gage had to use some of his alpha command voice to settle them down. *Listen up, assholes!*

They quieted immediately, whimpering a little. Even Jak bent his head a little with that tone in Gage's thoughts.

Mason has the prize. Jak dropped him north of us, near

the top of the ridge. We've got ten minutes to scent and recover the prize or Mason keeps it for himself. Gage looked up at the half moon. It was a decent amount of light in the meadow, but the forest would be slow traveling. *Wolf form only until we're done.*

They all yipped agreement, including Jak.

What's the prize, Jak?

Come on, tell us!

You idiots will just have to find out when you get there, Jak responded.

Their complaints were half-growl, half-groan, but Jak was glad to have an excuse to keep his thoughts quiet and focused on the hunt.

Time to go, Gage thought. He led the pack away from the van, quickly working up to a fast lope. The run felt good—cool air in Jak's ears, soft grass on his paws. The moon bathed them in silver light.

Once they dived into the murk of the forest, Jak took the lead. *Drop off point is about a quarter mile ahead.* He could get them there, but all bets were off after that—Mason could have gone anywhere with the prize. The pace was slower, with fallen logs, unsteady footing, and undergrowth in the way, but soon they padded into the clearing for the turnoff from the main road. The pack quickly fanned out, scenting for Mason.

Johnson yipped from back in the forest. *I've got him!* The rustle of his pounding paws, charging off on the scent-trail, followed. The rest of them scrambled after, making sure to stay in thought-range and not lose him. Jak and the others quickly caught the scent as well, and soon they were a force of fur, black and brown and silver-frosted by pockets of moonlight, trampling the undergrowth in the heat of the chase. Their thoughts were tight and focused. *Mason, Mason, Mason.* Jak was flush with the feeling of *belonging* that was part of being *pack.* He reveled in it, let it permeate his mind… and tried not to think about losing it.

A splash ahead and ripple of moans showed Mason had crossed a stream.

Lost him! Billy complained, but Sampson had already leaped ahead, splashing down the stream. The rest followed after, fanning out at the edges, scenting for Mason as they went.

He could have gone upstream, idiots, Jak thought. Billy circled back and joined Jak and Gage in scenting upstream. Even though Jak had set up the game, he had no idea where Mason would go… and half the goal was not so much claiming the prize as keeping Mason from getting it. Just as Jak was about to lose telepathic contact with the wolves downstream, a rapid-fire thought-argument resolved into a series of *This way!* thoughts that had half the pack charging off in a single direction again.

Jak and his cohort quickly circled back and loped after them. They only caught up as the pack broke from the forest into another clearing. On the far side was a tree that stood alone… and in the upper branches sat Mason, fully clothed next to the keg of beer that was today's prize. The moon glinted off the silver metal, but even from this distance, Jak could see Mason's grin.

Bastard broke the rules! was the resonant thought cycling through the pack, but Jak just wore a toothy wolf smile as he, Gage, and Billy trotted toward the front of the pack. Rules were *all wolf* for the game… but for the chasers, not for the chased. Jak had no idea how Mason had hauled the keg up into the branches, but staying human was the only way he could move the prize, so the *all wolf* rule didn't apply to him. However, the trees were off-limits precisely because wolves couldn't climb.

Make a pyramid! Gage ordered. It was a decent way to make up for the fact that they had paws not hands, but Jak could see there was no way they would get far with that. Still, they piled one on top of another, claws digging into furred backs to form a wolf pyramid that would at least reach the lowest branches. While they could hold on with their razor-sharp claws, they'd just rip the bark right off the tree if they tried to scale it.

Coming through! Jak threw a thought out into the pack. As a beta, his order carried a lot less weight than one from Gage, but the pyramid of fur tolerated his climb up their backs well enough to get him to the top.

He paused. *Boys, when your enemy breaks the rules, you've gotta to do the same.* He shifted right there, taking a leap as he did to catch the next branch up.

"Oh, shit," Mason said as he saw Jak coming, buck naked in the moonlight, climbing hand-over-hand up the tree. Yips and howls from down below cheered him on, and so far, Gage hadn't called foul on his move.

When he reached the branch Mason was perched on, Jak saw he had carved a notch into the thick wood with his claws and lashed the keg to it with a rope he must have secreted away in the forest prior to the hunt. Jak braced himself to fight Mason for the prize, but he just looked defeated as he watched Jak climb up next to him.

"Hidden rope," Jak commented casually. "Nice touch."

"You're the game master," Mason said, grumbling. "I didn't count on you breaking the rules."

Somehow that stabbed Jak in the heart. He was going to miss Mason. All of them, really. Now that he was human again, his stomach was back in knots.

"We could just keep it for ourselves," Jak said, patting the tap on the keg.

Mason's face lit up—his reddened cheeks looked like he had already taken a few slugs to drink. "Yeah?"

Jak just laughed. The pack was howling their impatience below, now that Jak was just cozying up to the keg like Mason. "No. But it was a respectable try." His smile faded. "Maybe next time, I'll tell Gage to make you game master."

Mason's grin was ear-to-ear then.

"Let's lower this thing down," Jak said. "I don't want Billy breaking his damn neck trying to get up here."

As they worked the rope, the clench in Jak's stomach just grew. Breaking the rules was all fun and games within the pack, but the truth of his words plowed into him like an avalanche: *his enemy had already broken the rules.* The rules of being alpha. Of protecting your own. Of caring for your mate. Jak hadn't been born alpha—he was the last in a brutal line of brothers competing for dominance in their tiny pack—but even he knew that a dark alpha like Mace was a betrayal of everything their kind stood for. Being alpha meant doing everything for the ones you loved. Everything for your pack.

Mace had broken the rules.

And Jak would do the same to take him down and give Arianna the alpha she deserved.

Chapter Twelve

SATURDAY NIGHTS... ARIANNA DREADED THEM EVEN more now.

The weekends were when Mace came home with another girl's scent on him, usually ready for a drunken round two. If she were asleep when he arrived, he would just awaken her—and half-asleep was no state to deal with her alpha. She needed all her wits about her to get through it with the least amount of pain, physical and emotional.

But now... now that Jak had promised an escape... it was almost unbearable to contemplate another Saturday night with Mace. Whatever dark art deal Jak was making with the witches to free her, no matter how painful that might be to endure, it would eventually be *over*—unlike the purgatory she lived in now. Like she told Jak in the forest, he had given her *hope.* But back in Mace's house, the mating bond still hung over her, wringing her with guilt and fear about even the possibility of leaving Mace. She felt feverish, running hot with anger and cold with fear, one moment contemplating taking a butcher knife and plunging it into Mace's heart, the next curling up on the floor in a ball of self-loathing for even thinking of raising a hand against her alpha.

Hope was a dangerous, volatile thing. If Jak didn't free her soon, she might go mad with it.

Arianna paced the house, tidying things that didn't need tidying, straightening her dress, reapplying her lipstick. It helped when she looked like she had been waiting for Mace: that seemed to appease him or perhaps flatter him. But she could hardly look in the mirror anymore. Just as she was heading up the stairs to the bedroom, to make sure everything was in order there as well, an insistent tapping sound drifted in from the kitchen.

Jak. Her heart seized, and she prayed she was wrong.

It took her three heart-stopping seconds to race to the kitchen, but it was him: hands pressed against the glass of the door's window, looking handsome and sexy with his wind-tousled hair and half-open shirt.

She threw open the door. "Are you *insane?*" she gushed out. "Mace could be home at any time."

Jak held up his hands. "He's not. I just got back myself, and I know Mace's pack is still out at the clubs."

Her hammering heart slowed even as her heaving breath was finally catching up. "How can you… Jak, someone will *see* you."

"It's all right," he said. "They're all heading to bed. I just… I had to see you. Please, just… come outside with me for a little while."

She shook her head vigorously. She couldn't even chance his scent drifting into the house. "I can't."

"Just for a few minutes. Just so I know you're free of… *him.*"

"I can't." She tried to close the door, but he shoved his hand against it. "He'll be here any minute." The terror was making her voice squeak. If Mace even suspected anything… on a Saturday night… a full-body shudder made her hand on the door quiver.

"Okay, okay!" He eased back but still held the

door open. "I just needed to tell you that… well, plans have changed."

Her heart dropped to her stomach. *He's changed his mind.* She blinked, feeling lightheaded and suddenly unable to speak.

"The witches can't do the spell the way I thought they could," he said.

She almost couldn't hear his words over the rushing of blood in her ears. *He's changed his mind. He's not going to rescue me. I'm stuck, trapped here.* She braced herself against the door, holding on, so she didn't tip over with the sudden nausea tearing a hole through her.

"Arianna, honey? Arianna!" The panic in his voice finally brought her back. His face was etched with concern. "Are you okay?" He was on the edge of coming into the house.

She couldn't let that happen. "I'm fine, I just… need a moment." She held up her hand to stop him from coming in. "I understand." She couldn't keep the sob out of her voice. "I should have known it wouldn't really work…" Then her throat closed up completely.

"What? No!" He reached for her, but she backed away. "Arianna, listen to me: I *am* going to get you free of Mace. I promised I would, and I will keep that promise."

Her gaze wandered up from the floor to meet his dark eyes. "I don't understand. You said—"

"I said the witch's magic isn't going to work." He paused then stood straighter in the doorframe. "I'm going to kill Mace myself."

She shrunk back from the doorway, fear hammering her heart. *"What?"*

"Arianna, it's the only way—"

"You can't do that!" Her voice was screeching now… too loud, someone would hear her… she brought it down to a hiss. "I will *not* let you die for me, Jak." There was no way he could kill Mace without his pack taking Jak down. Even his own alpha wouldn't be able to tolerate it—he might have to kill Jak himself, a mercy killing, just to make it fast. Unlike Mace's betas who would… she couldn't even think about it. A sob reached up and choked her anyway.

"I have no intention of dying." Jak gave her a small smile.

For a brief moment, Arianna thought maybe he was losing his mind. This was crazy talk, pure and simple.

"Besides," he said, and the smile was stronger

now. "I want to make sure you're taken care of—the *right* way—once Mace gets what he deserves. I'll need to be around and breathing to make that happen."

He was serious. She could tell by the look in his dark, smiling eyes that he had a plan to make this actually happen. And Jak was *so* smart… maybe, just maybe, he could pull this off without dying in the process. He certainly seemed determined to try.

He was really going to kill her alpha.

Her wolf recoiled so strongly from that thought, Arianna had to retreat another step from the door, wrapping her arms around herself.

"Arianna." There was pain in Jak's voice and worry in his eyes. And she didn't want that either, but she couldn't help herself, not while she was in Mace's house. Not when he was minutes away from being home.

"You need to leave," she said softly.

"Arianna, please… I just need to talk to you for a little bit. Explain what I've got in mind."

"You need to go." She dashed toward him but only to grab the edge of the door and try to close it. He held it open, but she pushed hard enough that he finally relented and let her close it in his face.

She had to wrench herself away from his sad look on the other side of the glass.

She stalked out of the kitchen and nearly ran up the stairs to the bedroom.

Could she do this? Could she let Jak take that risk? What if it didn't work? Jak would be dead, she would be to blame, and Mace… Mace would make her pay in ways she couldn't even imagine.

Arianna ran to the bathroom, getting there just in time as the contents of her stomach emptied out. Which only made her panic more: Mace would not be happy to come home to a house that smelled of vomit. She briefly considered feigning illness: maybe he would leave her alone for a night. Only wolves didn't get sick, not that way.

Before she could figure out what to do, the front door opened.

Her heart quivered so badly, she couldn't do anything but curl up on the floor and pray that Jak had gotten away before Mace arrived at the house. Mace stomped around downstairs for a while, probably getting another drink. He took long enough that her racing heart started to calm. Taking deep breaths to quell the shaking in her hands, she grabbed the sink and hauled herself off the floor. She had to clutch the sides not to go tumbling back to the tiles. She flushed the toilet and was just splashing cold water on her face when Mace tromped into the bedroom.

"Arianna?" His voice had a bit of a slur, just enough that she knew he had been drinking. "What the hell's that smell?"

She grabbed a hand towel to wipe her face. Her lipstick smeared all over it. She had to look like hell as she stumbled out of the bathroom.

Mace gave her a look of disgust. "What happened to you?"

"I… I don't know," she said, floundering. "Maybe it was something I ate, I just… felt sick."

His fists curled up, and Arianna felt the blood wash out of her face with the murderous look on his. "Do *not* tell me you're pregnant."

"What?" she said, genuinely shocked. "No! I know you don't want that, Mace. I know it. I take my pill every morning."

He narrowed his eyes at her as if he thought she would actually do that—have pups against his wishes. His scrutiny made her stomach churn, and she pressed the towel to her mouth, but she managed to keep more from coming up.

"I think it was just that fish I had for dinner,

that's all," she managed to mumble through the towel.

He must have had a fair amount to drink because the suspicion didn't last long. He grunted and gave her a short nod. She finally had a chance to look at him: his shirt was rumpled and half-untucked, and it wasn't hard to figure he had already had his pants down once tonight. She prayed it would be enough. He turned away from her, toward the closet, and she sighed in relief. He wouldn't bother changing if he wanted sex tonight.

"Well, whatever it is, get rid of that smell," he called from the closet. "And if you're going to be throwing up all night, use the bathroom downstairs."

She stumbled on spaghetti legs down to the kitchen to get some disinfectant and deodorizer. Her sense of smell was inundated, but she had to get the mess cleaned up quickly before Mace decided it annoyed him even more. She hurried back upstairs and scrubbed the bathroom floor, toilet, sink, everything that might have even the tiniest residual… then sprayed the air with deodorizer. It was the scentless kind, the one that captured the airborne molecules and deactivated them. It should act quickly.

Mace had changed into sleep pants with no shirt. She wasn't sure what that meant in terms of sex, but she had to get rid of her soiled clothes, so she quickly changed out of her sexy dress and into a nightshirt she hoped wasn't too appealing. By the time she emerged from the closet, he had flopped down on the bed, lying on his back and rubbing his temples with his eyes closed. She hoped all the cleaning chemicals weren't giving him a headache and crept toward the bed. When he looked at her, she froze.

"Are you going to throw up some more?" he asked.

She shook her head.

"Then come to bed." He patted the white comforter next to him.

She shuffled over, but she had no read on him: she couldn't tell his mood at all. And her body was still shaking from being sick… and the stress of Jak's visit.

Jak. He was going to try to kill Mace. The tremulous hope that she could actually be free was crushed as soon as Mace's hands found her body next to him. He was her alpha. She *belonged* to him. Yes, he was horrible in many ways, but as long as she did what he asked, he wouldn't kill her. Or Jak.

It was only wanting to be free that put everyone at risk.

Arianna shuddered as Mace palmed her breast and seemed to be warming up for more.

Surprisingly, he stopped caressing her. "Are you *sure* you're not going to be sick again? Because I do *not* want you throwing up on me, Arianna." There was less menace in his voice than normal. Maybe the liquor had softened him. That happened sometimes. He usually wanted sex when he was drunk, even more than normal, but sometimes… sometimes the alcohol seemed to deaden some of the anger he flung around like scattershot.

"I'm okay now," she said quietly.

"Should I call a healer?" he asked. There was almost a hint of concern in his voice.

"No. I'll be fine." She swallowed down the last of the bitterness in the back of her throat and took a deep breath.

Mace was quiet a moment. "Apparently those bounty hunters who were after you have gone on the run. Fucking Jak let them get away, and now they've cleared out."

Arianna perked up a bit. Mace rarely shared information with her… unless there was a need for her to know. And even Jak hadn't told her about finding the bounty hunters.

She edged up on her elbows to look at Mace. "Are they gone for good?"

He frowned like it was a puzzle his alcohol-fogged brain couldn't quite put together. "I guess. They're probably not stupid enough to try hitting the same wolves twice."

"So… what does that mean? For school, I mean?" She knew better than to straight-out beg to go. She needed desperately to talk to Jak, to convince him this was crazy, his idea of killing Mace to free her… but there was no way she would be able to leave the house again if Mace thought she was still in danger. He didn't love her, not the way an alpha should love his mate, but she knew the last thing he wanted was to lose her. She was too important to his position in the pack. But she had to let him think going back to school was *his* idea.

His frown grew deeper. "The old man thinks you should go back."

"What do *you* think?"

"I think it's a fucking stupid idea." He turned to her, taking her cheek in his hand. It wasn't entirely rough, but it was firm. "And if anyone tries to take you from me again, I won't let them slip away into the dark like cockroaches. I will *crush* them."

She nodded her head. The movement wasn't much since he had such a grip on her, but her heart was thudding in her chest. Her wolf was responding to his alphaness, whining and tucking her tail, but Arianna knew Mace wasn't protecting *her*… he was protecting his position in the pack. She had no doubt he would hunt down and kill Jak if he took her away.

Mace was staring into her eyes, licking his lips.

"Those hunters wouldn't stand a chance against you," Arianna whispered, and it had the effect she hoped, flattering Mace's ego.

"Damn straight." He was eyeing her lips. She could smell the scotch on his breath.

She wasn't sure what he intended, but she wanted to take advantage of this moment, this brief period when he seemed softer than normal. Maybe it was her sickness or the scotch… or the close-call, almost losing her to the bounty hunters. She didn't know.

"Maybe I *should* go back," she said softly. "I don't want to get behind in my classes. I want to make you look good, Mace."

He nodded, absently, his eyelids drooping. He

was tired. Maybe that was it. "I'm going with you this time. And I'm bringing Beck, not Alric. I want no fuckups with this."

Arianna nodded quickly, but her heart sunk. How would she meet with Jak if Mace was watching her every move? "Whatever you think is best. Like you said… those hunters wouldn't dare mess with an alpha like you."

Mace grunted, but she could see he was flattered again. He released her face and eased back on the bed, letting out a long sigh. She lay still next to him, waiting to see if he would turn his attention back to her. But before long, he started snoring. She wrapped the edge of the comforter around her, trying to calm the shivering in her body while not moving too much and waking him.

Mace might want to guard her for a while, but she knew he would bore quickly with that. Eventually, he would let others guard her again… maybe even Jak, once Mace was sure the bounty hunters had fled. The only question was if she would get a chance to see Jak before he took matters into his own hands.

Chapter Thirteen

Jak checked the time on his phone for the third time in as many minutes.

Professor Nalik didn't notice, still going on about his test results and the laser apparatus. Jak nodded at all the right times, but his attention was on the clock, counting the minutes until Arianna's class started. Visiting Silver Quick's lab was a decent excuse for being on campus, in case his plan went sideways, but if the timing wasn't as precise as Nalik's laser setup, the whole thing could unwind.

And Jak wasn't ready to go fang to fang with Mace. Not yet.

"The calibrations are certified," Nalik said. "We are quite certain there are no errors in our measurements. Besides, the optical memories would be less if there were any such decoherent effects in the crystal."

"No system is error free, professor," Jak said. But he really needed to make an exit if he was going to get where he needed to be on time.

The diminutive Indian man's spine stiffened. "We've accounted for all the stochastic interactions that could be reasonably interfering."

Jak nodded, but he wasn't reassured by the man's defensiveness. If he wanted funding from Red Wolf, he was going to have to be more forthcoming about the holes still left in the technology. Gage was all about taking risks in the market, but not with tech guys who were too afraid to show their faults to allow them a realistic assessment of the risks involved.

"All right, look." Jak made an obvious glance at his phone this time. "I have another appointment. How about I come back with one of our managing partners, and you can go over this all again with him? But we need to know *everything*, Pradeep. Keeping secrets is not going to win you any investors."

The professor's eyes narrowed at Jak's use of his first name… but he had to understand who was in the driver's seat with this.

"Perhaps," he said archly, "we will find other investors with more confidence in our ability to run our own lab."

"Yeah, good luck with that." Jak grabbed his jacket off a lab bench. "It's not that I don't trust you, Pradeep. It's that we're talking lots of investor money, and I'm your tech guy. If I don't have full confidence in your setup, I can't sell it to my boss or our other investors when we try to leverage a buy-in on this. And if you managed to find an investor who doesn't care about due diligence, I'd be worried, if I were you. As in *violation-of-patent* worried."

Pradeep's prickly demeanor deflated as Jak slipped on his jacket and headed for the door. Just as he was about to step out, the professor held up his hand.

"Wait." He seemed to be physically swallowing his pride. "Bring your managing partner back next time. We'll have all the information you want."

Jak held his smile in check and just gave him a sharp nod. "Glad to hear it. I think you really have some industry-busting stuff here, Nalik. You just need to give me the information to prove it." With that, Jak turned on his heel and hurried out of the lab, down the stairs, and across the quad.

The day was relatively clear, but the wind was starting to pick up, lifting the fall leaves in tiny whirls off the pavement and sending them dancing into the air. He had just two minutes to get to Arianna's classroom, so he picked up his pace.

It had been an agonizing four days since she had slammed the door in his face late Saturday night. He'd been over it in his mind again and again, but he just couldn't tell if it was the mating bond that had sent him packing or if she truly didn't want him to free her anymore. He couldn't believe that was true, but he hadn't had a chance to meet with her since. She'd returned to school on Monday, but Mace and his beta, Beck, were doing guard detail now. And Jak was clearly not in the rotation. On top of that, Mace hadn't gone out drinking all week, which was not the norm, and Gage had been keeping Jak busy at work: there had been literally no time when he could go over and yank Arianna out of Mace's house to have a real talk with her.

He would just have to sneak into her life.

Dashing across the red pavers of the plaza, he arrived at Kane Hall just as the other students were starting to trickle in. Jak stepped down his pace and played it cool, hoisting his backpack up on his shoulder and strolling like he was just another eager student arriving early to class. He was afraid Arianna might have been early too, but he'd left plenty of room: fifteen minutes before class ought to be more than Mace would be willing to do. And Jak knew Arianna's schedule: she only had the one class today, just like the first day, when Jak had been her bodyguard. Which was also the day he first realized how much trouble he was in with her.

Amazing that it had only taken a week for her to change his life.

Jak put up his hood and kept his head down while surreptitiously scanning the few students in the hall and then in the classroom. None were her… and more importantly, he'd managed to slip into class before Mace arrived. Jak was counting on Mace staying outside in the hall—if he walked Arianna into the classroom, Jak would have to pull his hood down over his face and pray he could slip past Beck and get the hell out before he was recognized. With any luck, Arianna would come in alone.

Jak hung out at the top row of seats: the classroom was one of those theatre-style ones that could hold hundreds of undergraduates. He would have been ridiculously suspicious in a normal-sized classroom, but lurking with his hoodie and bent over his phone… he was one of a dozen students milling around the classroom, coming and going before they settled down for class.

He pretended to be engrossed in his phone while actually keeping his eye on the door. His heart lurched when he saw her: gorgeous, long brown tresses spread over her fall jacket; tentative smile, brightening more the farther she walked into the classroom; and a backpack banging lightly as she pattered down the steps, scanning for a seat.

She walked right past him.

He didn't breathe again until he was sure Mace wasn't following or watching. Then he trotted down the steps, dropping into the seat next to her just as she sat down. She startled a little, smile going a little uncertain but still bright, until her eyes worked their way up to his: then they flew open wide.

"Shhh," he said very quietly. He still had his hood up, peering at her from underneath it as he dug around in his backpack for a paper pad. "I'm just another student who happened to sit next to you. Nothing special."

She had already turned into a mannequin, stiffly staring at her swing-arm desktop then turning to dig into her own backpack. "What are you doing here?" she asked harshly.

A small pain tore through his chest. Maybe this was a mistake.

Arianna had failed utterly in keeping her voice down. The guy in front of them turned slightly but didn't say anything before apparently deciding it was none of his business. He moved over three seats.

"I had to see you," Jak said quietly. "But if you don't want to see me… anymore…" He was having a hard time getting the words out. His whisper faded at the end, and that feeling in his chest was stabbing him again. He stared at her hands, turning white as she clutched her notebook.

"Jak." It was just one word, but it was his name in a whisper full of emotion.

He lifted his gaze: her eyes were glassy with tears. If she told him to stay away, he could still blame it on Mace and the mating bond—her alpha had to be just outside—but that wouldn't stop it from ripping a hole in his heart.

"All I want is you." Her words were barely audible. A tear slipped from the corner of her eye, and she ducked her face away.

Jak's heart was soaring.

He glanced at the top of the classroom: the door was closed. He turned back to Arianna and reached for her face, lifting her chin with one finger so she would bring those beautiful blue eyes back to him. She blinked more tears, and he gently brushed them away.

Her lips quivered. "But I'll die if you're hurt because of me."

He leaned as close as he dared. "You're not going to die. And neither am I." He pulled back and held up his notepad. "Notes only. Okay?"

She sniffed back the rest of the tears and nodded. If he had to pick one moment as the exact instant when he fell in love with Arianna Stefan, he would have to say that was it: when she had nothing to go on but his word, but she trusted him anyway. All while being amazingly brave in the face of what they both knew was a ridiculously dangerous idea: breaking her free.

All the more dangerous to be plotting it here under Mace's nose. Although Jak's heart was still flying from her words and her trust… now that he had that, nothing would stop him from being the one to set her free.

The instructor had arrived on the stage at the bottom of the room, and all eyes were on him. Jak bent over his notepad and scribbled out his first flush of thoughts. He would have the whole length of the class to write out all the details of his plans for Saturday. But he had other things he had to tell her first.

You're all I think about. Everything I want. I made a promise to you. I'm going to keep it. And soon… Saturday, my love.

He slid the pad to where she could see it, still on the swing-arm desk of his stadium seat, but close enough for his scribblings to be legible.

She read it then bent over her own pad, and a moment later, held out a note for him. *The submission ceremony? The whole pack will be there. Too dangerous.*

He suppressed a grin. *I'll be the last thing they expect,* he wrote.

This time, it took her several scratched out tries before she wrote back. *Too dangerous.*

I'll need your help, he scribbled on the pad. *You'll have to signal me at just the right time.* He dug into his backpack again. The instructor was telling them to get out their textbooks which led to a flurry of iPads being withdrawn from backpacks and covered his shuffling pretty well. He drew out a small phone, the tiniest he could find on the market. It was a burn phone, but it had text capability. That was all she would need.

He passed it to her under the tabletop. When

her fingers brushed his, the warmth of them surged his senses. But her hand was gone an instant later, whisking away the phone before he could do more than wish to hold her hand.

My number is programmed in, he wrote on his pad. *I'll spell it all out for you, step by step. It will work. I promise.*

Maybe we can just run away? she wrote back. The phone had already disappeared into a pocket deep inside her backpack.

He paused to look at her. She kept her eyes glued to the instructor rambling below them, avoiding Jak's corner-of-the-eye stare.

It was tempting. He could just wait until Mace was out screwing someone else in a club in Seattle. Then Jak could simply drag Arianna out of his house until she would come with him willingly. Of course, the magic would still hold. It was strongest when she was near Mace, or in his territory, but no matter where on Earth Arianna went, she would always carry Mace in her blood. And he would never stop searching for her, never stop wanting to reclaim his mate. She and Jak would have to constantly look over their shoulders. One day Mace might catch up to them… and then Arianna's fate would be worse than it was now.

Much worse.

Not to mention that simply running away would mean she could never mate again.

She would never fully belong to him. That thought struck at a nagging fear: what if, once she was free of Mace, she didn't choose to be with him? Once Mace was dead, his magic in her blood would die along with him… and the mating bond would be cleared from her mind. What if, in that clarity of mind, she realized Jak wasn't really worthy of her? He was only a beta. And she was young and beautiful, smart and unmated: she could have her pick of any alpha on the planet. The likes of Mace only got hold of her by force. If she was free, she could choose to be with anyone… and, if she was at all logical, she wouldn't pick a beta like Jak to mate with. To raise a family with. It wasn't just tradition or pack ritual—it was primal. He knew her wolf would be drawn to the strongest alpha around. It was the instinct of their species, the way to ensure the strongest bloodlines. Survival of the fittest.

She could fight the instinct, of course, make a different choice. But would she?

Jak wasn't even sure that she *should.* In any event, she would need the protection of being mated to *someone.* An escaped captive female who was still mated… she would never find another pack who would take her in. Jak would protect her with his life, but she would always be at risk of being hauled back to Mace by some wolf who thought he was doing the right thing.

Or a bounty hunter in it for the cash. Or the parts.

Arianna snuck a look at him: he was taking too long to respond. But that innocent, trusting look in her eyes decided it for him: whether she wanted him or not, he was going to wrench her free of Mace. This wasn't about having Arianna for himself—this was about freeing her to make her own choice. No matter what that choice might be.

He finally wrote on his pad. *I would run away with you in an instant. But as long as Mace lives, you will never have another mate. Or a pack. You deserve better than that. You deserve a wolf who will claim you with his heart as well as his bite.*

He watched her face as she read his words. The tears slowly leaked down again, working a strange magic on him. They loosened a need to touch her that couldn't be denied. He reached under her table, his fingers searching out hers. When he found them, her hands were soft and warm, and there was a tremble in them that he tried to soothe by lacing his fingers with hers and slowly running circles across the back of her hand with his thumb. He didn't think his heart could soar any more, but when she squeezed his hand tight, it practically lifted him out of his chair.

She trusted him. She said she wanted him, at least for now. That was all he needed.

He spent the rest of the hour detailing their plans, step by step, so she would know exactly what to expect on Saturday. They promised each other they would try to find a way to meet before then, but even if they couldn't, everything was set. An entirely new life was crafted with paper and pen on the pads before them. Jak would be sure to destroy all of it before they left, but it was all inscribed on their hearts anyway. All they needed was a little luck, and within two days, Arianna would be free. Then they would leave Seattle for their new lives. Together.

Neither of them spoke for the rest of the hour.

Jak held her hand until the very last moment of class… then reluctantly let her go.

Chapter Fourteen

"You have got to be kidding me!" Mace shouted into the phone.

Arianna flinched in the passenger seat next to him. He veered out of one lane and into a faster one. Their speed crept up, and Mace's face turned red as the phone call progressed. She wasn't sure who was on the other line, but it had to be someone from work.

Mace had been taking all kinds of work calls while acting as her guard this week. She knew he hated watching over her at school, but he was too stubborn to let anyone else do it without him. Or maybe too afraid someone else would make him look bad, on the off chance the bounty hunters came back and managed to capture his mate. It was already Friday, and Arianna was starting to give up hope that he would ever let her go to school without personally guarding her himself… although this morning, he sent Beck to Red Wolf. Apparently, work was piling up on some project, and senior Mr. Crittenden was starting to complain about them falling behind.

"Well, call them back!" Mace shouted again, making a rude hand gesture to a nearby car as he swerved toward the exit to UDub.

Arianna gripped her passenger side door.

"Why the hell would you set up a meeting for this morning?" His voice was turning dangerous, and Arianna's heart was pounding, both from his tone and the high speed they were taking the exit off the freeway. "You *know* I'm busy guarding Arianna. It's on the damn calendar."

They lurched to a stop at the end of the exit ramp. "Shit," Mace said under his breath. He ran a hand over his face then glared at Arianna, which sent her pulse racing even faster. She shrank against the car door. "Okay, fine," he said into the phone, his gaze holding her in a lock she couldn't escape. When her alpha captured her like that with his eyes, she couldn't look away. "No, I'll be there." He clicked off the phone and tossed it into the compartment under the armrest.

Arianna knew better than to say anything.

Mace growled, pounded on his steering wheel once, then rolled the car forward with the change in the light. Silence hung heavy as they wound their way toward the university.

Arianna waited, letting him sort it out.

"I have a meeting I have to go to," he said eventually. It was half growl. "You'll have to miss class today."

Her heart sunk. "We're already almost here. Maybe you could just drop me, and Beck could pick me up later?"

"*Beck*… I swear to God, I am surrounded by incompetent assholes!"

She wasn't quite sure what that meant, but she zipped her lips shut. Mace took the turn-off to head into the university. She struggled to bat down the hope that he might let her attend by herself, maybe catch a taxi back home… she didn't dare suggest that.

"Beck is in the same meeting," Mace grumbled, the anger still simmering hot under his breath. "He was supposed to handle it himself, but that idiot promised the client I would be there."

"I'm sure it would go better with you there," she said carefully.

He grunted but still seemed pissed. "You'll have just run in and get notes or something from the professor."

"It's a really big class." She swallowed. Did she dare even suggest this? "The professor's already said he won't hand out notes. Or let us share. He expects us to attend." Mace growled audibly, so she rushed to add, "Maybe there's someone else who can pick me up? Maybe one of Gage's wolves isn't too busy?" She didn't trust herself to say Jak's name… and besides, that would only be suspicious. She held her breath, clenching her hands in her lap, hoping Mace would be willing to at least try.

He let out a long sigh but pulled into the Red Square parking garage rather than circling back toward the freeway. Once they were parked, he dug out his cell phone again and dialed.

"Yeah, it's me," he said into the phone. "Look, I'm at UDub, but I have a meeting. Do you have someone you can send to watch Arianna?" There was a pause. "Do you think I haven't thought of that already? Beck's tied up, and Alric's off on a site visit. Do you have someone or not?" Another pause, then his voice dipped into sarcasm. "Fuck. That's just perfect." He sighed. "No, I'll take him. But if he fucks up, I'm taking it out of his hide. Personally." Another pause. "Right. We're there now." Then he hung up.

Arianna's chest hurt from holding her breath so long. She tried to let it out calmly and without drawing attention to herself.

"Apparently, Gage and his idiot beta are on campus on some kind of site visit. He's sending Jak over. I'll drop you off at class, and he'll bring you home."

Arianna's heart spasmed, and she could hardly believe she had heard him correctly. "Jak?" Her voice was whispery, and her eyes had gone wide.

Mace snorted. "I know, right? I'd be better off leaving you with Alric, for Christ's sake." He turned to her, and his face softened a little at her expression. "Look, I'm sure the bounty hunters are long gone. Jak's an asshole, but even he can handle this." Mace held open his jacket and showed her a gun he had holstered under his arm—one he'd apparently been carrying all week without her knowledge. Her heart raced at the sight of it, retroactively ramping up her fear for when Jak had snuck into her classroom. And the fact that they were about to go see him again.

"With this," Mace said, "even an idiot like Jak can keep you safe, all right?"

She nodded rapidly and with what she hoped was enthusiasm. As they climbed out of the car, her fears and tremors settled a little. *She was going to see Jak.* Although, once Mace saw her and Jak together in the same room, she was afraid their sins would be written clear as day on their faces. How could Mace miss it? Her heart lurched again.

Due to Mace's speeding, they were actually early for class. By the time they crossed the plaza and entered Kane Hall, there were only a few students trickling into the classroom. Mace lingered, keeping them out in the hallway, apparently waiting for Jak to show up.

When he appeared around the corner, Arianna did everything in her power to keep her eyes down and her face frozen. She was afraid to even look at him: she was just sure she would give them both away. But she couldn't help peeking up as Jak's hard-soled shoes rapped against the tiled floors.

He hurriedly stalked up to them, his face furious. "I have better things to do than take care of your business, Mace," Jak said, his voice low but harsh.

"Apparently not." Mace's smile was gloating.

"But I'll tell you what, *beta*—you screw this up, and Gage won't be able to keep me from tearing you into pieces."

They were attracting some notice from the other students in the hall. Arianna was convinced she would have a heart attack at any moment.

Mace lowered his voice, his smile vanishing. "All you have to do is get her back in one piece." He clapped a hand on Jak's shoulder and dragged him closer. He lifted the gun from his hidden holster and jabbed it into Jak's side, just under his coat jacket.

Jak's face went hard.

Arianna couldn't breathe.

"You fuck this up," Mace said in a menacing whisper, "and I'll be using this on *you.*" Then he turned the gun sideways and pressed it into Jak's chest.

His face inscrutable, Jak took the gun and quickly shoved it into the back of his pants, hidden under the jacket. Arianna sucked in air and flitted glances around them. She didn't think anyone had seen the gun.

"I'm not the fuck-up around here," Jak said coolly.

"Keep telling yourself that, beta." Mace's sneer was back, but he turned his hard gaze on Arianna.

"Call me from the house when you get back. I want to know whether Jak needs an ass-kicking or not."

Arianna nodded, not trusting her voice to speak. Jak glared at Mace's back all the way down the hall until he disappeared around the corner. Arianna didn't dare move for several more seconds. Finally, Jak turned to her, a grin wide on his face.

"You. Are. Amazing," he said, drawing out the words as he stepped close. Then he dropped his voice to a whisper. "How did you manage to arrange this?"

With Mace gone and Jak smiling, Arianna could finally breathe again. "I had almost nothing to do with it. What are you doing on campus?"

"Doesn't matter." Jak's grin just grew. "The question is, what are *we* going to do with an hour on campus alone?"

"Jak." She felt the heat rush to her face. "I have *class.*"

He scoffed. "As much fun as it was to sit next to you in class, I have something a little different in mind." Then he grinned wickedly, and with one last look down the hall where Mace had just left, Jak grabbed her hand and towed her in the opposite direction.

They quickly left Kane Hall and dashed a short

ways to a majestic building with Gothic architecture. Its tall stone columns loomed over them, and the arched entranceways were topped with terracotta figures that looked very scholarly.

"The Suzallo Library was one of my favorite places to hang out," Jak said breathlessly as he towed her up the stone steps and inside the building. Stone staircases swept off to the side, and a reading room that looked like the inside of a medieval church filled most of the building, but Jak hurried past those to a help desk in the center.

Jak rained a sexy smile down on the short, rail-thin girl manning the desk. "Hi! My name's Jak. I was hoping you might help me with something." She had to be one of the students, and Arianna could tell she was dazzled by Jak's trim suit, tailored to fit perfectly over his well-muscled shifter body, not to mention that gorgeous smile he was favoring her with. Arianna felt a small pang of jealousy, but more than that, she felt sorry for the girl. Whatever Jak wanted, she was sure the girl would happily give it up… but she'd never get what she hoped for in return.

"I, um, sure… what can I help you with?" The girl's eyes grew wider as Jak placed a hand on her desk and leaned forward. Shifter pheromones worked best up close—and Arianna knew human females were even more susceptible to them than wolves. The girl had no chance.

"You see, I used to love going down in the stacks," Jak said in a sexy half-growl. "All those old books, you know, the smell they have? It was like being absorbed into all the stories, all the great characters…"

The girl was nodding. Arianna rolled her eyes.

"But I hear they closed them down," he said. "Restricted access only now."

"Yeah, it's really sad," the girl said, leaning forward, entranced. "Only the staff are allowed down there these days."

"That's a terrible shame." Jak bit his lip.

Arianna swore the girl was about to drool on her papers.

The librarian dropped her voice. "Sometimes I go down there and just pull a book at random and read."

"I know, right?" Jak said. "I mean, everything's a treasure. You never know what you can find." He sighed. "I mean, I get it, you want to keep out the people who don't understand. The ones who don't *get it.* But the people like us, who really appreciate what's down there…"

The girl was eating this up. Then she glanced at Arianna. She tried to put on her brightest smile but kept quiet, letting Jak work his magic.

"Look, I know this is asking a lot, but..." Jak glanced at Arianna and gave her a soft smile. Arianna *knew* it was all an act, and she *still* melted inside. Then he leaned forward to whisper in the librarian's ear. Arianna couldn't hear what he said, but the girl's eyes went wide, and a small smile crept onto her lips. She flicked a look or two at Arianna, but mostly she bit her lip and grinned.

When Jak finally pulled back, the librarian smiled wide. "I don't think it would hurt anything."

"You're the best," he gushed.

Arianna had no idea what he had just told her, but two seconds later, the girl was fishing out her keys from her desk and beckoning them toward a special-purpose elevator. She keyed them in, and it was quickly apparent that they were heading down to the Restricted Access Only stacks.

It was all Arianna could do to keep her grin in check.

The girl stayed in the elevator when they stepped off. "Take your time. You don't need a key to come back up, just punch the call button."

Jak grinned and squeezed the girl's hand lightly. "Thanks again. I really appreciate this."

She smiled, and the elevator door closed, leaving Jak and Arianna in a giant room with dozens and dozens of shelves lined with books. Everything was a hundred years old by the musty smell, and the stacks stretched what looked like the length of the building. There wasn't another soul in sight or signs of anyone down here with them.

"What did you *say* to her?" Arianna asked, her grin finally let loose.

Instead of answering, Jak swept her into his arms and kissed her thoroughly. She felt as dazed and light-headed as the librarian must have been by the time he stopped.

"I told her I wanted to propose to you, and I needed a very special place in which to do it." His grin was wide. "Wouldn't have worked at all, but she's new."

Arianna laughed as Jak towed her away from the elevator. "So you're saying you've proposed to other girls before, down here in the stacks?"

"Oh… only a few," he said, still grinning. "Less than ten, for sure."

"You are awful!" She swatted him on the shoulder. He was still dragging her past shelf after shelf, searching for something. Then he seemed to find it and veered down one row. At the end was a heavy wood-carved table with two chairs, clearly set up for the scholars and their work in a previous era. He clasped her hand and brought her to the table, twirling her around and backing her up against it. He kissed her again, and she could feel his cock growing hard as he held her against him.

Then he pulled back from the kiss and just held her in his arms. "However… I've never been here with someone I actually intended to spend the rest of my life with."

Her breath caught, and she stared up into his dark, shining eyes. "You do?"

He brushed her hair back and lightly kissed her face, starting with her cheeks, then her nose, then finally, her eyelids. At last, he swept a feather kiss against her lips. "I know it's fast," he whispered. "I know it's crazy. But I want to spend the rest of my days giving you everything you deserve, Arianna. If you'll let me."

Her heart felt like it might burst with his words. "I already told you," she whispered. "You're everything I want."

Suddenly, all the gentleness was gone from his touch. Jak's hands roamed her body, his fingers tugging at her clothes, his commanding touch igniting a fire between her legs. Her backpack and jacket were gone first, discarded to the floor, but her shirt went next. She grabbed at his, trying to get to his bare skin, but she wasn't fast enough. He shucked them off quickly and set Mace's gun down on the table. Then he came back to her, his mouth nipping at her neck as his hands worked her bra free. He groaned as her breasts met the bare skin of his chest. Then his hands attacked the buttons on her pants, working them down. He hoisted her up on the table, pressing his cock, still straining against the fabric of his pants, against the ache between her legs. Her wolf whimpered for him to go faster, to take her *now*.

"God, I need you, Arianna," he said hoarsely. "Now and again and again. Forever."

"Take me," was all she could manage to get out before his mouth found her breasts and his hand slipped between her legs. Her words became moans and then gasps as he pulsed pleasure through her body like only he knew how to do. She grasped at his pants, trying to clear the last of his clothing, and when his cock finally sprung free, she wanted nothing more than to take it into her mouth and pleasure him the way he was pleasuring her. But he wouldn't allow it.

He held her tight to the edge of the table and thrust into her, gasping as he did so. The table cried out in protest just as she cried out in pleasure. The fullness of him, the hot shocks of heat that raced through her with every pound against the table… it quickly crashed an orgasm through her. She clawed at his back, arching hers in pleasure and gasping her way through it. As it peaked, she kept calling his name, and he kept murmuring *my love, my love, you're mine,* over and over. It was such sweet music to her ears, filling her with such lightness, she scarcely could breathe. He kept going, building to his own climax, and his touch on her, stroking her with his fingers while filling her with his cock, was quickly building another orgasm inside her, tight and low and hot.

She cried his name again as she came, and his groans matched hers. Then he slowed, but didn't stop, the steady beat, working her body with his. When she could breathe again, she held onto him tight and whispered, "What you do to me, Jak…"

He pulled back to look into her eyes but still slowly stroked into her body. "And what do I do to you, Ms. Stefan?"

She was still breathless—with pleasure, with the look of love in his eyes. "Everything."

"Not everything." He grinned. "Not yet. I still have an hour."

She laughed, lightly, but that was soon lost in the joining of their bodies, hot and hard and secret among the dusty tomes of forgotten books.

Jak was everything to her: freedom, pleasure, hope.

Soon, all of it would be hers forever.

Chapter Fifteen

SATURDAY NIGHT. THE CEREMONY. TIME TO KILL Mace.

Only… not quite yet.

Normally, Gage and Mace would have their submission ceremonies in different parts of the Olympic mountains. There was no love lost between the brothers, no reason to have a family ceremony. But this time, they were staying at the estate, which meant carving out different sections of the sprawling landscape in order to still have a sense of separation. Gage's pack would meet at the south end of the main house, Mace on the north, in the clearing near his house. Jak had gotten all the details of how Mace normally ran the ceremony from Arianna, and he wasn't surprised to find it different from the way Gage ran things.

Jak's alpha always used the submission ceremony as a time to draw the pack together. Even Gage's two mates were brought into it, with everyone submitting to their alpha under the full moon at the same time. Then, the pack usually ran, including the females, in some sort of game, bonding them further together. Later, after the festivities, Jak was sure Gage went home to claim each of his mates… maybe in turn, maybe together. That part was none of the pack's business, and Gage never made it so. It was private.

Apparently, Mace's goal was to humiliate everyone.

According to Arianna, Mace fought each of the three members of his pack—Beck, Alric, and Thomas—individually in a sparring match. They started human then shifted, wrestling, biting, drawing blood… eventually, when Mace had pummeled them sufficiently and had their throats in his mouth, they would submit. He would take each of their submissions in turn. When all the fighting was done, and Mace had a hard-on the size of Manhattan at how much of an alpha he was, then he would take Arianna. The rest of the pack would wait… and watch… while she submitted.

Jak needed to know the exact order of events, but it had taken him several tries to get out of her what precisely happened. And Jak could see why. Mace, bastard that he was, didn't fight Arianna… he just forced her to have sex in front of the rest of the pack. She said he did it while in wolf form, once she had submitted, but still… just because she was covered in fur didn't mean the pack didn't get off on the show.

It made Jak want to retch. And eased any guilt he had about putting a bullet in Mace tonight. Jak had one of the pack's guns holstered under his arm, loaded and ready. It felt heavy and hot, warmed by his body and the tension of carrying it. But the timing would have to be just right to pull this off: Jak needed to catch Mace in wolf form. If he died that way, it would be a lot easier for Jak and Arianna to make their escape—they didn't need to have a murder charge trailing after them. In case Mace was carrying a weapon, being in wolf form would mean Jak would have crucial seconds to make their getaway before Mace could to get to it.

Plus killing Mace at all required Jak to be free of his own submission bond to Gage. Jak could feel the effects waning already, as the night wore. Jak needed to push it as far as he could, get as free of his commitment to Gage as possible before pulling the trigger. Just in case any of a dozen things went wrong.

Timing would be everything.

Jak paced the floor of his room, his phone in his hand, waiting for Arianna's signal. The wolves of Gage's pack were starting to scuffle out in the hall, gathering to head over to the far side of the estate… farther away than Jak wanted to be when Arianna's text came in. Plus, he would need an excuse to leave, and that would be tough when in the middle of his own submission ceremony. Which he couldn't, under any circumstances, actually complete. The last thing he wanted was to fight his own alpha… which wouldn't even be possible if he submitted. Jak had to stall as long as he could.

A rapid knock sounded at his door.

Jak lifted the phone to his ear as if he was talking to someone. He covered the microphone and shouted at the door, "Be there in a minute!"

The doorknob turned, and Gage stuck his head in. Every muscle in Jak's body tensed.

"Hang on," Jak said to his imaginary phone caller. "What's up?" he asked Gage.

"What's up?" His alpha gave him an exasperated look. "Did you forget we're having a ceremony tonight, Jak?"

"No, I just..." He held the phone out. "I've got these jokers from Silver Quick on the line. They're giving me some bullshit about the numbers being different than what they were showing us yesterday."

"On a Saturday night?" Gage asked, skeptically.

"They had some grad student working late, and he found something... I'll be off soon, I promise." The gun under Jak's arm felt like a heavy indictment of the betrayal he was about to commit. Was *already* committing...

Gage frowned. "All right. But we're ready to go. The guys are going out afterward, and I'm sure they're anxious to get to the party phase of tonight's activities."

"Yeah, okay." Jak nodded then pretended to talk into the phone again. "Hey, I'm back." He waved to Gage. "Okay, fine, but tell me how that changes anything..."

Gage shook his head and retreated from the room.

As soon as he was gone, Jak drifted over to the window, still holding the phone to his ear, in case someone else decided to pop in on him. The moon lit up the entire estate, turning the grass into a silver-frosted carpet and the trees into dark sentinels protecting the perimeter. Mace's house still had its lights on, but that might not mean anything. He was only going out into the meadow in back to do the ceremony. Jak ground his teeth as he realized Mace had every intention of forcing Arianna to have sex with him in front of his pack in the middle of the estate.

Not tonight, asshole.

The rustling sounds from the hallway settled, and the distant thumping of boots on the stairs said most of the pack was heading outside. His time was growing short. A couple more minutes, and Gage would be back in Jak's room, insisting he call the university nerds back later. Jak really needed a backup excuse for delaying further. Maybe he should take this moment, when everyone was heading out, to slip outside on his own and just lurk around Mace's house until he got the signal from Arianna that Mace had shifted. The problem was, Jak didn't know who was still straggling behind in the house like him.

Or if Gage was waiting just outside his door.

Just as Jak was about to pace the room again,

and try to come up with a backup excuse for delaying, a movement over at Mace's house caught his eye. Shadows moved across the blind-covered windows, and a breath-stopping ten seconds later, he saw long shadows cast by the moonlight of something moving at the rear of the house. Jak glimpsed five figures just briefly before they moved deeper into the meadow where he couldn't see them. But that had to be Mace, his three pack members, and Arianna.

Come on, come on, come on.

Jak pulled the phone from his ear and looked at the face of it, willing Arianna's text to come. Just at that moment, Mason stuck his head in Jak's door, jolting surprise through him.

"Hey, are you done?" Mason asked. "Gage is getting pissed."

Jak shook his head and quickly put the phone back to his ear. *He needed more time.* "What do you mean, the basement's flooded?" he said harshly into the phone. He held up a finger to Mason, indicating he needed another minute.

Mason just crossed his arms and leaned against the doorframe.

Shit.

"Well, yeah, but I don't see why that would shut

down your hoods," Jak said into the phone. He shrugged to Mason and held up his hands like he was helplessly stuck on the phone then waved off Mason like he should leave.

Mason just shook his head and stayed put.

Meanwhile, Arianna could be texting him any second.

Dammit. Jak covered the microphone and whispered to Mason, "Dude, I'll be there. Just start without me."

"No can do," Mason said, not moving an inch. "Gage says not to come back without you."

Jak stalked across the room, still holding his hand over the phone. "Look, just give me two seconds, all right?" He uncovered the phone. "Yes, I'm still here," he said into it. "I've got to go, so can we—yes, I know that's a problem." Jak took his free hand and shoved Mason out the door. He closed it in Mason's face before he could get a foot back in. Jak leaned against the door to hold it closed. He sighed in relief. At least Mason would be out of the room when Arianna's message came in, but now Jak was stuck in a major way.

He glanced at the phone. *Still nothing.*

Jak would have to take Mason out somehow. Once the message came in, everything went into play. Jak had to be ready to move. The last thing he wanted was to have to shoot Mason, not least because it would be *too soon* for shots to be fired and send everyone into red alert. And because he actually liked Mason. His stomach knotted up even more than the ball of extreme tension it was already. Jak would have to knock Mason out or come up with some excuse—

His phone pinged.

Morgan Media.

What the hell?

Ice ran through his veins. Why were the witches calling him?

He swallowed and answered. "Hello?"

"Well, *hello.* Damn, you even sound sexy on the phone." It was Circe, Hecca's sister. The witch who he had hoped would break Arianna free of her mating bond, only to find the spell would break *him* instead.

"Look, I'm a little busy right now—"

"I'm sure you are, lover," she purred. "Full moon and all. Isn't that when you boys get together and tuck your tails between your legs—"

He gritted his teeth. "What do you *want?*"

"The question is what do *you* want, hot stuff? I've been waiting for your call. You left me hanging, and that's something you promised you wouldn't do."

"I didn't promise you shit," he said, but his heart was hammering. He had left the coven without making it absolutely clear he wasn't interested in Circe's offer of exchanging her dark art spell—which would free Arianna but kill him—for a round of wolf-on-witch sexploits.

"Well, you did brag quite a bit about your prowess, Jak dear," Circe chastised. "You got me all hot and bothered. I was hoping you would take me up on my offer."

Mason banged on the door, making Jak's heart lurch.

"This really isn't a good time," Jak said, quiet but harsh into the phone. "And I'm not interested in your offer. I've made other arrangements."

Her voice turned from smolder to ice in an instant. "Have you, now? Well, then, I'm glad I called. Because, darling, you see, you really don't have a choice. Not if you want to keep secret this little yearning you have for an *already-mated* wolfy playmate."

"What?" Jak pushed away from the door, locking it so Mason couldn't barge in. He stalked to the window and peered out, looking for Mace and his

pack. He couldn't see anything. "What exactly are you threatening me with?"

"It's not a threat, Jak darling, it's an opportunity." Her voice was back to purring. "You have something I want—namely your smoking hot body in my bed. And I have something you want—a little tidbit of information about that female you're so hot for. I propose a trade."

"Wait, what?" A chill ran through him. "What do you know about Arianna?"

"Oh, just the names of the people who sent those bounty hunters after her."

Jak's chest grew tight. He wanted to know who was after Arianna, but at this point, it was more important to get her free of Mace. And his plan to do that was seriously in jeopardy the longer he was on the phone with this witch. He was tempted to hang up.

"We can discuss that later."

"I'm sorry, darling, later doesn't work for me," she said, her voice cool again. "In fact, maybe I'll call that alpha of yours right now and let him know what his beta has been up to in his spare time."

"No!" Jak's breaths were starting to heave out of his chest. He rubbed a hand across his face. "Just… give me a little time."

"I have a taste for wolf tonight, Jak." Her voice dropped dangerously low. "And you don't want to leave me hungry."

He swallowed. "All right. I'll meet you in an hour."

"That's what I like to hear." Her voice was back to the sex-drenched tone from before.

It churned his stomach, but in an hour, he planned to be in his car, heading for the state line with Arianna by his side. The witch could go to hell, then. He just couldn't have her screwing things up for him *right now.* But if he left her high and dry, he had better make sure they were leaving the area in a serious hurry. And any information he wanted from her, he had better get it now.

"Now tell me what you know about the hunters," he said.

"In an hour, lover," she teased. "If you're good."

"Now."

Mason banged on his door and rattled the knob. A cold sweat was breaking out on the back of Jak's neck.

"You don't want me coming to bed angry, do you?" he said into the phone. "Besides, you'll still have my little secret to hold over me to make sure I show up."

She paused. "Well, all right. No harm in it, I suppose. But you're not going to like it, lover."

"Circe…" he warned.

"It's the girl's family," she said. "They want her back."

Chapter Sixteen

THE PHONE WAS HEAVY IN JAK'S HAND, THE WITCH'S words ringing in his head.

It's the girl's family. They want her back.

He let the phone fall to his side. A tightness seized his chest. Circe's voice was squawking from the dangling phone, but his mind was racing ahead. He hung up on the witch and ran a hand across his face.

Arianna's family was behind the bounty hunters. They weren't trying to harm her: *they were trying to rescue her.* And Jak had foiled their attempt. Jak's family had always been a cruel freak show, but he couldn't imagine Arianna's family was anything like that. She was too sweet and brave and kind to have come from that kind of hot-mess family situation. Besides, they wouldn't risk working with bounty hunters to rescue her if they didn't love her.

They want her back.

This completely foiled his plans to take Arianna and head for the state line.

He scoured his memory for anything he knew about her family. They were a small pack from rural Washington. She had a mother and brothers. Mace had captured her while they were visiting the Olympic mountains: packs often ran into each other there, for better and worse. Usually worse. The only reason Mace managed to take her was because her pack was so small. They couldn't fight the combined Red packs. Even if her family managed to rescue her now, they would have to flee the area... or Mace would hunt them down, reclaim her, and probably kill them all.

What were they thinking, coming back for her?

A pounding on the door startled Jak out of his shock. Mason was on the other side, impatient for him to join Gage's submission ceremony. Jak shoved his phone in his pocket. He couldn't wait any longer for Arianna's signal that Mace had shifted and the ceremony had begun. He had to move *now.* After he had broken her free of Mace's hold, then they could talk about what to do next. If she wanted to return to her family, Jak would make sure she was still protected, but he wouldn't stand in her way.

He had already decided that freeing her was more important than keeping her.

Jak strode to his bedroom door, wrenched it open, then punched a very surprised Mason in the face. He went down, cursing and sprawling on the carpet. Jak didn't waste time trying to make sure he stayed down… he just needed Mason out of the way. Jak's attire—jeans, fall jacket, sneakers—was designed for their escape tonight, and he made almost no noise as he sprinted down the hall.

He took the steps two at a time, down to the main floor, then raced out the back door of the main house. If Mason was chasing after him, Jak would have heard something. But he didn't slow down or look back as he raced toward Mace's house.

The moonlight had turned everything a whitish gray, stealing the color of the night. Jak's breath rushed in his ears as he sprinted across the expanse of lawn, past the winding road of the estate, then down the long side of Mace's suburban-looking home. He stopped when he reached the back corner, peering around to see if Mace's pack was in the clearing.

They were. Unfortunately, there was a good hundred feet of empty lawn between the house and the pack, which meant Jak would have no cover whatsoever. No element of surprise.

And he could see now why Arianna had never texted him.

Mace and his pack—Beck, Alric, and Thomas—had formed a circle with Arianna in the middle. The men were all naked, having already shifted at least once, but Arianna was in wolf form, already in the submission pose with her tail tucked low, legs stretched forward, and head bent. Her clothes lay in a heap at the edge of a circle. Beck and Alric were tossing something small and silver back and forth between them. It glinted in the moonlight as it arced through the air: *Arianna's phone.*

She had been caught with it.

Alric caught the phone, then held onto it, examining it. A moment later, Jak's phone pinged. He shoved his hand in his pocket and turned off the ringer before it could give him away. Meanwhile, Mace had strutted to where Arianna crouched in the grass. He stroked himself as he loomed over Arianna, obviously getting off on the whole sick ceremony. Jak gritted his teeth and drew his gun out of his holster. He gauged the distance, but there was no way he could sprint across the lawn and get close enough to shoot Mace before they all saw him.

Shit.

Jak holstered the gun, his strained breath steaming the cool night air. He started to calmly walk toward the group. If he could just get close before they realized what he was up to—

Suddenly, Mace shifted and started rubbing his snout against the side of Arianna's face. Then he clamped his jaws on the back of Arianna's neck, forcing her submission deeper, and even from the fifty feet or so away, Jak could hear her wolf whine. Jak's own wolf was snarling and stomping to be released.

He lurched into a run, one hand on his gun underneath his jacket. If he could just get close enough to shoot Mace while he was in wolf form… Beck noticed Jak first, barreling toward their pack. He snarled, and then Alric turned as well. Meanwhile, Mace was working his way behind Arianna, moving into the claiming position. He clearly meant to take her any second now, in the middle of the lawn, with Thomas smirking and watching.

There was no way in hell Jak was letting that happen.

He pulled his gun. "Get away from her, Mace!" He held it in front of him with both hands while still running toward the pack. Mace whipped his head toward Jak. For a split second, long enough for Jak to get a few feet closer, Mace did nothing. Then he roared and leaped away from Arianna, toward Jak. Which was exactly what he wanted. Alric and Beck had already shifted and were charging toward him, closing fast. Jak waited a heartbeat longer, just long enough for a clean shot at Mace without endangering Arianna.

He squeezed the trigger just as Mace's betas reached him.

Jak shifted, twisting away from their snapping fangs and leaving a mouthful of jacket in his wake. While Alric and Beck tangled with his clothes, Jak charged toward Mace, who was snout down in the grass. Jak's bullet must have found its target. His heart surged with hope, but before he could reach Mace to make sure, Thomas, the third beta, finally clued in and intercepted him. Thomas lunged in front of Mace, protecting his alpha and going for Jak's throat.

They went down together, rolling across the

lawn, snapping and clawing and drawing slashes of blood. Jak yelped as Thomas's teeth sunk into his side, but then he rolled hard and flung Thomas free. Jak scrambled up, veering to avoid Beck and Alric who were after him again, and lunged towards Mace. He was still down, but he was moving.

And then he shifted to human form.

Goddammit.

Jak leaped over Mace's body. The moonlight and smears of blood made it difficult to see where the bullet had gone in, but apparently, Jak had only clipped his shoulder. And given Mace's enhanced shifter healing, without a clean shot to the head or through the heart, he would live. Jak wrenched his gaze from Mace's cringing form and loped to Arianna's side, just to make sure she was okay. She was still cowering in her wolf form in the submission pose.

Arianna! he sent a thought to her even as he dashed to the side, evading the betas chasing him. *You need to shift!*

Now that Mace was back in human form, she should be able to. And he needed her in human form to escape—otherwise, the mating bond would be too strong. With his first shot only wounding Mace, running was now their only option.

Arianna whimpered, but she managed to shift. Jak couldn't circle back to her—he was too busy zigging and zagging through the open space, trying not to get trapped by Mace's betas. He circled back toward his clothes, praying he could get hold of the gun, but Thomas was already there, in human form, rifling through Jak's clothes. Jak galloped toward him, but Alric and Beck caught him from behind. He roared and snapped at them, but they sunk their teeth deep into his legs and dragged him down. Pain streaked white-hot through his body. He was kicking and biting, but they had two sets of flashing razor-sharp teeth, slicing through his flesh. Just like a hundred times before, when his older brothers had pinned him, Mace's betas were ripping him to pieces until the agony overtook him, and he had stopped fighting. But Jak wasn't giving up, not this time, not until he was dead. He raked a claw across Beck's eyes and tore a piece out of Alric's ear. Their yelps of pain and anger were enough for Jak to break free of their grips and scramble to his paws.

Just as he lurched forward, a gun went off… and something slammed into him with enough force to fling him back against Alric's flea-bitten hide. The searing pain hit a half second later, blossoming across his shoulder and sending him rolling to the side. The world went white for a moment. He blinked through it, bringing the night back in focus just in time to see Arianna in wolf form, leaping through the air and snapping her jaws on Thomas's arm. The gun went off again, which made Jak's heart spasm. He struggled to get to his paws, but one whole side was useless and screaming with pain. Beck and Alric were at his back, but he couldn't fight them this way. He shifted human, praying Arianna was all right as he struggled to his feet.

She was still wrestling with Thomas, on the ground, she in her wolf form and him in his human one. But a moment later, she shifted human. And when she came up, standing over Thomas in all her naked beauty… she had the gun pointed in his face. He just looked up at her, confused.

Jak almost laughed. It was the most gorgeous thing he had ever seen.

Alric and Beck had shifted human behind him, but they just stood there with dumbass looks on their faces. Arianna stepped away from Thomas then swung the gun to Alric and Beck.

"Stay back!" she yelled. "Don't touch him!" She meant Jak, which flushed him with joy… until he realized how much her hand with the gun was shaking. The smile fell off Jak's face, and he lurched to her side, leaving Alric and Beck still staring and Thomas struggling to get up off the lawn.

Jak's body was screaming in pain—his shoulder and legs were a bloody mess—and a wave of dizziness almost made him lose his footing, but when he reached her, he took the gun from her trembling hands. He only had one good hand left. His other one dangled uselessly at his side. Flashes of numbness ran up and down it, and he could feel the blood gushing out of his body. His breath was becoming labored, and he shuddered violently in the cold night air. He was fairly certain he was going into shock.

Not good.

His hand shook even more than Arianna's, but at least he stood between her and Mace's betas now. And he had a chance of getting her out of there.

"Move!" Jak ordered Thomas away from the heap that was Jak's clothes.

Thomas shuffled toward Alric and Beck, hands up.

More gently, almost in a whisper, Jak said to Arianna, "I need my phone. Right pocket."

Arianna bent down and rifled through them. Mace was still moaning and holding his side, but he had managed to get to his knees. He must be hit badly because he wasn't saying anything. But when Arianna stood up with the prize of Jak's phone, Mace's face came back to life.

"What are you *doing?*" he screamed at his betas, who were all clustered together with Jak's gun trained on them. "Get him!"

Jak swung his gun to point at Mace. "Move a muscle, and I'll shoot your alpha." The three betas snarled and clenched their fists, but he knew with their submissions fresh, they wouldn't do anything to endanger Mace. They would sacrifice themselves in a heartbeat, but at this range, there was no way they could reach him before he could pull the trigger. And Jak wouldn't miss a second time.

Arianna huddled at his side. He was sorely tempted to simply kill Mace, but as things stood, keeping him alive was their only way out. If Mace died, his betas would make sure Jak was close behind. And Arianna would be on her own again: which meant one of the betas would claim her, and that was almost worse than Mace. Besides, Mace was in human form now. If Jak shot him, they would have more than a pack after them, they'd have all of Washington's law enforcement agencies.

Arianna wouldn't be able to make a new life, not that way. And neither would he.

Jak slowly backed away from Mace and his betas, edging toward the forest. He didn't dare turn his back on them, just kept moving and holding them at bay while he and Arianna made their slow escape.

"Jak!" The word ripped through the air, carried on a command from his alpha. It stopped Jak in his tracks.

He kept his gun trained on Mace, but he couldn't help searching for the source of the voice. Gage stood twenty feet away, Mason by his side, both of them looking aghast at the scene in front of them.

"What the hell are you doing?" Gage's rebuke was harsh. Jak felt it through to his bones, but it didn't have the power to hold him. He glanced up at the moon. It was close enough to full. His submission bond to Gage wouldn't stop him from leaving. He started his slow backward march again, Arianna at his back as they crept toward the forest. Even if the bond wouldn't stop him, the pain of walking away from Gage was worse than the physical agony ripping through his body.

"I have to do this," Jak said to Gage, his voice

rough but strong. "I can't let him hurt her anymore." It felt good to say the words out loud. It was the truth of why he was here, why he was taking her, and why the rest of it—the shooting, the betrayal, the breaking of pack law—didn't matter. Because Mace had violated everything that made pack law decent and right. He had steeped darkness into the mating bond, the one that should be sacred above all.

Jak's words carried across the cool night air, met only with silence.

He prayed Gage would figure it out and see that Jak was doing the right thing. But if he didn't, that also didn't matter. All that mattered was righting the wrongs done to Arianna. And setting her free.

Gage's brow scowled deeper, and Jak figured he was putting together what had actually happened here; what had been happening all along. Between the six of them—Mace, his three betas, Gage and Mason—they could stop him. They might not be able to stop him from shooting Mace, but they could keep him from leaving with Arianna.

But Gage just stood and watched as Jak drew farther and farther away.

Mace growled when he realized his brother wasn't going to help. He lurched to his feet. "Arianna, come here!" It was a full command. Jak could feel the strength of it, even though Mace wasn't his alpha.

Arianna whimpered behind him and clutched his shoulder. Her claws came out and dug into his flesh. It hurt, but nothing like he imagined the fight she was waging inside, disobeying her alpha so she could leave.

"Stay human, baby," Jak whispered. "Stay with me." If she shifted, he would lose her. The bond would be simply too great to overcome.

He groaned as her claws dug deeper into him, but the rest of her stayed human. And they kept marching, slowly backward. They were far enough now that they might have a decent chance at escaping just by flat-out running. But their chances would be better if they reached the forest first.

Seconds ticked with each step closer to freedom.

Jak had to look away from Gage's broken expression.

Mace snarled but didn't move. His betas did likewise. Mace must know by now that, if he tried to stop Jak, he wouldn't hesitate to finish the job.

If Mace let them go, he would live.

Mace glared hatred across the growing expanse between them. Jak knew this wasn't over. Mace would search the ends of the earth for Arianna and kill Jak, if at all possible. Jak would just have to make sure he never got that chance. He and Arianna kept inching backward until they reached the forest.

Then they turned and fled into the darkness.

Chapter Seventeen

Arianna felt like her mind was ripping in two.

Her mate, her *alpha*, was furious. *Furious.* As she backed away from Mace, fleeing with Jak, Mace's hatred reached across the night air and choked her. Part of her knew this was wrong—this vile, deadly hatred shouldn't come from her own alpha, the man who was supposed to love and protect her—but her wolf whimpered to return to him, all the same.

It took every ounce of *human* inside her to withdraw her claws from Jak's shoulder and still remain by his side. And seeing his injuries, his blood-covered body, made her tremble even more. She hated that she had added even a tiny scratch to his pain… because Jak was her *savior.* He may be a beta to the world, but in her eyes, he was all alpha. The good kind. The kind who, before her eyes, was giving up everything, risking everything, including his own life, to free her. Even with the turmoil in her mind, her love for him glowed like the sun.

Her inner torment lessened with more distance from Mace. And once they turned into the darkness of the forest, it eased considerably. She and Jak were running now, Jak leading her but keeping close by her side. He still held the gun so he couldn't hold her hand. His other one was slick with blood and hung at his side in a way that made her stomach clench. His chest and legs were also drenched with the dark red stain—she was amazed he could still walk, much less hurtle through the forest as they were now, with all the blood he had already lost.

"It's going to be okay, baby," he kept saying over and over. "It's going to be all right."

She kept a hand on his shoulder, claws retracted, so she could gently squeeze it in response. Her throat was too thick for words, and her breath too ragged. It seemed to take forever, but eventually, they reached the fence. She handed Jak's phone over to him. Everything had gone wrong with their plan up until now: she half expected Jak's program to deactivate the security system with a special app on his phone to fail utterly. For them to be trapped. Breath heaved out of her as she waited, but with a few swipes on his phone, the hum of the electrified fence ceased.

"Can you climb it?" Arianna asked as he handed the phone back to her. She couldn't imagine how he could in this state.

"Not much choice, have I?" He gave her a lopsided grin, half filled with pain.

It wrenched her heart.

"You first," he said.

She almost insisted that she help him up, but she knew he would fight her on that, and that would only slow things down. They needed to get off the estate before Mace changed his mind and came after them with guns. Arianna clamped the phone in her mouth and quickly scaled the chain link fence, dropping down the other side. Her heart thudded as Jak tried to do the same, only one-handed, with a gun held in his mouth and a body slick with blood.

He groaned several times, each one piercing her heart. When he reached the top, she didn't know if he would make it. He handed the gun down to her and stayed there for a heart-stoppingly long moment before rolling off his perch. She couldn't help crying out when he hit the ground. She rushed to him, hands out to do something, anything, to make sure he was okay.

He groaned again, longer and deeper. "Let's not do that again." His voice was wheezy.

She let out a short, shaky laugh through the tears threatening to spill and helped him to his feet. But he was considerably less steady now. He paused to swipe at his phone, and the electric hum of the fence started up again. Jak had thought of everything, including closing off their escape route, in case Mace came after them.

She shuddered. She knew that would happen eventually.

The tromp through the rest of the forest was considerably slower now. She carried the gun, and Jak draped his arm over her shoulder, but she could tell he was barely making it.

When they broke free of the trees, Jak's car was waiting for them. Arianna sighed in relief. They were going to make it. They were actually going to get free.

As they lumbered toward the car, Jak said, "Baby, I think you need to drive."

"Really?" she said, trying to keep her voice

light. "I thought you might take me for a tour of the nightclubs in Seattle."

He chuckled, but it just ended in a cough. She helped him into the passenger seat and hurried around to the driver's side. Once she was inside, she tucked the gun under the seat.

"You need a healer," she said, reaching to the back seat and pulling up the stash of clothes Jak had put there. She didn't bother with pants, just threw on a t-shirt so they wouldn't get pulled over for indecent driving.

"I know one downtown." Jak wheezed, and she hated the sound of it. "The address is on my phone, under Richter. Just plug it into the GPS." Then he seemed to melt into the car seat with exhaustion, eyes drifting closed.

Arianna scrambled to do as he said, then started the car and put distance between her and the Red pack estate. It almost seemed like a dream, like they were heading off to UDub for class, not running away, never to return. After a few blocks, she pulled over. Jak was shivering, and the car wasn't warming up fast enough. She brought more clothes up from the back and struggled to get a t-shirt over his head. He resisted, but without much force, not even opening his eyes. He just mumbled some protests then lolled his head to the side and let her work. She got the t-shirt on, but just draped his jacket over the rest of his body, hoping it would keep him warm.

She threw the car into drive and barreled toward downtown. It was killing her not to speed the entire way, but they couldn't afford to get stopped. She hoped the GPS wasn't leading her astray—this part of downtown was run-down and shady-looking. Probably filled with city shifters in low-life gangs. That was one reason her family stayed to themselves, just a small pack out in the country. The biggest "city experience" she'd had so far was attending UDub. But Jak needed a healer, and this was where the healer lived. She would just have to act like she had a clue about what she was doing and get through it.

The address of Jak's healer was an apartment in a decrepit tenement, number 3B.

She parked and struggled into the rest of her clothes before going around to the passenger side. Jak had fallen asleep on the ride over, but she wasn't alarmed until she couldn't wake him back up. Kneeling on the edge of the passenger seat, she tried to gently shake him, calling his name… nothing worked. Tears blurred her eyes, but there was no time for that. Hands shaking, she pressed two fingers to his neck. He still had a pulse, and she could see his chest rise and fall, but it seemed to be in jittery movements. Her shifter genes gave her more strength than your average college girl, but even she wasn't going to be able to haul Jak out of the car and up three levels to the healer. Not to mention that he might get hurt along the way.

Biting her lip, she tucked the jacket tighter around Jak to keep him warm and reached over him to grab the gun from under the driver's seat. She tucked it into the back of her pants, which seemed ridiculous, but openly carrying it seemed to flash a neon sign to the darkened street, inviting trouble. Then she locked Jak into the car and strode up to the apartment with her head held high.

You're a shifter, and you're armed, she told herself. *You can do this.* She kept her head up as she climbed the concrete steps and buzzed the door for 3B. She couldn't help looking back to the car, checking on Jak, but he hadn't moved.

There was no answer.

Come on! Her heart lurched and jumped around as she buzzed the apartment again and again. What was she going to do if the healer wasn't home? It was the middle of the night, but who knew? Maybe he was out at the clubs. That's what Mace and his pack did every Saturday night. Something banged inside the apartment complex, startling her, and she stopped buzzing. There was no window to peer in, but she heard some kind of rapid pattering, maybe someone coming downstairs, so she held off on buzzing again.

She waited.

Nothing happened.

Just as she was about to push the buzzer button again, the door cracked open. Inside was a woman in flannel pajamas and a thin tank top. Her pink fuzzy robe was hanging off one shoulder, crooked like she'd just thrown it on, and her hair was mussed.

"Who are you?" the woman asked.

"I… I'm a friend of Jak's," Arianna said, surprised at the shakiness of her own voice. She cleared her throat. "I'm looking for Richter."

The woman lifted an eyebrow. "Well, you found her."

Arianna was speechless for a moment. All the healers she'd known were men, all shifters with some kind of medical training. It wasn't that female shifters couldn't be healers… it was mostly that they were so rare that Arianna hadn't met many others. Especially out in the country.

She had better make sure, just in case. "You're a healer, right?"

The woman narrowed her eyes. "I'm out of the business now. Shifters bring nothing but trouble into my life."

Arianna didn't know what to make of that, but it didn't matter right now. "Jak's hurt. Badly. He needs a healer… please. He gave me your name and said you could help."

The woman bit her lip and peered around Arianna. "Jak, huh? Where is he?"

Arianna stepped back and gestured to the car. "I couldn't move him. Besides, there's so much blood…"

The woman sighed as she peered at the car. "All right. I'll be right back. Need my kit." The door slammed in Arianna's face, but she only hesitated a second before sprinting back to the car. The street was dark except for a few buzzing streetlamps. If this healer woman was going to work on Jak in the car, she would need some light. Arianna hopped in the driver's seat and edged the car forward, so it was directly under the white glare of the lamp. Then she parked and checked Jak's pulse again. She could feel it, but his skin was clammy and cold. He mumbled something when she touched him, but he wasn't really awake.

The healer returned a minute later, a black leather bag in one hand. She peered in the passenger side window then opened the door.

She pulled the jacket away from covering his body, then wrinkled up her face. "Jesus, what a mess." She looked at Arianna. "We need to get him in the back seat. Easier to work there."

Arianna jumped out of the driver's seat and raced around to the passenger side. The woman pulled off Jak's blood-soaked t-shirt, then together, she and Arianna wrestled Jak out of the front seat and into the back. He was still only partially awake, and his flailings got in the way more than helped. The healer climbed in the back, practically on top of Jak… who still had no pants on. Arianna felt her face heating, but there wasn't any room for modesty right now. Not that Jak would probably have minded having the petite, blond healer perched on top of him. Arianna slipped back into the front and watched the healer go to work, wiping away the blood, probing his wounds.

"Do you have a first name?" Arianna asked.

The healer glanced at her then went back to examining Jak's wounds. "Sarra. You?"

"Arianna."

She nodded. "All right, Arianna, I'm seeing a bullet wound to the shoulder and deep lacerations in his thighs and side. No major organ wounds that I can tell, but one of the slashes in his leg nicked an artery, and he's lost a lot of blood." She finally looked at Arianna. "Anything else I need to know about?"

Arianna shook her head. "It was a bad fight."

She wrinkled up her nose and turned back to Jak. "Are there any good ones?"

They didn't speak as Sarra dug a needle and thread out of her bag and started with the gaping bullet wound in Jak's shoulder. The pain of the stitching must have started to rouse Jak. He groaned a few times, his head moving a little. When she plunged the needle into his skin again, he tried to sit up, pushing Sarra's hands away with his good arm, even though his eyes were still closed. Sarra shoved his chest down into the seat with one hand and smacked Jak on the face with the other.

"Hey!" he said, his hands flailing up in front of his face.

"That's for messing up my stitch, Jak Roberts." Her voice was frosty.

Arianna held her breath. There was more than just a messed up stitch charging the air.

Jak creaked his eyes open and peered at her over his raised arm. "Sarra?"

"I'm trying to stitch up your sorry ass." But her tone had warmed a little. "Lie down."

He obeyed, but a half second later, he was up again. "Arianna!" His frantic gaze swept the car.

"I'm right here," Arianna said quickly, and his gaze found her face.

He breathed a sigh of relief and eased back down to the seat.

Sarra lifted one eyebrow, taking in the whole exchange, then went back to sewing up Jak with renewed speed.

He winced as she dug into his wound. "Lost your gentle touch along the way, Sarrabear?" He breathed through his teeth.

"Only for guys who don't call the morning after," Sarra said coolly. "Those get *special* treatment when they show up at my door covered in blood and towing a new girl along."

Jak grimaced. "Oh come on, Sarra. It wasn't like that."

Sarra tugged on the stitch, keeping it tight, but also causing Jak to grunt. Arianna bit her lip, hating to see him in pain, but knowing the stitching was the only thing that would stop the bleeding. Jak's normal shifter healing ability was useless without enough magic-filled blood to make it work. Arianna gripped the edge of the front seat, watching Sarra's needle dip back into Jak's shoulder.

"So that wasn't you who rocked my world for a couple weeks and then disappeared? That was some other hot shifter?" Sarra asked coolly. "Good to know. By the way, who's the new girl?"

Jak let out a pain-filled breath, and Arianna could see him sneaking looks at her. He didn't need to worry about anything. She knew a handsome shifter like Jak would have had lots of girls before her. She also knew he had just given up everything to save her. There was nothing Sarra, or anyone else could say or do that would change that. Or change how Arianna felt about him.

"Arianna is…" He paused, sucked in a breath. "If I could make her my mate, I would, Sarra. Just like I would have with you if you hadn't been so stubborn."

"Oh, *that's* how it was, huh?" But her voice was teasing, and she snuck a glance at Arianna. "Well, your new girl's pretty tough, hauling your sorry ass into this part of town. I'll give her that."

"She was in a bad situation, Sarrabear." Jak winced again at Sarra's stitching. "I had to get her out. And she needs a place to stay. Just for the night."

Sarra sighed. "I figured that out as soon as I saw the mess you made of her car. You have any idea how much blood you've lost?"

"A lot?"

"A shit ton." Sarra shook her head. "I honestly don't know how you keep avoiding actually dying, with all the trouble you seem to find."

"That was a long time ago," he said.

"And yet here you are, about to bleed on my carpet again."

He smiled at that. And Arianna felt a gush of relief at seeing it. She was keeping quiet, letting them have their banter, hoping that would mean Sarra would fix everything that needed fixing. And let them stay, at least for a little while. Jak would heal fast once the stitching was done, but there could be complications. It would be good to have a healer nearby, just in case.

Sarra moved down to his legs and started stitching there. The gashes were deep and ugly and oozing blood even faster than the bullet wound. Jak was naked, but Sarra didn't seem to notice. Or at least she didn't say anything, just lapsed into a quiet focus on her work.

It wasn't until Jak was stitched and able to stumble up to the apartment—with Arianna's and Sarra's help—that Arianna finally let herself believe he would be okay. Jak collapsed on the bed in Sarra's spare bedroom. It was more of a studio really, filled with canvases and paintings of the forest. The bed was just a small cot, barely a foot off the ground, and Jak took up most of the space.

Arianna watched as Jak fell asleep almost as soon as he lay down. Sarra disappeared and returned with an armload of blankets and sheets. One was for Jak, but there was a second set for Arianna.

"The couch is pretty comfortable," Sarra said.

She bit her lip and looked down at Jak. He was already snoring. She didn't want to leave, but she also didn't want to offend Sarra, given how much help she was graciously giving her ex-boyfriend and the girl he showed up with.

"Or you can sleep on the floor in here," Sarra said softly. "Probably better to have someone watching him overnight."

Arianna met her gaze. Tears pricked her eyes. "Thank you. For everything."

Sarra gave a small smile. "Jak's a special guy. I hope you know that."

Arianna nodded vigorously. "I do. I promise."

Sarra gave her a nod, then ducked her head and closed the door on her way out. Arianna settled on the floor next to the cot, edging as close to Jak as she could. She ran her fingers lightly through his hair, softly, so he wouldn't awaken. Then she laid her hand on his chest so she could feel it moving. Even in his sleep, he snuggled into her touch. She closed her eyes, and drowsiness swept over her.

She was quickly drifting into dreamland, but she already felt like all her dreams had come true.

Chapter Eighteen

THE SUN PRIED OPEN JAK'S EYES.

He blinked rapidly, but it still was blinding him. Then he moved his head, just slightly, finding a different cool spot on the mattress below him, and the flood of light dimmed. Only thin slices of sunshine made it into the room through the slatted blinds, and one had just happened to land on his eyes. His mind was still swimming up from the deep, hard sleep he had been in, but now that he could see again, he realized he must be in Sarra's studio. Apparently, she was still painting, something that made his heart glad even before the events of last night came rushing back.

He'd failed to kill Mace.

That thought made him cringe… and it meant things were well and truly fucked up now. At least Jak had managed to get Arianna away from him. But Mace was still out there, and he would be coming for them. Then the rest of the night's events came flooding back: the witch, Arianna's family, his injuries, the escape, Sarra's stitching, and finally… he felt a soft hand move against his chest. Arianna was on the floor next to him, buried in a blanket up to her nose, but with her delicate fingers touching him, keeping contact with him.

She was watching over him.

His heart swelled with that simple fact. The vision of her angelic face, sleeping by his side, made it feel like his heart might actually burst. And it fired a need to have a lot more of her body pressed against him. He shifted on the cot, stretching and testing to see if everything had healed the way it should. Sarra was the best healer he'd ever known—he had no doubts about her work—but she'd said he'd lost a lot of blood. That could slow the recovery, or at least make him pay for it in aches and pains for a while. There were a few twinges, especially in his shoulder, but other than that, he was pretty well healed. Well enough to do something constructive with the morning hard-on raging underneath his blanket.

He reached down to gently tug the blanket from Arianna's face. When she didn't move, he took the opportunity to trail his fingers through the tossed strands of her hair. She stirred slightly. He slid his finger down her cheek. That brought her eyes open. Her lips parted, and her chest filled with sucked-in breath. He wanted all of it: her cheeks, her lips, her gorgeous breasts, all pressed against him.

"Good morning," he said, softly.

She blinked, squinting up at him, still waking. "Jak," she breathed. Then she shook herself awake and sat up. "How are you feeling?" Her gaze searched his chest, looking for the gaping wounds he no doubt had the night before.

"I don't know," he said, trying to hold in the wolfish smile that was threatening to break out. "I think you better come up here and check my wounds."

Her serious look deepened into a frown, and she struggled to her feet. She bent over him, gently pulling the blanket back from his chest and running her fingers lightly over the spot where the bullet went through. Of course, it had mostly healed. Her touch was so soft it almost tickled.

"It looks much better from the outside." Her

frown was a growing crease on her forehead. "Does it hurt on the inside?"

He could hardly keep his smile contained. "I think you need to look closer." He took her hands and drew her down onto the cot with him. Her eyes went wide, and she nearly tumbled down on top of him, but he caught her at the waist and hoisted her to straddle him. He winced as pain shot through his shoulder from the strain, but it was worth it to see the look of shock and a hint of a smile on her face: there were a blanket and her soft sleep pants between them, but she had to feel his rock-hard cock as she sat on it.

"Well, some parts of you are apparently in working order." Then she smacked him lightly on the chest.

He laughed, softly, but it bounced them both on the springy cot. Which just ground her against his cock and killed all the smiles in a need to have much more of her. Now.

He slipped his fingers under her t-shirt and caressed her breasts with both hands. She had apparently never put on a bra since the night before. Her nipples stiffened quickly under his touch, making his cock twitch against the pressure of her sitting on him. Her eyelids dropped to half mast, and this time, when her lips parted, it was in pleasure.

"God, I need you, Arianna," he said, his voice suddenly hoarse.

He lifted her t-shirt, but he couldn't get it free by himself. She pulled it up and over her head. He cupped her breasts, then slid his hands to her back, pulling her down to him and taking one tight nipple into his mouth. She exhaled a shuddering breath, and it about undid him. He pinched the other nipple, pulling a gasp from her, and she started grinding against his cock.

He moaned with the raw pleasure of it. And the need for more.

She pulled back, glancing at the closed door. "Maybe we shouldn't… not here…"

He brought her sweet body back to him, cupping her other breast to his mouth and nipping gently at it. "I'll keep my moans quiet if you can." Then he tipped his head back to look into her eyes. "Arianna." He moved one hand up to her cheek, holding it and hoping she could see the love in his eyes. "The fact that you are here with me, that you resisted the bond, that you came with me and cared for me…" The words were locking up his throat.

Arianna beamed and dipped down to kiss him, but before he could get a proper hold on her, to plunge into her mouth and taste every part of her, she lifted away and bounced up from the cot. He gave her a quizzical look, but she just stood before him, half-naked, with a wicked grin on her face. Then she hooked her fingers in the waistband of her sleep pants and inched them slowly down her hips, swaying them as she worked the pants lower and lower in a slow tease. He propped himself up to watch, letting his wolfish smile run free. His inner wolf was panting hard, voting a hearty lust-filled growl in favor of this show. She was bare underneath the sleep pants, her panties apparently never making an appearance out of the clothes he had packed. He licked his lips in anticipation of tasting the sweetness between her legs. She stepped free of her sleep pants, now pooled on the floor, then captured his gaze with her beautiful blue eyes.

Then she shifted.

It caught him by surprise, and he held her gaze through the whole, quick transition. He had no idea where she was going with this. He'd had plenty of sex with human females, and a few dalliances with unmated female wolves looking for fun before settling with a mate, but never in wolf form. It wasn't a common practice for shifters, if only because the positions and creativity of making love in wolf form were fairly limited compared to what could be done in human form.

But he was definitely game for whatever turned her on.

She stretched her forelegs in front of her and lifted her rear into the air. Her tail dipped down between her legs. Only when she finally ducked her head, lowering her gaze from his, did he realize what she was doing: *she was submitting to him.*

His mouth fell open, and a split second later, the magic hit his bloodstream like a flashfire. The power of her submission filled and lifted him. He bolted upright on the cot and swung his legs over the edge. His chest was tight, but only from trying to contain his heart, which was swelling with the gift she was giving him. Her submission… it was literally making him an alpha from the inside out, super-charging the magic in his blood with her devotion. The last of his aches and pains vanished, swept away by the clean fire of her bond to him.

He stared at her for a long moment, uncertain, then realized he had only felt half of the true power of her gift: he was still in human form. He quickly shifted, landing on soft paws on the floor next to her. His blood surged with the fervent strength of her submission, two or threefold over the intensity of a moment ago. The room was small, barely leaving room for both of them on the floor, muzzle to muzzle amongst the paintings of the forest and the bed behind him. He loomed over her: she was still crouched in the submission pose.

Rise, my sweet, sweet Arianna, he thought, words he never imagined he would have the right to: the words of an alpha.

She popped up from the submission, nuzzling him from underneath. He rubbed his face with hers, tasting her, scenting her, filling his every sense with the feel of her. He was stronger, more powerful, than he had ever been in his life, all because of her.

Jak, you are my alpha, she thought, and he felt his heart might break with the love he had for those words. *You're the alpha I've always dreamed of having. The one I want to give every part of my soul to. The one who deserves every bit of love I have to give.*

His need for her couldn't be contained. *Shift,*

Arianna, he thought. *Shift for me now.* He made it a command, because he *could,* and because it charged the magic in his blood. He felt her respond to his thoughts, a magical surge between them that was filled with passion.

His wolf was desperate to claim her: water was pooling in his mouth. But of course he couldn't have her that way—he would *never* have her that way—but he would do everything short of actually claiming her. He would take her and pleasure her like an alpha should.

She shifted in front of him, and he changed with her.

As soon as they were both human, he pulled her to him, threading his fingers into her hair to hold her tight as he devoured her with a kiss. He used the other hand to hold her delicious body tight against him, his rock-hard cock between them. He walked her backward until they met the wall. He seared his body to hers, pressing her into the wall and plundering her mouth with his tongue. His heart beat so madly, he was sure she could feel it, skin-to-skin where they touched. He broke the kiss. Her lips were swollen with it, her eyes half-lidded. Her arousal perfumed the air, calling to him. He wanted to make her shriek with pleasure, but that wouldn't do with Sarra, their host and healer, on the other side of the wall.

He slipped a hand between Arianna's legs, dipping into the honey dripping between them, then nipped at her neck, tasting her and working his way up.

"I'm going to make you mine," Jak whispered in her ear as he teased her entrance with his fingers. "I'm going to claim you with my love and with my cock. I'm going to make you want to scream my name. But you will be quiet. Absolutely quiet. Do you understand?"

She whimpered and squirmed against his hand. He smiled, enjoying her torment, knowing it would make her climax all the better. He grabbed one of the wooden-handled paint brushes off the easel nearby.

"I have something for you to do with that delicious mouth of yours." He gently placed the smooth handle across her parted lips, urging her to take it. "Bite." He smirked as she bit down on it, then ran a thumb across her cheek. "I'm going to miss hearing you pray my name."

He took the hand rubbing her already-swollen nub and thrust two fingers inside. She groaned, but the paintbrush did its job of keeping the sound contained, a guttural, animal thing inside her throat. It was wild, her wolf speaking, and it made his cock twitch. He reached down behind her knee and lifted it over his hip, opening her up more to his hand plunging inside her. His teeth nipped at her breasts, first one, then the other, all while he pumped his hand faster and faster. He could feel her tense around his fingers. Her hands clutched at his bare shoulders, digging her fingers in deeper with the building pleasure of each thrust. Her head fell back against the wall, and she moaned and panted around the paintbrush. When she came, it sent a glorious flush across her chest that he chased after with his tongue. Then he couldn't stand it anymore. He had to claim her in the only way he could: his body owning hers, filling her, driving her to ecstasy against the wall.

He lifted her sweet bottom with both hands, pulling her from the floor and wrapping her legs around his back. Then he thrust hard and deep inside her. Her paintbrush-muffled-shriek sent electric shocks straight to his cock. She was so sweet and tight—being inside her was like being buried in warmth and love. He held still for a moment, wanting to stay there, but his girl needed more than that—her hands were begging for it, gripping his shoulders and urging him on. He pulled out almost all the way, then thrust hard. Again and again. Her whimpers grew to gasps, then to shrieks. Their thumping, wallbanging passion was shaking the easel next to them. Brushes fell. Her cries grew louder.

Jak growled and panted out the word *Mine* between thrusts, each one searing his love for her with the heat of his body and the pleasure of hers. His climax was coming. He felt it coil deep inside him. Her body squeezed down on him, milking his cock with her orgasm. It tipped him over the edge, and he spilled inside her, a long groan carrying him through.

When it had peaked and subsided, he calmed his motions, still inside her, holding her softly against the wall. Using his teeth, he gently pulled the paintbrush from her mouth. It was scored deep with her teeth marks. He tossed it to the floor and kissed her, lightly. His fangs were out, craving to claim her, so he was careful to keep them well away from her sweet, tender flesh.

He lifted her from the wall and carried her, legs still wrapped around his back, to the bed. He wished he could make love to her again, right away. And then again, endlessly. He wanted nothing more than to stay buried in her, enveloped by her love, forever. But he knew they would have to re-enter the real world soon.

A world where they were on the run from an alpha who would like to see them both dead.

Chapter Nineteen

Arianna's bliss couldn't be any greater.

She was snuggled up with Jak, under the covers of their too-small cot, all tangled limbs and happy afterglow from their lovemaking. Her submission bond to him was an absolute wonder to her. Unlike her bond to Mace, which always fuzzed out her mind and her will, her submission to Jak was a warm, comforting blanket wrapped around her mind, calming her and lifting her up. It was magically filled with love, and with it, she felt that anything was possible. They had escaped Mace, and Jak had lived! If that wasn't defying the impossible, she didn't know what was. Even though she wasn't free of Mace's mating bond, it had become buried under her love for Jak and the fresh strength of her submission bond to him. She wished she could be free of Mace forever, of course, but if this was all she could ever have—this hot shifter by her side, loving her, commanding her with his sexy growl voice—it would be enough.

Jak snuggled closer to her side, burying his face in her neck and dropping delicious kisses there. If he was ready for more lovemaking, she was more than ready to help him out with that. Her hand floated over the rippled muscles of his chest, traveling down to his stomach. He groaned when she reached his cock, which was just growing stiff again.

She would be happy to help with that, too.

Just as she started to burrow under the blanket, eager to take him in her mouth and hear his moans of pleasure, a chirp started sounding in their room. Jak groaned, but in frustration this time, and his gentle hands stopped her progress. The sound was coming from the pile of clothes Sarra had brought in from the car. Jak dug through it and came up with his phone.

He frowned, swiped a few things, then stabbed at the face of it. "Shit."

Arianna frowned and sat up, gathering the blanket around her. "What's wrong?"

He gave her a mournful look, tapped off the phone, and tossed it back in the pile before answering her. Then he came back and took her in his arms, pulling her close, her back to his chest. He snuggled his face through the mop of hair on the side of her head, nuzzling her cheek. She thought he might not answer her at all, until he finally said, "We have to talk, my love."

She turned in his arms to face him, touching his cheek with the tips of her fingers and gazing into his eyes. They were so serious, it made her stomach clench. "No matter what it is, I will always be yours."

His shoulders dropped with that, and the look in his eyes made her heart glow. He took her cheeks in his hands and kissed her gently. Once. Twice. When he pulled back, the serious look had returned.

"I have something to tell you that…" He paused. "I'm not sure if it's real or not, but you deserve to know."

"What is it?" Her hands found his, holding them even though the two of them were only inches away.

"The people who sent the bounty hunters after you. I think they might be your family."

Her eyes went wide. Her brothers were trying to

rescue her. It was foolish and crazy and reckless… and just the kind of thing Marco would do, especially now that he was the alpha of their family since their father died.

Arianna grinned. "That's great!" She glanced at his phone. "We have to call them."

Jak bit his lip and dropped his gaze.

"What?" Arianna asked, her heart sinking.

The look in his eyes was so gentle. "I said I *think* it might be your family. I'm not sure."

She frowned. "But it doesn't matter. Thanks to you, I'm free now." She smiled wide. "Kalis will be so happy. And my mom…" She stopped, choking up. "Oh, Jak, I've missed my mom so much."

Jak looked pained, like her every word was stabbing into him. Which she didn't understand at all, but she knew he wanted nothing but the best for her.

She tamed her smile and reached for his face. "Tell me, Jak. I don't understand. Why is this bad?"

"First, just tell me: do you *want* to go home? Is it safe for you there?" His eyes were intense, but his words and his expression just puzzled her.

"Of course, it's safe for me there."

He nodded, thoughtfully, dropping his gaze. "I had to ask. My family is… well, let's just say someone would probably end up dead if I went back." He looked up. "But even if you *want* to go home, Arianna, it's not safe for you there. Not yet. It's the first place Mace will look for you."

Her heart lurched. "Oh no. Are they… will he go after *them?*"

Jak pressed his lips together. "He might. As soon as he recovers, he's going to start looking for us. I thought we could just make a run for it, just me and you, head for Canada and never look back." He had a wistful look in his eyes like he still wanted to do that.

And she would, too, if it weren't for Mace. "There's only my two brothers and my mom." She lifted her hands, palm up. "I'm amazed they even thought they could come to get me. Marco's the alpha of the family now, but Kalis… he's still just a kid." Her throat grew tight thinking about Mace going after them.

Jak took her cheeks in his hands and rested his forehead against hers. "I'm not going to let Mace get near them. I promise." He pulled back. "I need to return a phone call and see what I can do about this."

She nodded. She trusted Jak with her life. She knew he would keep her family safe, too.

Jak rose up from the bed, pulling her up with him. "Let's get dressed and go apologize to Sarra. Then I'll make my call."

She felt her face get hot. "We made a lot of noise, after all, didn't we?"

Jak chuckled as he hunted through the pile of their clothes. "To be fair: it was mostly you."

She swatted him but quickly got dressed. It wasn't as if they had taken showers or anything. Sarra would scent the sex on them. But that was different than having to listen to it. Guilt speared through Arianna. She had a sense that Sarra had real feelings for Jak, and here Arianna was, having wall-banging sex with him in her studio.

She tried, unsuccessfully, to get the grimace off her face.

Jak held the door of the bedroom for her, hand at her back, but she still could barely force her legs to walk through the door. She crept out, guilt all over her face.

Sarra sat at the kitchen table in the small apartment, sipping from a giant mug that said *Keep Calm and Kick Ass* while reading something on her e-reader. She looked up and sized them up with her bright blue eyes. "Feeling better, I see? I could tell by the pictures falling off my wall."

Arianna cringed and fought for something to say.

Jak didn't even have the decency to look sheepish about it. "You could have let me bleed a little longer."

"Yeah." She snorted. "Like a dead shifter in my front yard would have been less trouble."

Arianna was frozen, torn between her desire to effusively thank Sarra and her need to sink into the floor due to extreme mortification. Jak just grinned at Sarra and left Arianna's side to stride over. He bent to place a kiss on the top of the petite girl's blond head. She peered up at him, and they exchanged a moment of soft smiles that Arianna knew she should feel jealous of, but she just couldn't. Instead, it warmed her heart that Jak was forgiven. And hopefully, she would be as well.

Sarra sighed, then peered at Arianna over her cup. "She's the one, isn't she?"

Jak smiled at Arianna with such love that her grimace finally faded away. "Yeah. She's the one." Then he gave Sarra another soft look. "I'm going to step out to make a call. Can you keep her company for a little bit?"

Sarra's eyebrows scrunched up. "Whoever

you're calling, don't bring them here. I've had enough party for one night."

Jak grinned again, dropped another kiss on her head, and strode toward the door.

"I'm not in business again, Jak!" she called after him, but he just waved on his way out.

Arianna stood awkwardly, still right outside Sarra's studio.

Sarra beckoned her over to the table. "Well, c'mon. Sit down. You're probably hungry."

"I'm fine, really, I don't want to put you out." Arianna shuffled over and took a seat at the rickety wooden table. It was pretty cheap, like everything in the apartment, really. Except for the paints and easels in the guest room. Those seemed top quality.

"I'm not much of a breakfast person either." Sarra got up, went to the tiny kitchen behind her, and returned with another steaming mug. This one said *Keep Calm and Paint On.* "I hope you like tea. No coffee in the house, sorry."

Arianna took the mug. Just holding it was reassuring to her. "This is perfect."

Sarra settled into her seat and took a sip from her mug, but her eyes never left Arianna. The awkwardness was creeping up Arianna's neck again.

"He really loves you," Sarra said. "I hope you know that."

"I do." Arianna let out a sigh of relief. "I hope… I'm sorry about…" She glanced back at the studio.

Sarra just chuckled, set her mug down, and leaned back in her chair. "Jak's a sex machine. Believe me, I know how he is. If he hadn't woken up and wanted some, I would have been worried I didn't stitch him up right."

Arianna felt heat rising to her cheeks, but a smile as well. It was true. Jak couldn't seem to keep his hands off her. Not that she exactly minded.

She peered shyly at Sarra. "The two of you were together, weren't you?"

Sarra sighed and gave a lingering look to the door Jak left through. "Three amazing weeks. If you think he's a sex machine now, you should have seen him as a hormone-raging teen wolf."

"Did you grow up together?" Arianna asked. Maybe that was it… childhood sweethearts.

But Sarra just snorted. "No. And thank god for that. Jak's family almost killed him."

Arianna drew back. "What?"

Sarra raised one eyebrow. "He didn't tell you? Interesting." She studied her mug. "Jak stumbled into my apartment, torn to shreds by his own brothers when he was only sixteen. His brand-new alpha brought him. I stitched him up. I hadn't been a healer long, and I was terrified I would miss something. But he was a strong wolf, even then. He almost died." Sarra looked up at her. "He stayed for a few weeks. I don't think we left the apartment more than a couple of times." She smiled, but it was in a sad way, then she just shook her head and sipped her tea.

Arianna sipped hers as well. There was more to that story, but she wasn't sure she should ask. Or if she really wanted to know. She knew she had Jak's heart now… but it felt like she should know more about where this brave, selfless shifter had come from.

"Jak said he wanted to make you his mate," Arianna said, recalling his exchange with Sarra, in the car the night before. "But you said no. Was it because he was a beta?"

Sarra laughed outright, setting down her tea, so it didn't spill from the jostling. Arianna glanced around the apartment. It was clear that Sarra lived alone. And she was Jak's age, probably twenty-four or twenty-five. A female shifter, unmated at her age… it had to be by choice. And

Arianna couldn't imagine turning away someone like Jak.

"No," Sarra said, amusement high on her face. "I would have had Jak for a mate in a heartbeat. If I was… normal."

Arianna dropped her gaze to the table. "I'm sorry, I don't mean to pry. It's none of my business." She gripped the mug with both hands and peeked up.

Sarra had a soft smile on her face. "I can see why he likes you. You're kind-hearted. Soft. Jak needs more of that in his life."

The heat rose in Arianna's cheeks again, but she didn't want to feel embarrassed. Not about loving Jak. It was one of the best things she'd ever done, no matter what pack rules had to say about it.

Sarra's lips drew into a tight line. "I'm a shifter who can't shift, Arianna."

Realization dawned. "You're a half-breed." Then she grimaced. That wasn't exactly a complimentary term. "Sorry, I didn't mean—"

Sarra held up her hand. "That's exactly what I am. Might as well call it what it is." She took a breath and let it out. "I was on the losing end of a pairing between a bastard of a shifter and a human girl who couldn't wait to drop her panties for him."

Arianna drew back a little. Sarra was talking about her parents. It didn't sound like she had the best childhood either.

Sarra continued, "Not all half-breeds are non-shifters. Some are just like full-breeds in all their abilities. But I didn't get enough magic in my blood out of the deal, so no shifting for me. And a female who can't shift? Not exactly sought after as a mate. I don't bring the right, shall we say, genetic material to the bargain. My blood isn't fit for parenting. At least not with shifters, and really, probably not with humans either."

Arianna's heart was breaking, and she didn't even really know Sarra. But there was something that still didn't make sense. "Did Jak know?"

Sarra's life-hardened face softened a bit. "Oh yeah. He knew. Even back then, even when he was just a kid, Jak was full-on ready to rescue me from my fate. But I knew he deserved better. I'd stitched him up and shared his bed and, dammit, I fell hard for that boy. But I knew I wasn't the right one for him. He deserved someone who could give him pups and a home and everything he didn't have with that fucked up family of his. I told him there was someone out there, someone who would be The One for him." Sarra captured her with her blue-eyed gaze. "He rescued you from something bad, didn't he?"

Arianna nodded, a lump in her throat.

"And you're not broken, like me, right?" Sarra held her gaze steady.

Arianna had to look away. "I'm still mated to another wolf."

"Oh shit." Sarra leaned forward, rubbing her hands across her face. "I take it back. Maybe Jak has a taste for hopeless cases." She laughed a little, but it was sad.

Arianna's chest was squeezing tight. "I can't give him a family, either." She looked up at Sarra with tears in her eyes. "Not strong ones, with the protection of a mating between us. Not like he deserves."

"All right, look here," Sarra said, her voice rising. "Forget everything I said. That boy loves you. *Do not* send him away just because you can't have magic puppies together."

Arianna dropped her gaze to her mug. Was she making a terrible mistake?

"Arianna look at me," Sarra demanded.

She wiped at her eyes and looked up.

"He thinks you're *The One.* If you care for him

at all, you stay with him and figure out how to make it work."

Arianna nodded through the tears making their way down her face. "I love him so much," she whispered.

"Then you'll figure it out." Sarra gestured to her. "If nothing else, you're still mated, right?"

Arianna nodded again.

"Then, as much of a bastard as your mate, no doubt is, you've still got that magic in your blood. Your pups will have that going for them, even if it's not Jak's magic." Sarra pinched up her face. "I know that's not what you want. But if you break Jak's heart, I swear to God, I'll have to find you and beat you down. I don't care if you can shift. I've got a black belt that says nobody messes with my Jak."

Arianna smiled through the tears now flowing freely. She didn't miss how Sarra called him *her Jak*. Her love for him was as clear as anything, and it was the purest kind. The selfless kind. The kind Jak gave to her freely. And Sarra was right. Whatever else happened, Arianna would rather die than do anything to hurt him.

Even if she had to carry Mace in her blood for the rest of her life.

Chapter Twenty

JAK PACED THE SIDEWALK OUTSIDE SARRA'S apartment, phone to his ear.

He had five messages from Circe, the witch who wanted his body, each more threatening than the last. He had *planned* on being well out of her reach by this time today, not just barely recovered from his completely failed attempt to kill Mace. But now he needed her… and pissing off a witch was not the best way to start a negotiation.

The phone was ringing.

It rang four times before Circe picked it up. "Yes." The chill in that word could freeze the sun.

"Sorry I didn't make our date," Jak said hastily, hoping the immediate apology might help. He added a bit of low growl to it, just in case that might help.

"I hope you were dead." The frost was still in negative temperatures. "That would be an acceptable excuse."

"Well, if you called my alpha to expose my little secret, you would know that wasn't far off."

"Oh?" She was warming a little. "Did you boys get a little over excited with the full moon and nip each other to death?"

So she hadn't called Gage. Jak blew out a silent sigh of relief. Not that it mattered if she spilled his secret to his alpha—*ex-alpha*—but he didn't want Gage to know about his connection to the witches. It might get back to Mace and make for trouble with his plan. Which was a terrible plan, but it was the only one he had. And making sure Arianna was forever free of Mace was still more important to him than keeping her for himself.

"No, *little witch*, we're not quite that stupid," Jak said, putting more of the sexy in his voice. He needed to get this witch to play nice if his plan was going to work. "However, I did do a rather stupid thing last night that almost cost me my life. Otherwise, I would have returned your calls."

"Hm," she said, and she was definitely warming up now. "What flavor of stupid were you?"

"I tried to kill an alpha."

"And that didn't go well? I'm shocked." Then she paused. "Wait… this was the alpha of your little pet, wasn't it?"

"Yes." He sucked in a breath through his teeth. This was the hard part. "And that didn't work out. So I'm back to needing your help, Circe."

"Are you, now?" She was warming up to a full purr.

"I need to know if you were serious about Arianna's family sending the bounty hunters after her."

"Your wolfy affairs don't interest me enough to *lie* about them, Jak," she said with disdain.

"How did you know it was them?" he asked.

"Well, that's for me to know and for you not to worry your pretty little head about."

"I *need* to know, Circe," he said. "All deals are off otherwise." He had his suspicions: the bounty hunters knew exactly where to find him and Arianna. When pressed, they squawked Hecca's name. And now Circe knew who really hired the bounty hunters. That was way too much circling for the bounty hunters and the witches not to be connected. Which mean Circe was somehow connected to Arianna's family.

Circe was quiet on the phone. "And what do I get in exchange for this information?"

"I'm willing to make you a very happy witch for a very brief period of time." Jak swallowed down the choking in his throat. This was a trade. A barter. And he didn't have many other options.

"I like the sound of that."

"I thought you might," he said. "Now tell me: how do you know that Arianna's family hired the bounty hunters?"

"Because, my sexy little plaything," she said, "I hired the bounty hunters for them."

Jak stopped his pacing and braced a hand against his car. "*You* hired them."

"Well, they were offering quite a bit of money to get their beloved sister back."

The gears clicked fast through Jak's head. "You used Hecca's name to make some easy money while ratting out your sister's favorite pack." What he didn't understand was *why?* If he could figure that out, maybe he could use that—

"When you put it that way, it sounds so underhanded." But Circe's voice was smug, not worried.

"Maybe this is something Hecca might want to

know," he said. If the sisters were fighting, maybe he could pit them against each other, rather than having to get down and dirty with Circe.

"Nice try, *little wolf.*" Now she was irritated. "But once you left the office, I made sure Hecca was aware of my little arrangement."

Dammit.

"And I disposed of the bounty hunters," she sniffed.

He choked. "You what?" *Jesus.* How did he forget that witches were not to be messed with? But again: short on options.

"Oh, it's wasn't that bad," she said with a sneer. "A simple forgetting spell and a bus ticket did the trick. I don't need the inconvenience of bodies floating in the bay."

"Glad to hear that." But he still didn't understand what her motivation was in this. "So if this isn't some kind of sister-spat, then why? Why help out Arianna's family when it might jeopardize Morgan Media's contract with Red Wolf?"

She sighed into the phone. "Let's just say I don't like wolves who kidnap women. You're tremendously hot, little wolf, but your kind can be so barbaric. Helping to liberate a sister, even of the wolf flavor, has its satisfactions, even if Hecca can't see the merits of getting involved."

Jak wholeheartedly agreed, but he was honestly surprised that she cared. Maybe she was lying, but it didn't seem so—her voice had lost that haughtiness it carried most of the time. And if she meant it, if she was telling the truth, then getting her to help might not be as difficult as he thought.

Time for the big ask. "Circe, I need to meet the family."

"And I need a little hot wolf action in my office." Her temper was rising.

"I think we can both get what we want," he said carefully. "Call up the family. Have them come to your office. I get to check them out, and you get to put your desk to a use for which it was never intended."

He could practically hear her licking her lips. "Getting them here may be a bit difficult."

"Make it happen, Circe." He couldn't keep the anger out of his voice. If he was going to have to pay up in witch-on-wolf sex, she better not fight him on the details.

"Why exactly do you want to meet the family, little wolf?" Suspicion was creeping into her tone.

"That's for me to know, and for you to not care about while I'm fucking you in your office."

She laughed softly. "All right, then. Give me an hour."

"I'll be at your office in half that." He had no idea how long it would take Mace to start looking for them. He could already be on the hunt, for all Jak knew. "We can take care of our bargain, then I want to meet the family."

"Fine." Her voice was tense again. "Half an hour."

Jak tapped off the phone and ran the back of his hand across his mouth. He could still taste Arianna on his skin… and he was about to trade sex for favors with a witch. The thought made his stomach turn, but he needed to make sure her family understood the stakes. And would be able to take care of Arianna.

After he was gone.

He took a deep breath and tapped the phone on again. He dialed Sarra's number. She answered on the first ring.

"Hey," she said. "What's taking you so long? We made you tea, and it's getting cold."

"I have to run an errand, Sarra."

His good friend and ex-lover snarled into the

phone. "The hell you do."

"Please, Sarra, just watch over her for a little bit longer. I need to do something, and Arianna can't be part of it. When it's safe for her, I'll call you. Then you need to bring her to me."

"What are you up to?" Her voice was a whisper now and muffled. She must be hiding her concern from Arianna. Jak smiled: he knew he could count on her.

"I'm going to break her mating bond. She deserves to be free. But don't tell her yet. I will. At the right time."

"I don't like the sound of this." Her voice was a little louder now.

"Please, Sarra, I'm begging you."

She sighed. "All right. How long?"

"An hour. Maybe more. I'll keep it as short as I can."

"All right. We'll be waiting."

"I love you, Sarrabear."

"Yeah, shut up with that already. I've got a reputation as a badass, and you're ruining it."

He smiled so hard his cheeks hurt. "Thanks," he choked out. Dammit, he couldn't afford to get emotional right now. There would be time for that later.

"Don't be stupid." She hung up.

He clicked the phone off, took a deep breath, and climbed into the car.

THE DRIVE INTO DOWNTOWN TO WHERE THE Morgan Media offices were didn't take the full half-hour, so Jak stopped at a coffee shop nearby. He started and then deleted, unsent, a half dozen text messages for Arianna. She didn't have her phone, of course, so it would have to go through Sarra, and he just couldn't bring himself to say the things he wanted to. The things he needed to say before all of this went down.

He would just have to find the right time to do it later.

With about five minutes left, he strolled out of the coffee shop and into the underground parking garage next door. There wasn't much parking downtown, but he knew this area fairly well. A large, familiar-looking van was parked next to his car that hadn't been there before. As he rounded the back of it, his shoes screeched on the concrete flooring of the garage.

Gage. His alpha leaned against Jak's car, waiting for him.

Jak held very still, wishing now that he'd brought the gun… although he couldn't imagine pulling it on his alpha. *Ex-alpha.* Jak reminded himself that his bond had been wiped away with the passing of the full moon.

Gage unfolded his arms and stepped toward Jak with his hands in the air. "I just want to talk, Jak."

Jak darted his gaze all around the parking garage, realizing now that the dark van looked familiar because it was a *pack* van. But there didn't seem to be anyone else nearby. Gage had come alone. Jak's heart thudded as he realized how: the GPS in Jak's car.

Gage had tracked him.

Which meant Mace could as well.

Jak turned and strode away. He would have to take a taxi from here on out. He looked at his phone and shoved it in his pocket, making a mental note to ditch that as well and get a burn phone.

"Jak, wait!" Gage was hurrying up behind him.

He wasn't using a command voice, and Jak wasn't under any obligation to stop, but years of habit, and the fact that he actually loved Gage like a brother, had him stopping in his tracks anyway.

He turned to face Gage. "No talking can fix this." He was acutely aware of time ticking past. He had to wrap this up and somehow get to Morgan Media *without* Gage in tow.

"Jak, what are you doing?" The pain on Gage's face ripped a hole right through him. "We can fix this. Just bring her back, we'll make it all right."

"Bring her back," Jak repeated, disbelieving. Then he saw something with a sudden clarity: something he should have known all along. Gage *let* this happen: he knew what kind of alpha his brother was. He *knew* what happened in that house. And he let it happen.

Every. Damn. Day.

"Mace is out for blood," Gage continued. "If he finds you, I won't be able to stop him. You have come back now, right now. Bring the girl in, and I can make it right with him."

Jak's rage was building to a frothy peak. "Do you know what I'm doing here, Gage?"

Gage gave him a hard look. He obviously wasn't used to back-talk from his beta.

"I'm doing what an *alpha* should. What any decent alpha *would.*"

Gage's face turned red, and his fists clenched.

Suddenly Jak didn't fear having to fight him anymore. Because Gage was *wrong.* Dead wrong.

"You saved my life," Jak said through his teeth. "All those years ago, you risked your life to stop something that was *wrong.* What happened to the alpha who pulled me out of the forest?"

Gage's jaw worked. "You may not want to be my beta anymore, Jak. But that doesn't mean you can steal my brother's mate."

Jak curled a lip in disgust. "You *know* what he does to her."

Gage's cheek twitched, and he had the decency to drop his gaze to the floor.

Jak wasn't letting him off that easy. "When did you become the kind of alpha who looks the other way?"

Gage kept his focus on the floor. "He's my *brother,* Jak."

"He's an *asshole.* And he'll have to kill me to get her back."

Gage winced but looked up again. "He will, Jak. He's coming for you."

"He can fucking try." Jak pointed to the garage exit. "I'm walking out of here. Right now. Don't try to stop me."

Gage's brow wrinkled, but he didn't say

anything. Jak turned on his heel and marched out. His heart pounded like a jackhammer in his chest as he broke out into the sunshine. He checked the time on his phone before dumping it in the trash can and walking on. Morgan Media was a good couple blocks away, and he was already late.

He picked up the pace and ran the entire way there.

He was so winded when he arrived, he had to bend over double during the elevator ride up, trying to get his heart to stop pounding out of his chest. Leaving Gage and his pack was going to be hard—Jak knew that going in. But somehow this was worse. This knowledge that Gage had let all this happen. It was his duty as an alpha to stop things like this, where it was within his power. And even sometimes when it wasn't. There were some things that were worth dying for… and protecting the innocents of the world, people like Arianna, was one of the things.

It was everything that being alpha meant.

The magic of Arianna's submission bond pulsed through his blood, and his inner wolf howled agreement. How could Mace feel that and ever harm her? How could Gage, powered by the submission bonds of his entire pack, not do everything in his power to right the wrongs happening in his own estate?

Jak braced his hand against the edge of the elevator as it arrived, and the doors opened. The run had flushed his face, but the thing that truly stole his breath was the knowledge that he had to go pleasure a witch to save the woman he loved. There were few things he wanted to do *less.* But it was just one of the sacrifices he would make to keep her safe. To right the wrongs that had gone on too long. It started with his mother. It would end with Arianna.

If there was anything decent in the world, anything like fates smiling down on him, Arianna would never have to know. If not, he prayed she would understand.

He stormed past the receptionist and through the frosted glass doors of Morgan Media. He knew exactly which office was Circe's. A wave of witch heads turned to follow him as he strode toward it. He threw open the door, and there she was: leaning against her desk, arms crossed, looking disgruntled at his tardiness.

But her eyes lit up when she saw him. "Little wolf," she breathed, a smile on her face.

He closed the door behind him.

Chapter Twenty-One

JAK HESITATED AT THE DOOR OF THE WITCH'S office, now closed behind him.

He was trading sex for her cooperation—with Arianna's family, with the spell to break Mace's hold on her, and with everything that was going down in the next hour. He had to leave Circe more than satisfied to get the things he needed. His chest was still heaving from the run over to Morgan Media, but that wasn't what cinched it tight: it was the idea of fucking a witch to save the woman he loved. A woman who had just strengthened him to the core with her submission, giving herself completely to him. It wasn't the fact that the witch could kill him with a touch of her dark-magic fingers—it was breaking his heart that Arianna might find out. If not now, if not right away… eventually.

He prayed she would forgive him for all of it.

He swallowed down the sourness in the back of his throat and tried to picture Circe as just another hookup at the club. Sex with her didn't mean anything. He'd get it up, get it done, and get out. And wash away any trace afterward, hoping to God Arianna wouldn't scent the witch on him before he could carry out the rest of his plan.

Jak strode across Circe's office to where she stood, leaning against her desk and licking her lips. Her blue eyes were lit up, and she was checking out his package like she had x-ray vision that could see right through his jeans. Her eyes grew wider as he approached. He didn't waste any time, simply grabbed hold of her hips and lifted her up on the desk. Her legs spread, and her filmy red dress rode up her bare thighs. He shoved his crotch against hers, hoping to jump-start things there. Getting it up might not be as easy as it normally was.

Circe let out a little squeak of surprise, but he figured that's what she wanted: she had a hunger for sex with a wolf for a reason, and it wasn't because she wanted *gentle.* He held her tight against him, crushing her ample chest to his, and started feasting on her neck. A strangled moan and pricks of daggered nails clawing at his back told him he was headed in the right direction. He slid a hand up her thigh, shoving aside the silky fabric and going right for the heat between her legs. She was bare—either witches went commando all the time, or she had already discarded her panties, knowing he was on the way. She arched her back and gasped as his fingers found her nub.

He lifted his head from nipping at her neck. Her eyes were already hooded with lust, lips parted, and a flush was creeping across her cheeks. She was actually insanely beautiful—all witches were. If they weren't so deadly, and generally would prefer castrating wolves to fucking them, he probably would have slept with one already. As it was, he had to work to convince his cock to pay attention to the scent of her arousal, which was quickly filling the room. He palmed her breast, hoping the heavy weight of it in his hand might help. Her head dropped back as he worked her stiffened nipple through the thin sheath of her dress. She was definitely curvy in all the places that would normally gain his cock's attention: full, perky breasts, begging for his lips; ample hips for a good grip while he slammed into her. Her face was beautiful and harsh, like a terrible angel—all angled lines, high cheeks, and perfect skin that was now flushed a delicate pink. Gasps came through her parted lips. He was a little relieved to find his cock straining against his jeans, finally responding to her obvious lust.

He gave her a moment more of pleasure, teasing her entrance with his fingers until she was bucking against them, then pulled back: he needed to make sure they were clear on their agreement before they got too far. He took one of her hands from where it was digging into his shoulder and pressed it against his cock, through his jeans. The contact was enough to make it twitch in response. He rubbed her hand up and down the length to make sure he could deliver… and to make a not-so-subtle promise. She moaned, and her eyes drifted closed.

"Is this what you want, little witch?" he whispered, his voice even huskier than he had intended. Maybe he could do this, even if the idea sickened him. He shoved that thought away.

"Oh God, yes," Circe breathed. She grasped hold of his cock through the jeans fabric, stroking him and making him harder. "I want all of you. Now."

He grabbed her hand by the wrist and pulled it away. "I'm going to give you everything you want and more." He growled out the words, which just made her squirm against him. "But first, I want to be absolutely clear about what you're giving *me* when we're done."

"I already called the family. They'll be here soon." She clawed at his pants, trying to slip her hand inside. He pulled her hand away again then pushed her body flat against the desk, hauling her bare sex against the rough fabric of his pants while holding her hands over her head with one hand. It was the perfect position to torment and tease her, and his cock stiffened even more in response. Circe gasped with it as well, arching her back and shoving her breasts up.

"Take me now," she breathed, straining against him.

"First, I want your promise," he said, even as he ground against her and made her whimper. "You'll help me with the family, you'll do the spell, and you'll speak nothing of this to Arianna. Ever."

Circe's panting slowed a bit, and she lifted her head to look at him. "Spell?"

Jak dipped his head to peer into her eyes. "The spell we discussed before? I do *you,* then you do the spell? And not a word to Arianna."

Circe frowned and stopped grinding against him. "Please tell me you don't mean that dreadful spell where you end up dead on my floor. Because you're far too delicious to waste with something like that." She seemed to be scanning his face and the air all around him. Her frown grew deeper.

"I'm sure you can find another wolf to threaten into your bed." Jak gritted his teeth, but all this talk of him dying was having a serious negative effect on the state of his cock. He started moving it against her sex again.

Circe dropped her head back to the desk and moaned. She was silent for a moment, clearly enjoying the contact between her legs. But then she groaned in a way that sounded more like frustration than pleasure. Jak startled when she seemed to slip her hands free of his hold without any difficulty whatsoever. Then he jumped when she slammed both fists against the desk, one on either side of her body.

He stepped back and frowned, not sure what was happening.

Circe sat up, looking grumpy. She glared at Jak

as she straightened her dress. "Why did you have to..." She waved at him. "...tell me all that?"

"Tell you what?" He thought it was clear he was here for the spell. But apparently not, judging by the look on her face. Was it more complicated than he thought? Maybe there was something to the spell that made her hesitate to go through with it.

Instead of answering him, she made a harrumphing sound and eased down from the desk. She tugged her dress into place then crossed her arms. "You're willing to die for this girl."

It wasn't exactly a question, but he said, "Yes," without hesitation. He was still confused. "What's the problem? You get what you want first. All I'm asking is that you don't tell her that we..." He gestured to the desk. "That there was a certain exchange involved. Is that so much to ask?" There had to be more to this.

Circe let out an elaborate sigh then leaned back against her desk. "I'm sure you think all witches are heartless and evil."

He knew better than to say anything, opting for a small shrug.

She waved at him again, gesturing at something around his head. "Your aura is screaming your love for this girl. You're willing to die for her, for magic's sake. I may want your hot shifter body, little wolf, but even *I* know better than to risk the karma of messing with a love bond that strong."

"I… don't understand." Jak clenched his fists. "Will you do the spell or not?"

She sighed again. The lust in her eyes had cooled ten degrees. "Why not just give her to the family? They've wanted nothing more than to have her back all along. Or, hell, run away with her! Are you so territorial that you'd rather die than have another wolf's magic in her blood?" She wrinkled up her nose at this, like he had suddenly turned into a distasteful beast that might soil the carpet.

Jak just shook his head, mystified. Did he really need to explain his reasoning to this witch? "Why do you care?"

"Performing dark arts is a tricky business," she sniffed. "And a deadly one. Why are you so eager to die, little wolf?"

"I don't *want* to die." He ran a hand through his hair and stepped back farther. This witch was confounding him. "I'd like nothing more than to run away with her. But as long as she's tied to her mate, she'll never have the things she deserves."

Circe shrugged. "She could still have pups. What does it matter if they're not yours? So to speak."

Jak growled and took two menacing steps toward her. He stopped before reaching her when her look changed from annoyed to glacier cold. She could kill him if she wished. And now that she wasn't, for some reason, clawing at him for sex, she just might do it out of frustration.

He dialed back his own frustration and said softly, "I would happily run away and spend all my days loving her. I would like nothing more than to make a family with her. But in the end, it would all be for selfishness. Because Mace wouldn't stop hunting her. And one day, he would find her—then he would claim not only her but her pups too. Our babies…" Jak swallowed down the thickness in his throat then looked away to hide the water glassing his eyes. "He would have every right in pack law to claim them all. I would die before I let that happen, but I might not be able to stop it. Arianna would always live in fear of that." He took a breath and looked back to Circe, whose face had opened in surprise. "This way I can ensure that it never comes down to that. No matter how much I want her for myself, the most important thing is to simply get her free from him."

Circe pressed her lips together, but Jak could tell something had changed. There was a look on her face, a concerned look, that made the sharpness of her features soften.

She nodded slowly. "You may not think much of witches, little wolf, but even we are not so heartless as to stand in the way of something so… *noble.*"

He raised his eyebrows. "That sounds suspiciously like a compliment."

She scowled at him. "Something you will not speak of again and will take to your grave."

He smirked. "Of course." But the smile was fleeting. "Will you do the spell, Circe?"

Her scowl darkened. "Yes. But it's not something we can do in my office. And you'll need to be in wolf form at the end. I prefer not to dispose of human bodies."

Jak swallowed, the reality of that sinking in. "Understood." Then he blew out a sigh of relief and gestured to the desk. "I'm still not sure why we're not…"

"Having amazing sex on my desk?" She smirked and eyed his body. "Make no mistake, little wolf, it would have been one of the best experiences of your life."

He cocked his head to the side. "It seems I'll never know."

She let out a wistful sigh. "It would have been delicious. But you were much more fun to bed when you weren't quite so nobly rescuing the woman you love."

He frowned. He had no idea such things *mattered* to witches.

She folded her arms. "Hecca would say I'm foolishly romantic. I think she's just had one too many dark-art spells worm their way into her heart. But regardless… I'll help you for the same reason I agreed to help Arianna's family from the beginning. Because I don't like to see a woman held captive and turned into a slave of the worst sort."

His eyebrows hiked up. He did remember her saying that before, but now that he had a moment to think about it, he could see that Circe had been trying, in her own way, to free Arianna all along.

Just like him.

He tipped his head to her. "You and I might have more in common than I ever suspected, little witch." He gave her a small smile and stepped forward, close enough to touch her, but he didn't.

"Thank you." Her eyes widened as he gently pressed a chaste kiss to her cheek. When he pulled back, that pinkish tone was coloring her face again. He surprised even himself with how genuine his smile was.

She shook her head, as if the whole thing was hopelessly foolish, then reached for her phone lying on the desk. "It's a damn shame to have to do this spell, little wolf. A damn shame." Then she tapped something up on the phone and spoke into it. "Have they arrived yet?" She paused to listen. "No. I'll meet them in the reception area when they get here. I'll be out in just a moment." She hung up the phone.

Jak's pulse quickened. "The family?"

She nodded. "They'll be here soon. But we can't do this at Morgan Media."

He nodded, ready to get down to business. "Understood. But first I need to talk to them. I need to make sure they can take care of Arianna after I'm gone."

Circe nodded, biting her lip. "Arianna's a lucky girl to have so many people love her so thoroughly." She gestured to the door. "It seems fitting that you should all meet before she loses one of you."

Jak didn't think he would ever feel actual gratitude toward a witch, but there was no denying the warmth in his gut with those words. He nodded, then strode toward the door of her office. The warm feeling lasted exactly three seconds—until he opened the door to a different and decidedly more furious witch. Hecca's dark-eyed glare was like a physical force. Jak stumbled back across the threshold, nearly bumping into Circe.

Hecca quickly turned her fury on her sister. "Circe, why is our receptionist on the lookout for a pack of wolves coming to meet you?" She gave Jak a disgusted look. "And what is *he* doing here again? I thought we were done with this business."

Circe breezed past Jak, hooking her arm through his along the way. She fluttered her fingers at Hecca. "Nothing for you to be concerned about, sister dear."

Hecca was hot on their heels.

Circe sauntered toward the front, towing Jak with her.

"The fact that you *don't* find this concerning," Hecca hissed, "is *exactly* why I'm concerned."

Circe whirled on her sister, and the humor was gone from her face. "I'm having a little *fun*, Hecca. Be a dear and don't ruin it."

Hecca wrinkled her nose up in disgust. "With *all*

of them? For the love of magic, Circe, you're taking this obsession of yours with these… *dogs*… a little too far."

Jak let out a low growl, playing along and bolstering Circe's cover. Slipping out for a wolfy orgy wasn't exactly an unbelievable lunchtime activity for Circe if he had to take a guess.

Hecca narrowed her eyes at him. "Don't growl at me, wolf. Not in my own coven. Not unless you want to end up as ash."

Circe tugged him closer, protectively. "Get your own playthings, Hecca." She said it loud enough for the entire office to hear. They certainly had everyone's attention.

Jak tried not to flinch as Circe ran her hand up his arm, squeezing his muscles lasciviously as she went. Hecca's disgust turned to loathing, but before she could start spitting spells at them, Circe turned them away and sauntered toward the front of the office again. Jak peeked back, but Hecca wasn't following after them anymore. Circe cuddled up to his side as close as she could get, her hand still roaming and getting a good feel.

Jak dipped his head to hers and said softly, "You enjoyed that, didn't you?"

Circe smirked just before they reached the

frosted-glass doors of the office. "Whipping Hecca into a froth is one of life's small, sublime pleasures."

Jak chuckled as they stepped across the threshold into the reception area. Soon he would meet Arianna's family… and, if all went according to plan, his fate as well.

Chapter Twenty-Two

ARIANNA PACED THE SMALL CONFINES OF SARRA'S living room, from the weathered leather couch spilling out stuffing to the shelves filled with art books at the end near the studio. She'd had three cups of tea already, and she and Sarra had lapsed into a heavy silence. They were waiting for Jak to return from whatever "errand" he had to run, but Arianna couldn't help feeling something had gone wrong. Every moment he wasn't calling inched up her back like a glacier of dread.

While Arianna paced, Sarra calmly read the newspaper.

Arianna glanced at Sarra's phone. It had been an hour since Jak called. "Something has happened," she said without slowing in her pacing.

Sarra didn't look up from her paper. "Nothing has happened."

Arianna didn't have a phone—Jak had given her one, but Mace had taken it—or she would have called Jak already. What errand could he possibly have to do that was more important than getting out of Seattle? Or reuniting with her family, now that she knew they were looking for her? At least, she thought they were looking for her—Jak hadn't been sure. Maybe that was the errand? Was he finding out if it was true? And even if it was, he said it wasn't safe to go there… that it was the first place Mace would look for her. Which was no doubt true. Something about the phone call Jak had to make sent him off on this mysterious errand… was he going after her family to keep them safe?

Her nerves were stretched so tight, she was about ready to snatch up Sarra's phone and call Jak herself. It called to her from the spot where it sat on the rickety kitchenette table next to Sarra's tea mug.

"What did Jak say about this *errand* he's running?" Arianna asked for the third time.

Sarra sighed but still didn't look up from her paper. "Just that it would take an hour and he would call when he was done."

"It's been an hour."

"It's been thirty-four minutes." Her voice was tight. Arianna couldn't tell if she knew more than she was saying or if she was just getting annoyed with Arianna. Which she could understand: Jak was Sarra's ex, and here she was, having to babysit his new lover. Arianna bit her lip as she paced. She hated to make it worse for Sarra, but worry about Jak and what he was up to was making her wolf stomp and snort. She was about to crawl out of her skin with it.

Arianna clenched her fists as she paced. "He's gone and done something stupid, Sarra."

Sarra turned the page of her paper. "Most of the things Jak does are stupid."

Arianna grabbed a chair at the table, turned it around, and sat backward in it. "He's gone after Mace. I just know it."

"Who's Mace?"

"My alpha." Arianna gripped the back of her chair to keep from popping back up and pacing again.

Sarra finally looked up from her paper with an inscrutable expression. "That would be stupid, even for Jak." But then the corners of Sarra's mouth turned down. She had to be thinking it was possible, too.

"Maybe he's going to slip back into the estate and attack Mace while he's still recovering." Arianna choked up. "Oh God, Sarra, what if he gets himself killed? I almost lost him once already…" Then she had to stop because tears were about to spill, and she had no time for that.

Sarra put the paper down and reached out to lay a hand on Arianna's white-knuckled ones. "Whatever he's doing, Jak's planning on coming back to you. He said he would call: he'll call."

Arianna glanced at the phone on the table. "Let me call him. Please."

Sarra sighed and pulled her hand back. She seemed to wrestle with the idea for a moment, then slid the phone toward Arianna. "Go ahead. Tell him I've got better things to do than wait around for him."

Arianna gave her a grateful smile then snatched up the phone. Sarra was quickly becoming one of her favorite people. Jak's number was the most recent incoming call, so she didn't have to troll through Sarra's phone book. Arianna was glad at least for that—she felt bad for all the imposition they had already made on Sarra's life.

Arianna pressed the phone to her ear, drumming her fingertips rapidly on the table top as it rang.

And rang.

And rang.

Finally, it went to message. She hung up without leaving one.

"No answer," she said, her voice tight.

"He's probably busy doing whatever he's doing." Sarra went back to reading the paper.

Arianna jumped out of the chair and paced again, the phone clutched in her hand. "He's in trouble. I know it."

"If he was in trouble, he would have picked up the phone." Sarra gave an elaborate sigh, setting the paper down again. "Jak's a smart man. He knows you're here, waiting. He's not going to leave you stranded. He just has something to do that he doesn't want you mixed up in."

Arianna stopped her pacing. "That only means it's dangerous."

"Or that he can take care of it better on his own. He said he would tell you all about it when it was done." Sarra's eyes narrowed. "Do you trust him?"

Arianna took a deep breath and let it out slowly.

"I do. I swear I trust him with my life, Sarra. I'm just not sure I trust him with *his.*"

Sarra frowned. "Yeah. I know what you mean." She shook her head and studied the pitted tabletop for a moment. "We'll just have to wait until he calls. Then we can stitch him back up or pick up the pieces or whatever he needs."

But that sparked an idea in Arianna's head. She shook the phone at Sarra. "My family is looking for me." At least, she hoped that was true. Even if it wasn't, she should alert them that she had broken free… and that Mace might be coming there next.

Sarra cocked an eyebrow. "You have a pack?"

"It's just my brothers and my mom. We're hardly a pack. That's why Mace was able to capture me so easily. We were outnumbered."

Sarra scowled, but Arianna was already pulling up the phone's number pad to dial. It had been a long time, but she had Marco's number memorized.

"If they're looking for me," Arianna said, "they might be nearby. If not, they need to know I'm out. And that Mace might be looking for me at home. At the very least, I can tell them where I am. They can clear out, maybe stash my mom somewhere safe, and come to get me. By the time Jak calls, they'll be on their way. Whatever his plan is, they can help."

Sarra was back to frowning again. "Are you sure that's what Jak wants? Maybe involving your family in this isn't the way to go."

Arianna looked up as the phone started to ring. "They're involved whether they want to be or not. And I'm not leaving Jak alone in this."

Sarra nodded in approval. "It would be better to have a few more fangs around, in case this gets ugly. Besides, I don't like where this is heading." She held up a hand. "But I do *not* want them coming here! The last thing I need is a parade of wolves through my door. I don't want people to think I'm back in the business again. Got it?"

"I promise," Arianna said quickly as the phone rang again. "We'll take it somewhere else. I'll arrange a meet." Her heart started to pound at the mere thought of seeing her family again.

The phone picked up. "Hello?" It was tentative —of course, her brother wouldn't recognize Sarra's caller ID—but it was definitely Marco's voice. It felt so good to hear it again.

"Marco! It's me, Arianna." Her voice was breathy with excitement.

"Arianna?" He was still tentative. "Why are you calling on this phone?"

"It's a long story." Arianna glanced at Sarra. "I'm in Seattle. But I'm not at the Red wolf estate. I ran away and—"

"Holy shit, it's really you!" Marco's voice took a swing up, enthusiasm kicking in. "Are you okay? How did you get out? What the… Arianna, oh my god… Mom is going to be so happy."

"I know!" She could hardly get the words out, she was grinning so hard. "I can hardly believe it myself."

"What happened?" he asked, the hope in his voice warring with concern. "Are you free of him, sis? I mean… is he…"

"No, he's not dead." Arianna blew out a breath. "And that's why I'm calling, actually. You and Kalis and Mom need to go somewhere safe. Mace is going to come looking for me, sooner or later. And I need your help, Marco."

"Of course. Whatever you need. We're practically in Seattle anyway..." She could hear Marco whisper something, covering the phone with his hand. After a moment, he was back. "Kalis is calling Mom. I'll have her go to Robertson's ranch for a while. He'll keep her somewhere safe until this is handled."

"Oh good." The tension in her body stepped down a notch. She always knew Marco would make a fine alpha someday… and in the six months since she'd been gone, he seemed to have grown into it even more. She could hear it in his voice. "Wait… did you say you're almost to Seattle?"

"Yeah." He seemed to hesitate a moment. "We're on our way to visit some witches."

"What?" Wolves and witches didn't mix. Not that she'd ever met one, but it was like a sixth sense… not to mention all the horror stories she'd heard growing up.

"We were desperate, Ari." That was what her father had always called her.

It made her choke up even more. "You were trying to get me back, weren't you?"

"Every day since the moment that bastard took you." He growled out each word.

Now she really was going to cry. She turned away from Sarra's curious gaze and said softly, "Oh, Marco. I've missed you guys so much."

"I know, sis. But it's going to be over soon. We're coming for you. Just tell me where you are."

His voice was full alpha-mode now, and it made her heart sing.

Arianna wiped her face, pushing away tears she didn't have time for. "I'm in a safe place, but you can't come here. Let me meet you somewhere. These witches… they were helping you, right?"

"Yeah," Marco said, hesitation back in his voice. "There's one that's… well, she's different. Decent. For a witch, I mean."

"Maybe I can meet you there," Arianna said.

"I don't know, Ari—"

"She's on our side, right? And besides… the last thing Mace would do is look for me in a coven of witches."

"That's probably true." He still sounded undecided.

"And it'll give me a chance to thank her for her help." Her heart was leaping with the fact that she would get to see her family again. Walking into a coven of witches wasn't exactly how she had dreamed of it happening, but that didn't matter.

"Right." There was still something off in his voice.

"What is it, Marco?"

"Mace isn't dead." The growl was back in his voice.

"Yeah." She already told him that.

"So you're still mated." Growl and anger, too.

"Right. But that can't be helped. And that's why we need to make a plan to get away. And there's something else you need to know. There's someone who's been helping me." She glanced at Sarra again. "A couple of people, actually. But the one who helped me escape… well, you need to meet him."

"Okay." But Marco seemed preoccupied. "Now that I think about it meeting at the witch's place is the way to go. We're almost there. We can figure out our plan once we meet up. These people who are helping you: do they have transportation? Can you get here on your own?"

Arianna glanced at Sarra. "Yeah. I should be able to. I'll bring one of them with me. Hopefully, the other one can meet us later. He's tied up at the moment."

"That's fine. I'll have Kalis text you the address when I hang up. And Arianna?"

"Yeah?"

"I love you, sis." His voice was choked. "There's not a day I haven't been trying to find a way to get you free."

She was tearing up again. "We'll have time to talk later."

Marco cleared his throat. "Later. Right. See you soon, Ari."

He hung up the phone.

"What is this business about a coven of witches?" Sarra was standing now, looking tense and staring Arianna down from her spot by the table.

Arianna winced. "I guess they're helping us."

Sarra looked askance at her. "Look, country girl, I don't know about where you're from, but here in the city, witches don't generally help wolves. Unless they're helping themselves to our body parts. Especially female wolves. Especially, *especially* mated female wolves."

"I know." Arianna handed back her phone. "But I trust my brother. If you just want to drop me off, I'd totally understand."

Sarra let out a dry laugh. "Jak would skin me alive, and rightly so if I dropped you off at a coven of witches. Um, no. I'll be going with you."

Arianna wrapped her arms around herself. "I'm sorry about dragging you into all this." It seemed like everyone she loved, and even strangers she had just met, were risking themselves, all to help her get free of Mace. She felt bad about that, but she couldn't help it either. It was either that or stay with him. And she'd already made that choice. Now she had to see it through.

"Looks like we're going on a road trip," Sarra said. "You might need a few things, just in case we're not coming back any time soon."

Arianna unfolded her arms and held her hands out. "Oh, no. No, no, no. I can't take anything from you. You've already given me too much help."

Sarra motioned her toward the bedroom. "Shut up and help me pack."

Arianna had no choice but to follow her and help in any way she could. And she couldn't help wondering what she did to deserve all this—Jak working to free her, Marco taking the risk to team up with witches to get her back, and now Sarra, giving her safe shelter, tea, and packing her up with things to go on the road. Which was probably where she was going to be—on the road, on the run—for a good long time. Possibly forever.

Arianna didn't know what she could ever do to repay any of them. But she would do everything in her power to live a life worthy of all the risks these people were taking to give her a chance to live one.

Chapter Twenty-Three

Jak and Circe spent five tense minutes waiting in the reception area of Morgan Media, subjected to the ogling and whispers of the two receptionists. Circe eventually banished them to the main office area of Morgan Media. A few minutes later, the elevator dinged, and two men stepped out. They were both tall, well-built males, clearly in possession of the shifter gene—the younger one was no more than sixteen, while the older one seemed closer to twenty. But what froze the breath in Jak's chest was the brilliant blue eyes, the dark brown hair, and the fresh-faced innocence of both.

There was no question in his mind: *they were Arianna's brothers.*

Circe quickly addressed the older one. "Marco,

nice to see you again." There was a purr in her voice that Jak recognized instantly as Circe-lusting-after-wolves. He wondered just what Marco had traded to earn Circe's help in finding his sister. Then again, maybe he had just paid her in money—the kid looked as innocent as Arianna, although he had that same world-weariness that didn't seem to belong on her face either.

Marco frowned, coolly taking in Jak's presence. "When you said you wanted to meet, Circe, I didn't realize you meant with *other shifters.* Who is this character?"

The younger one stood at attention like he was ready to brawl at a moment's notice, but he was just a pup. Jak could take him with one hand tied behind his back. The older one would take a bite out of him before going down, but Jak was fairly certain it wouldn't be much of a fight, either. He was seriously hoping it wouldn't come to that.

Circe arched her perfect eyebrows. "Marco and Kalis Stefan meet Jak Roberts. Jak is the wolf responsible for freeing your sister, at least in a physical sense, from Mace's hold."

Jak extended his hand, but Marco just scowled and ignored it. "*You* freed my sister?"

He clearly wasn't buying this, and Jak couldn't

blame him. It wasn't like he had brought Arianna along as proof.

"Yes," Jak said evenly. He needed to win these boys over and, at the same time, take their measure. They were Arianna's family, but as Jak well knew, that didn't always mean much. He had to be *sure* they were capable of looking out for her. And even if they wanted to, he was starting to wonder if they would be savvy enough.

"Look," Jak said, "I know you don't know me—"

"No. I don't know you." Marco's voice was clipped, and the younger one was still on high alert. "How about you clear out? I have a few things to discuss with Circe—"

He was cut off by the younger one batting his arm. Marco leaned over, and Kalis whispered in his ear. They both shot daggered looks at Jak. The hairs on the back of his neck stood up.

Marco straightened and growled out his words. But they weren't directed at Jak. "Circe, what kind of witch trickery is this?"

She narrowed her eyes, and her voice went cold. "What are you talking about, wolf?"

Marco flung his hand out at Jak. "He's *Red pack.* Did you expect us not to notice?" He snarled and tipped up his chin. "He was there when Arianna was captured, and now you've brought us here to meet with him? What is this, some kind of double cross? Are there more of them in the lobby? I thought you wanted Arianna free. Or was that just talk?"

Kalis had hauled out his phone and was yanking on Marco's sleeve. Marco stilled his brother with a harsh look.

The tension evaporated from Circe's slender frame. "No, you idiot." She sighed. "I swear, if you wolves weren't so sexy, I'd find the lack of a brain seriously unattractive."

Marco growled in response. "We're leaving." He turned toward the elevators.

Jak rushed out, "Marco, wait."

But he kept going, and Kalis was on his heels. The older one punched the elevator button then whirled on Jak as he approached. Both Marco and Kalis had their claws out and were snarling.

Jak put up his hands. He had maybe ten seconds before the elevator arrived. "Look, I would be suspicious, too. If I had a sister like Arianna, I'd tear apart anyone who looked sideways at her. But you have to believe me, I'm on your side with this."

The snarling eased up, but only slightly. And their claws were still out.

Jak rushed the rest out. "I watched for six months as Mace kept her caged like an animal in that house of his. It tore me apart every single day. And then, one day, I actually got to spend time with her, and I realized… someone like Arianna was worth risking everything for. I couldn't live with myself if I stood by while she slowly died—while everything good and beautiful about her withered away—all from being a dark alpha's mate."

Kalis was still giving him glares, but Marco's claws had retracted into his hands.

His blue eyes, so like Arianna's, were still squinted with suspicion. "What's in it for you?"

Jak blinked, nonplussed for the moment. *What was in it for him?* Redemption for not saving his mother? A chance to be an alpha, a true protector? It was simpler even than that. "I'm in love with her."

Marco's gaze still drilled into him. "Is that so?"

He could understand the skepticism. In the same position, with a sister like Arianna, he'd more likely go fang to fang than trust any wolf claiming to love her. Jak stood straighter. "I left my pack, betrayed my alpha, and risked my life all to get Arianna free."

Marco lifted one eyebrow. "So that was you? She said someone helped her."

Jak choked as he realized: Arianna had already spoken to Marco. She must have called them after he took off. "Yes, that would be me. I fought four wolves and betrayed my alpha to break her free of the estate. And now I'm prepared to do whatever I have to in order to break her free of the mating bond."

Marco's face opened with surprise before he shut it down again with suspicion. He threw a glare at Circe. "Did you tell him?"

The witch, for her part, looked amused. "No."

Marco leaned back, appraising Jak. He looked to his brother, the fresh-faced Kalis, and they exchanged a wordless conversation of pointed looks and head shakes. Jak didn't understand what it was all about, but the tension was ramping down. And when the elevator dinged and opened, neither of them made a move to board it.

After the door closed again, Jak asked, "Tell me what?"

Marco's lips were pressed tight, and Jak could tell he was debating whether to come clean about something. It was then that he saw how young these wolves really were. Arianna was twenty, but Marco was nearly the same age—maybe a year older or younger. Would he really be able to care for her after Jak was gone? But Marco's and Kalis's fierce loyalty to their sister, the risks they had already taken, contracting with Circe and the bounty hunters to get her back… Jak had to trust that once they were reunited, they wouldn't ever risk losing her again.

Finally, Marco looked to Circe, who nodded her encouragement. To Jak, he said, "We contracted with the witches to get Arianna back, but I'm not an idiot. I knew that wouldn't be enough. We're just two wolves, hardly even a pack. Against the Reds, we'd have no chance of keeping her free. The bond had to be broken, or her mate would keep hunting for her… until eventually, he would find her. And then things would be worse than before. Much worse."

Jak nodded, relief washing through him. Marco may be young, but he understood what was at stake. "Arianna would never truly be free. Even if you went on the run, you'd always be looking over your shoulder. All of you. Because Mace isn't just any mate—he's a dark bastard alpha. He'll tear through anything and anyone who stands between him and what he wants, and he really doesn't care who he has to kill to do it. And Arianna deserves better than to have the specter of him haunting her. She shouldn't have to go on the run for the rest of her life. And knowing Arianna, she'd never be able to live with that. She wouldn't want to bring that risk to *you.*"

Marco looked surprised. "That sounds like something Ari would say."

Jak smiled. *Ari.* It was a beautiful name, just like her. At the same time, it made his heart ache. He wasn't going to get the chance to dream up his own nickname for her. "The things she's been through with Mace… honestly, Marco, I'm not just in love with her. I'm kind of in awe of her. People like her —surviving the worst that life has to dole out, yet coming out as sweet and kind as she is, untouched by the darkness all around her—well, let's just say, those are the kind of people worth fighting for. Worth dying for."

Marco exchanged a glance with Kalis. "She needs someone like that looking after her."

"She does." Jak held Marco's steady gaze, and he could see that internal debate raging again as they both studied each other.

After a moment, Marco gave a short nod. "The witch has a spell. It will draw out the essence of her mate from her blood."

Jak glanced at the witch, who was keeping quiet. "I'm familiar with it."

Marco tipped his head to Circe. "I contracted with the witch to break Arianna free, not just because she could find the bounty hunters to do the job… but because she could help me break the bond."

Jak's eyebrows hiked up on his forehead. "Wait… *you* were planning on doing the spell yourself?"

Marco held him with a steely gaze. "Yes."

Jak hiked up one eyebrow and gave Circe a pointed look. "You know that spell will kill you, right?" This kid was either brave or stupid. Possibly both.

"Yes." Marco swallowed. "The question is, who's going to take care of her afterward? She would only have Kalis and our mother. But if you're in love with her the way you say you are…" Marco tipped his head up to give Jak another skeptical look. "The question is, can I trust you to take care of my sister after I'm gone?"

Jak smiled, and the last of the tension drained

out of him. This kid was definitely brave. And not at all stupid. Just like his sister. And clearly, he would do everything in his power to keep Arianna safe. He would protect her with his life. It was all Jak could ask for.

"You don't have to worry about that," Jak said to him. "Because you're not going to do the spell… I am."

A sea of emotions warred across Marco's face. Finally, he settled on a frown. "You said that before, that she was worth dying for. You really mean that, don't you?"

"I do. I'm just really glad she has a brother who understands what it will take to protect her afterward." Jak glanced to Circe. "That's why I asked the witch to bring you here."

Marco nodded, and Jak could see the uncertainty sweep away. "You had to be sure. About us."

"I had to be sure." Jak took a breath. "If you weren't up to the task, I'd have taken her on the run rather than do the spell. I couldn't risk stranding her, all alone, with no one to protect her. She could have fallen into even worse hands than Mace. But now that I know… well, that you're here… I can do what needs to be done."

Marco's frown carved deeper. "You really do love her."

"I do." Jak gave him a tight smile. "You can't tell her about any of this, Marco. Not until afterward. She'll never go through with it."

Marco's eyes widened slightly, and he nodded. "No, she wouldn't. I wasn't going to tell her myself until… well, until it was too late to back out."

Jak breathed a sigh of relief. "So you understand."

Marco shook his head. "No, I don't understand. Why are you doing this? I mean, she's my sister. I'd do anything for her. But you… you've just met her. You can't have known her for very long. Even if you're in love with her… it's not that I don't believe you. I'm just saying—I'm surprised."

Jak dipped his head, then looked up. "My mother was a captive mate. Let's just say I've been wanting a long time to right this particular kind of wrong." He hesitated—it was clear that Marco was an alpha if there ever was one. The good kind. He could rise to this… already was, in fact. Jak shuffled forward and put a hand on Marco's shoulder. He was talking to him brother-wolf to brother-wolf now. "I need your help in this, Marco. I need to know you'll be smart about this. Even with the mating bond broken, you'll need to move your whole family far away. So Mace won't be tempted. You don't know him like I do—he's one vindictive asshole. You need to find Arianna a good, strong alpha for a mate. Someone worthy of her. Who can protect her. It shouldn't be hard. She's everything any alpha would want." He paused, his heart breaking a little that *he* wouldn't be that alpha. "All I need is to know that she'll finally be safe. Can you promise me that?"

Marco's eyes were wide, but he didn't move away from Jak's brotherly hold on his shoulder. "I promise."

The kid was young, but Jak could tell this was a promise he would do everything in his power to keep. "And I need you to lie to her, just this once. Help me keep the secret of what the spell does until it's too late to do anything about it. And then… afterward… she's going to have a rough go of it for a while. But she'll get over it." He gave Marco a tight smile. "Like you said, she's only known me for a little while."

Marco nodded, still wide-eyed. "I won't say a thing. You have my word." Then, slowly, Marco lifted his hand and offered it to him. Jak took it, clasping him strongly like a brother would.

"Good man," Jak said, with a nod. "Now, I need to call Arianna. She's not far away, and she's probably going out of her mind, wondering what the hell happened to me and why I haven't called."

Marco gave a tiny smile. "Well, one thing you might not know about Ari is she's not exactly the patient type. In fact, she's on her way over."

Jak arched up an eyebrow and laughed a little. "That's right, she called you, didn't she? I told her not to. Obviously, that didn't stop her."

"Yeah, she doesn't listen to me, either." Marco smiled and released him from the handshake. "She did say she wanted me to meet the person who broke her free." Marco dropped his gaze for a moment then met Jak's stare. "I'm not sure I have the right words to thank you for this thing you're doing for my sister."

Jak smiled. "Hold up your end of the bargain, kid. That's all I need."

Marco gave a sharp nod. "You have my word."

Jak glanced at the younger one, Kalis—he was all wide eyes, keeping quiet while listening in. It stabbed Jak a little that he wasn't going to have the chance to get to know Arianna's kid brother. But he looked like the kind who would be a comfort to her.

Circe, meanwhile, was downright misty-eyed.

"Well, if this female wolf you all are so eager to die for is on her way, we might as well head out. No sense in bringing a mated female into the coven unnecessarily." She tapped the elevator button to call it again.

Jak had no idea where she was planning on taking them. But wherever it was, he hoped it was a decent place to die.

Chapter Twenty-Four

ARIANNA'S NERVES WERE STRETCHED TIGHT THE entire short ride to the witches' coven.

Sarra's battered Jeep looked like it had been stolen from an army surplus depot—after a tour overseas—but it was rugged and roomy. She said she was out of the healer business now, but Arianna could easily picture the Jeep transporting more than one pack of broad-shouldered shifters. The shocks were shot, making the ride pretty bumpy, but it served to take them from Sarra's down-and-out neighborhood to the sparkling towers of downtown Seattle. The address was for a place called Morgan Media, which sounded vaguely familiar. Mace didn't talk much about work, but she knew that Red Wolf worked with lots of businesses in the area, both as clients and as partners. That was probably where she had heard it.

But if it was really a coven of witches… it suddenly clicked in Arianna's head that Mace might have worked with the Morgan Media witches. He had a witch brought in when he was trying to mate with the Sparks pack female. And the Red pack had been involved with witches before—she seldom knew the details, but Mace often bragged about how the witches feared Red pack and not the other way around. Which she doubted was actually true.

But she suddenly worried about meeting her brothers there. If they were involved with the same witches as Mace and the Red pack… it just seemed a lot riskier for *all* of them to be there at the same time.

Arianna bit her lip as Sarra pulled into the parking garage. The Jeep lumbered into a spot barely large enough for it, and Sarra turned it off.

Arianna hesitated to leave the car.

Sarra frowned at her. "What's wrong?"

"I'm thinking that meeting at a witches' coven might not be the most brilliant idea I've ever had."

"Definitely not the safest move." Sarra smirked. "It is kind of genius though."

"I don't know about that." Arianna grimaced.

"My mate might not be as hesitant to come here as I thought."

Sarra heaved a sigh. "Okay. Then we get in, get your brothers, and get out. Yes?"

Arianna nodded her agreement.

They climbed out of the Jeep and crossed the parking garage's concrete floor quickly. Before, her excitement about seeing her family again had overwhelmed everything. Now, an awful anxiety itched up her back. She wanted to get them as far away as possible from anything that might be related to Mace.

As she and Sarra took the elevator up to the lobby, Arianna tried to settle her breathing, which was starting to hitch into panic mode. This was how her life was going to be from now on: running away from Mace, trying to keep her family safe. Always.

She might as well get used to it.

When they reached the glass-and-chrome lobby, it was beautifully appointed with plants, a mahogany receptionist desk, and sparkling granite floors. But the thing that stole her breath was the sight of three shifters waiting in the middle of the open-floored space: *Jak, Marco, and Kalis.*

Arianna broke away from Sarra, practically sprinting across the floor to the three men she loved most in this world… then she stalled out when she arrived in front of them, breathless. Words had forsaken her, tears were threatening, and she had no idea who to embrace first. She wanted to hug them all simultaneously, but instead, she stood frozen in front of them.

Kalis crashed through the awkwardness first, lunging forward to scoop her into a giant hug. He swept her off the floor and spun her around. She hugged him back, even as he was squeezing all the breath out of her. A smile nearly broke her face.

When he set her down, smiles had jumped to everyone's faces.

"Oh man, it's good to see you, Ari," Kalis said, his voice low and growly, so much deeper than when she saw him last. She had to reach up to ruffle his hair—he must have grown six inches, his shifter genes finally kicking in to turn her baby brother into a man.

It speared right through her heart.

She scowled at him and took both his cheeks in her hands, pinching them like their aunt Josie did before she passed. "Oh my god, it's my little Kalis!" she said in her best Aunt Josie impression.

He laughed and twisted his face out of her grip.

Then she dropped the fake voice and said,

"Jesus, Kal, seriously—when did you turn into the Incredible Hulk?"

He blushed and ducked his head, but she could tell he took it as a compliment. And that made her heart pound with happiness. Marco stepped up next, nudging their now-big baby brother aside to hug her. He held her for a long moment, and her tears nearly escaped her valiant attempts to hold them back.

When Marco finally loosened his grip, he still held her close and peered into her eyes. "Ari." His voice was thick. She knew him well enough—from running as a pack a hundred times, sharing thoughts—to know what was going through his mind. And she finally would be able to say all the things she'd imagined saying ever since Mace captured her… but never had the chance.

"It's not your fault, Marco." Her throat was closing up. "None of it was. Mace took what he wanted because he could. It's how he is. There's nothing you could have done except die trying to stop him. And I'd have never forgiven you for that."

She could tell he was tearing up, and she didn't want him to be embarrassed, so she grabbed him in another fierce hug. He held her tightly for another long moment before finally releasing her.

Only then did she turn to Jak—with a heart-twinge, because he was the only reason she was able to hug her brothers at all. If he was feeling neglected, he didn't show it: he was grinning ear-to-ear. She gave Marco's hand a squeeze before leaving his side.

"So *this* is your errand?" she said to Jak, teasing him and smiling just as hard. "Saving my life again?"

His smile faltered for just a split second, and she was afraid he somehow took her words the wrong way. So she flowed into his arms and hugged him tight.

As he buried his face in her hair, she said, quietly, just for him, "Oh my god, Jak, you brought my family back to me. Thank you."

His hands were on her back, holding her so tight, she didn't think he would ever let her go. For a long stretch of seconds, she just basked in the safety of his arms. Then thoughts of Mace wormed their way back into her mind: her family couldn't stay here, out in the open, exposed and vulnerable.

She eased back from Jak. He seemed reluctant to release her. There was such a mix of joy and pain on his face that it confused her. She was momentarily at a loss for words.

But then a voice spoke up, saying what she was thinking anyway. "We need to leave."

She turned to find the source—it was a strikingly beautiful woman in a red dress, tall and imposing, that she had somehow not noticed before in all the excitement. She had never met a witch before, but this woman was the perfect picture of one: an air of haughtiness, a magical beauty, and a powerful, glittering look in her eyes.

"This is all very sweet," she said, coolly, "but this isn't the place for a *pack* reunion." She threw an arched-eyebrow look to Jak.

"Arianna, meet Circe," Jak said softly, still holding her loosely in his arms. "And she's right. We need to move."

Sarra had already gone on full alert, holding back from the group, especially the witch. "In and out, Jak," she said, but she was really addressing the group. And keeping a hawk-eye on Circe. "That was our plan. Jeep's in the garage."

They didn't waste any more words, just hustled back to the elevator. Sarra was in the lead, with Jak and Arianna close behind. Marco and Kalis and Circe brought up the rear, which made Arianna frown: when did her brothers get so comfortable around witches? They kept quiet on the ride down.

It wasn't until they reached the Jeep that Arianna realized they should have some kind of plan before all piling in.

She pulled Jak to a stop with their clasped hands. "Sarra was super smart and brought some things for us to use on the road. But where do you want to head first?" She glanced back to Marco and Kalis. "Should we get my mom, too? I'm thinking if we're heading out of state—"

A gentle squeeze of her hand stopped her.

"We're not going out of state, my love," Jak said softly. He looked to Marco. "At least, not yet. Maybe after we're done."

Arianna frowned. "Done? What do you mean? We can't stay here. Mace will—"

"Arianna," Marco cut her off. "Let the man talk." He tipped his head to Jak.

That simple motion stirred all kinds of feelings around inside her chest: happiness that her brothers seemed to have already accepted Jak; irritation that Marco wasn't explaining what he was talking about; and a horrible dread, like black oozing tar dripping through her body. Something wasn't right here.

She turned to Jak. The pain in his eyes just clenched her stomach tighter.

"Circe is coming with us," Jak said, glancing at

the witch, who was holding back, watching them. "She's going to perform a spell that's going to break your mating bond with Mace."

"What?" Arianna wriggled out of his arms and took a step back. Then she glanced at Sarra, whose general wariness had gone up five levels of alarm. Arianna swung back to search Jak's eyes. He was serious about this. "I thought you said they couldn't do the spell."

"Well, I have to admit, I'd rather not do it," Jak said tightly. "Turns out I'll have to be involved and… it's on the painful side. At least, my part will be. When Circe first told me about what was involved…" He took a deep breath. "Well, it just seemed easier to get rid of Mace the old-fashioned way."

Arianna swallowed—if Jak would rather kill Mace to break the bond than do this spell, it had to be bad. Really bad.

"But that didn't exactly work out for you, did it?" Sarra's alarm level had settled into a fierce scowl. "And now you've got some hair-brained idea about using magic to break the spell. I swear to God, Jak—"

"Sarra." Jak's voice was full of alpha command,

and it almost made Arianna cringe, hearing it. For Sarra's sake.

Sarra pressed her lips tight, but the anger was clear on her face.

Which only made Arianna's anxiety shoot through the roof. "How bad is it, Jak?" she whispered. The black ooze was filling up her lungs, making it hard for her to breathe. She couldn't watch him get *hurt*… not over her. Not for anything. He'd already nearly bleed out in her car, all just to set her free.

The guilt was written all over his face. "It's really not that bad." He was lying to her. Completely.

"Tell me the truth." Her fear was rising up and making her angry. A terrified kind of angry. "Tell me the truth, or I swear, I'm marching right back to Mace's house."

He threw up his hands. "All right, all right." He glowered at her. "It will hurt. A lot. I'll probably pass out from the pain. I may scream like a little girl. I'm not exactly proud of this, Arianna. I should have just done this from the start instead of being… squeamish. I'm a shifter, for god's sake. It's not like a little pain is something I can't handle. It's just that…" He lowered his voice and dropped his gaze to the floor. Then he spoke softly, like he was confessing to something even more embarrassing. "It reminds me a little of when I was young. When my brothers used to slice me up for fun. I really didn't want to… well… revisit that." He took a deep breath and peered at her. "But it's going to be worth it. To get you free."

And that part had the ring of truth. She could feel it in her heart.

"Oh, Jak." She was back in his arms in a heartbeat, a fierce hold on him with her arms around his neck. But it was nothing like the hold he had on her like he couldn't get her close enough to him. She forced herself to let him go and gently pulled away, far enough to look in his eyes. "You don't have to do this. We can just run away—"

He put a finger across her lips, softly. To keep her from speaking, but also to trace them with his fingertip. "He'll find us, my love. And then I'll lose you and everything we have together. I can't let that happen."

His fingers wandered to her cheek, and a small, terribly sad smile lifted the corners of his mouth.

She kept her voice soft, just for him. "What did I ever do to deserve someone like you?"

His smile grew as he caressed her face. "You were just… you."

Arianna had the vague sense that the others were still there—her brothers, Sarra, the witch Circe—but it was as though they had faded away into the dark corners of the parking garage. So she gave into the urgent need to kiss Jak, pressing her lips to his. She meant for it just to be a soft kiss, a gentle touch so he would feel her love, but Jak's hands were instantly in her hair, his lips devouring hers. He was breathing her in, consuming her in a way she couldn't help but give herself over to—he was her alpha in every real sense of the word. She had submitted to him, and the magic of that bond flared between them, turning the kiss hotter and more full of love than anything she had ever experienced, even when they were deep in the throes of their lovemaking. It was like he possessed her in that moment, claiming her in a way that went beyond magic. She was his. She *belonged* to him. It left her gasping for breath when he finally broke the kiss, still holding her tight but only lightly brushing her lips with his.

He was breathing hard as well, but then he slowly eased his hold on her. The rest of the world came swimming back. Her lips were still tender with his kiss, but a rush of heat flooded her cheeks as she realized everyone was staring at them. Kalis was gawking in amazement. Marco's eyes were blazing, but he didn't make a move. Circe's smile was broad, which surprised her, but Sarra's gaze was averted… which made the heat in Arianna's cheeks flame higher.

She turned back to Jak. "We should probably leave," she said quietly, still absorbed by the kiss. "Where exactly are we going to do this… spell?" The black ooze started to creep back in with the thought of what Jak was doing for her. But it was his fervent wish to do this: that much she could tell. He wanted to break her free of Mace's hold forever—and then she and Jak would be free to mate. She would truly be *his* in every way, including magic. And there was nothing in the world that could make her say no to that.

Jak loosened his hold on her further, just taking her hand in his. He looked to Circe. "Did you have a place in mind?"

She was still smiling over them like her good humor was a benediction. "We have a few clients with unfinished construction projects downtown. One's on a temporary suspension of work due to a dispute with the city. Seems like a good place to conduct our business in private."

Jak gave her a solemn nod. Then he threw an apologetic look to Sarra. "Sarrabear, you don't need to be a part of this. Thanks for taking care of Arianna for me. We can find our way from here."

"Oh hell no." Sarra was still pissed. "I don't know what you're getting yourself into, Jak Roberts, but I have a feeling you're going to need a healer in your near future."

Jak opened his mouth to object, but he seemed to think better of it. He shut it again and tipped his head to the Jeep. "Still have the beast, I see. Maybe you could give us a lift?"

"Exactly what I was thinking." Sarra stormed off to the driver's side.

Jak frowned, watching her go.

"She'll get over it," Arianna said quietly to him. "I'll talk to her."

He turned back to her with a soft look on his face that confused her again: it was like joy and pain were warring across it like angels and demons were taking turns prodding his soul. She clasped his hand harder, trying to reassure him, even though her own heart was quaking. Would she be strong enough to let him do this? Could she watch him writhe in pain under the witch's spell without dying a little inside herself?

She pulled in a breath—if Jak could be brave about this, so could she.

Circe and her brothers were already piling into the van. They had left the front seat open, so Arianna and Jak took that for themselves. Even with the roominess of the Jeep, it was still cramped with so many people. Arianna had to sit on Jak's lap in order to not have her legs tangle with the massive stick-shift of the ancient car. In the back seat, Circe seemed entirely too happy to be sandwiched between Marco on one side and Kalis on the other. Marco glowered at her, but Kalis's mouth seemed to hang permanently open at Circe's beauty.

As they pulled out of the parking garage, the Jeep's lousy suspension made Arianna bounce on Jak's lap. With Sarra's eyes on the road, and the others stuck in the back seat, no one appeared to notice Jak's hands roaming her body. He didn't seem to be trying to arouse her, necessarily, although it definitely had that effect. He was just skimming his fingers lightly along her thighs, the backs of her knees, up across her stomach and along the undersides of her breasts. Like he was making a map of her body with just his fingertips.

She ducked her head close to his ear to whisper, "What are you doing?"

He adjusted her on his lap to pull her in for a kiss. Just a soft one this time. "Touching you." His smile was only half devilish smirk. The other half still carried some kind of pain.

She traced her fingertips along his cheek, mimicking his traveling touch. "Why?"

"Because I can." Then he pulled her into a more serious kiss.

She lost track of where they were going, the city towers whizzing past outside the window, and just kissed this man who was giving her the most precious gift of all: *freedom.*

Chapter Twenty-Five

Jak was so lost in kissing Arianna, he didn't realize they had stopped.

The bright morning sun glinted off the bare girders all around them in the construction site. Sarra had pulled the Jeep right up onto the bare dirt, next to the construction company's trailer and several ten-foot-high stacks of sheetrock and lumber. An enormous crane stood silent and unmoving in the center, with a half dozen lifts and diggers filling out the wide-open construction area and waiting for the contractor to settle their dispute and return to work. Half-constructed skeletons of buildings surrounded them on three sides, but at least one had the ground level built out. There were concrete floors and some sheetrock walls up: enough to give them privacy for the spell.

And there was plenty of equipment to bury him once it was done.

Jak was loathe to move Arianna even a centimeter off his lap, but the rest of the crew had already climbed out of the Jeep. He gently eased her down from the high seat of the car, keeping a hold on her hand as he followed her out.

Circe was giving disgusted looks to the dirt-packed ground, but she gamely was making her way in teetering heels toward the enclosed building. Arianna's brothers were following close behind, but Sarra was holding back, waiting for him and Arianna. And openly glaring at Jak.

She had to know something was up. She knew him better than anyone else here, and that was just the problem: she might guess what was happening before he could complete the spell. He just hoped she wouldn't say anything… until it was too late to stop it.

Then she could curse him as much as she wanted.

He laced his fingers with Arianna's and pulled her closer as they trudged toward the building. Not only did he want to touch her as much as possible in these last moments, but he had a feeling his love for Arianna was a kind of shield—one that would make Sarra hold her tongue.

He was right: Sarra's hot glare finally left his face and dropped to their clasped hands. Then she turned away and marched with stomping boots toward the witch and his fate awaiting in the construction building.

Arianna snuggled closer to his side. "Sarra's just angry because she doesn't want to see you get hurt." He could feel the tremors racing through her body, one small hand holding his, the other gripping his arm. "She's afraid."

He frowned down at her, his heart skipping a beat. He knew she was talking about herself as much as Sarra. "There's no need to be afraid. When I'm…" He swallowed down the lump growing in his throat. "When I'm going through the spell, your brothers will be here to take care of you."

She peered up at him with an earnest look full of love. Which just made his heart swell… and calmed the writhing tentacles of fear working through his body.

"I'm not afraid." She was lying; he could feel

the fear in every quiver of her body. "I trust you, Jak."

He blinked, a tsunami of doubt threatening to pull him under. He was lying to her. His last and final act with her would be a lie. He hated that—hated every part of it—but it was necessary. He prayed she would forgive him in the end. For now… he pulled her to a stop and kissed her once more, soft and sweet. Then he laced his fingers with hers again and picked up the pace toward the building. He needed to do this before he lost his nerve altogether. Or Sarra put the pieces together. Or anything else could go sideways to stop it.

Everyone was waiting, a tense circle of silence, when they arrived at the shadowy half-built building. The sun only penetrated in strips that painted the floor with prison-bar shadows that were really reflections of the girders. It gave an eerie half-light, half-dark feel to the concrete-and-bare-steel skeleton.

Sarra was still fuming.

Jak ignored her and turned to Circe. "So, how is this going to work?"

Circe's earlier smiles had faded. In fact, every face had a grim look to it now, which Jak supposed was fitting for the funeral most of them knew this was about to be.

"I'll need DNA from both of you," Circe said, beckoning Jak and Arianna with her long dagger-nailed fingers.

"How's that?" Jak asked. He really hoped they didn't have to draw blood or do anything painful to Arianna. That might undo him.

"Just a sample of your hair, you big baby," Circe said, but her voice was gentle and teasing. She stepped up to them, her heels clacking on the concrete. Using two fingers, she plucked one of Arianna's long black strands of hair, floating gently in the breeze. Then she reached for Jak's head, but he stopped her, opting to yank out his own DNA sample for her. She twirled the two bits of hair and follicle-root into a small ball in the middle of her palm.

Jak had seen Hecca, Circe's sister, do something similar with the Sparks pack female, trying to force her to shift. He also remembered that being far from a painless encounter for the girl. He clasped Arianna's hand tighter in his.

"Is this going to hurt Arianna in any way?" Jak asked.

Circe's voice was cool. "It won't be painful, so

much as… uncomfortable. Her mate's essence will not willingly leave." She turned to Arianna, towering over her and boring a steady gaze into her eyes. "This is a dark art we are performing, Arianna. You have essentially two wolves inside your blood—yours and your mate's. To extract one while leaving the other is a delicate thing… not unlike slicing out half of your soul while leaving the other half behind."

Arianna swallowed visibly. "Whatever it takes… is fine."

Jak could see her quivering. The witch was scaring her. "Circe." He put a warning in his voice.

Circe threw him a sharp look. "Do you want this to succeed, little wolf?"

He pressed his lips tight. She knew the answer to that.

"It's important for Arianna to understand what she will be facing," Circe said carefully, but he got the message: *Arianna had to be fully prepared for her side.* Especially if she was going to be kept in the dark about Jak's part.

"Fine," he said tightly.

Circe turned her attention back to Arianna, whose eyes had gone wide. Circe's voice softened. "The wolf essence of your mate will not want to leave. And your wolf will fight the separation as well. You must bring everything *human* that you have to this, Arianna. The part of you that wants to be free of your mate, that's the part that needs to be the strongest today. The spell *will* work… but there will be less, shall we say, damage, if you can lower your resistance to it and help force your mate's essence away from you."

Arianna sucked in a breath. "What do you mean *damage?*"

"It won't be a physical thing… more of a psychological trauma. And your wolf… she will suffer the most from this. You need to let her know you're doing it for her own best interest."

Jak had no idea how Arianna would do that, but she was nodding like she understood what Circe was talking about.

"It may not be as hard as you think," Arianna said with a soft smile and a peek at Jak. "My wolf has already submitted to Jak. She already believes he is our true mate. We both know it in our hearts."

The love on Arianna's face nearly broke Jak's heart.

Circe smiled, tightly, and placed her hand sweetly on Arianna's shoulder. "I'm sure that you do, dear."

Jak had to look away. They needed to do a whole lot less talking and get on with this, or he wasn't going to make it through. As he was avoiding the love and hope on Arianna's face—and her conviction that she and Jak were destined to be mates—his wandering gaze found Sarra's face. And she was red in the face with fury.

He whipped his gaze back to Circe. "We need to move this along."

She took a deep breath. "Very well."

But Sarra was already crossing the dozen feet of concrete floor between them, fists clenched at her side. Circe waved her hand over the tangle of his and Arianna's hair in her palm. It slowly began to smoke, and Jak could feel it tugging on him, deep inside, bonding him to Arianna. He edged closer to her, taking her hand once more.

Sarra had stopped just behind the witch, hovering there with a murderous look on her face, like she was ready to shift and stop Jak that way. But Sarra couldn't shift—that had been the problem all along between them, but really, only on her side. Plus her stubborn conviction that he deserved someone better than her, someone just like Arianna, for a mate. And maybe she was right in the end: he was right here, right now, doing the thing he was always meant to do. He could feel that in his bones.

And at this point, nothing could stop him, not even Sarra. She could try, but she wasn't capable of stopping him physically. And he would just have to ignore her words.

"Jak," Sarra hissed. "Can I have a word with you?"

"Little busy at the moment." He avoided looking at her.

The smoking ball of hair in Circe's palm had transformed into a tiny grayish cloud that hung just above it. She lifted her hand up to Arianna's face, holding her other hand above it as if cupping the cloud with both hands, while in reality touching neither. It was a ball of spell, and Circe was whispering incantations into it. Small lightning strikes appeared within the ball, sparking and crackling the air with magic.

Sarra shoved past the witch to stand right in front of Jak. She stared angrily up into his face. "I need to talk to you about this... *now.*"

"Sarra, please," Jak begged her. "If you've ever loved me..." If he ordered her away, would she go? He just needed another minute to make this happen. With each snap of lightning in Circe's spell, he could feel that twinge inside growing stronger, binding him closer to Arianna. He could already sense the two wolves within her: her own and Mace's. He needed to focus, to draw Mace out when the time was right.

And Sarra needed to leave him alone. But she was still in his face.

"If I ever loved you?" She was spitting angry now. "I love you *now*, Jak Roberts." She threw a pinched look to Arianna. "Not in the way *she* loves you. Or the way you love her. I don't mean like that. I love you like a *friend*… one who wants to know what the hell you think you're doing here!"

Jak didn't say anything, just ignored Sarra and turned to look at Arianna. The bond between them was intensifying. He met her gaze, and there were fine lines forming at the corners of her eyes as she squinted with it, too. It wasn't so much pain as… *discomfort.* Like Circe said. He hoped that was all it would be for Arianna in the end.

"Jak!" Sarra grabbed hold of his arm, forcing his attention back to her. She searched his face. He wasn't sure what she wanted to see there.

Marco had come up behind her. He gave a nod to Jak then laid a hand on Sarra's shoulder. It was a gentle touch, but she jumped from the contact, then threw suspicious looks back and forth between Jak and Marco.

"Oh my god," she said, almost a whisper. "You're in on this together."

She knew.

Jak closed his eyes briefly, then opened them to stare Sarra in the face.

"You stop this right now," she said, lips trembling.

"Jak?" Arianna's worried voice punched him in the gut.

He squeezed her hand and threw her a soft look. "It's going to be all right, Arianna. I promise." Then he turned back to Sarra. "You always knew this was how it would go, in the end, Sarrabear. You even said it yourself. I was meant for someone else."

Her eyes were wide, and her head shook back and forth in tiny movements.

He put his free hand, the one not holding Arianna's hand, on Sarra's shoulder. "This is the single best thing I'm ever going to do."

She shook her head more fervently.

He grimaced. The bond was squeezing on him. "Don't ruin it for me, okay, Sarrabear?"

She gaped at him, but he couldn't wait any longer. He swung to face Circe, who was watching him with a razor-sharp eye, the ball of magic twitching and sparking in her hand.

"Do it," he told her.

As fast as the lightning in her palm, Circe smashed her hands together then rent them apart, a piece of magic cloud in each. She quickly blew on each hand in turn, one long sweeping breath. The two clouds puffed over them, one into Arianna's face and one into Jak's.

Arianna gasped.

Sarra screamed, "No!"

Jak couldn't pay attention to either one because it felt like his soul was ripping in two.

The bond he had with Arianna shattered. He fell to his knees, not so much with pain, but the sudden disconnection was giving him massive vertigo. He reeled with the sensation of it. And yet… he wasn't entirely disconnected. He still held her hand, but more… he could feel tenuous threads, like straws piping something, some essence, from her into him. It was like a thick oil sludge dripping straight into his veins, and each drip brought with it a welling up from deep inside him. At first, it was an ache, like a toothache or a headache that nags at you all day, but never really makes its presence known. But it kept growing… and growing…

each drip making it stronger, until it was the pounding, skull-splitting kind, the headache that lays you out for an entire day.

He tried to keep the groans inside, but it was getting harder.

Still, the drips came, only now they were more of a pumping gush, filling him with a sludge that was drowning him, dripping into every tiny crevice of his body. Then the gushing stopped, and he could feel the entirety of it—almost like he had been wholly possessed by a dark spirit.

Mace's wolf.

Jak's wolf snarled and howled, but there was nowhere to turn, nothing to do. The enemy was *inside* him. He dropped Arianna's hand and clutched at his stomach. He fell forward but kept himself from falling on his face by bracing his hand on the cool concrete floor. He really didn't want to throw up. He wanted the end to come with some kind of dignity… but the pain was really starting to escalate now. His wolf was howling in his ears.

Jak felt hands on him, urging him to turn, to lie down. His body was starting to cramp up so he couldn't resist them. His vision was blurred, white stars shooting across it from the rippling pain that was tearing him apart from the inside out. He blinked so he could see the faces hovering over him.

It was Arianna. Beautiful Arianna, her face all squished up and worried for him. Tears raced down her cheeks, but he couldn't uncramp his hands to brush them away. Her lips were moving. She was saying something. But sounds seemed to come and go like he was moving through a tunnel and cars were speeding past him, taking their blaring horns and near-misses with them. He tried to focus past the blinding pain. Tried to hear the things she was saying.

Somewhere in the background, Sarra was cursing like a sailor. It would have made him smile, except his face was frozen in a grimace. He strained to shut out the background and just focus on Arianna's shining face above him. Her beautiful, brilliant blue eyes. If that was the last thing he saw in this world, it would be okay. It would be enough.

Her words leaked through the shrieking pain inside his head. "Jak… Jak… stay with me… please…"

He licked his lips. So dry, they cracked. It was such a small pain on top of the large one singing through his body—two wolves locked in a death dance at the DNA level. He tried to speak, but it was only whooshes of air, no sound. Just grunts… and he was afraid he wouldn't be able to get those last words out… the ones he wanted to say, but couldn't. Not until the very end.

He concentrated everything he had on forming words. He thought of Arianna's sweet hands, now on his face, holding his cheeks. Her tears dripping on him. And somehow he managed to get his lips to cooperate and make sound.

"You," he gasped, speaking it just for her. The one word felt like a triumph. He pushed for more. "You… are meant… for someone better than me." The words laced through the gasps, but he heard them. He hoped she could hear them too.

Her eyes went wide with alarm. And he knew that she *knew* at that moment. Knew that this wasn't something he was coming back from.

"No, no, no," she said, over and over.

But he wasn't finished.

"I'm just…" he gasped out, and she stopped her tirade, bending low, placing her cheek against his, wetting him with her tears and bringing her ear close enough for his whispers to reach her. "I'm just… the one who… set you free."

He heard her gasp. He saw her pull back, but the sounds were gone again. Everything was dimming… the bright morning sunshine of Seattle was darkening like an eclipse had turned everything into the blood red of sunset. Then darker still. A creeping blackness.

The sludge inside him was waning too. All of it was fading.

The last thing he saw was a single tear clinging to the edge of Arianna's sweet cheek. It clung, holding on to the bitter end.

Then it fell.

He wished he had the strength for one more kiss.

Then the world faded completely to black.

Chapter Twenty-Six

"I'M JUST... THE ONE WHO... SET YOU FREE." JAK'S words, broken by gasps of pain, whispered in Ariana's ear. Her tears were already sliding down her cheek, which was pressed against his so she could hear his achingly soft voice.

But his words... those were the words of a dying man.

She yanked back, the breath stolen right out of her body. *No. No, no, no.* She couldn't tell if her words were in her head or coming out of her mouth, but a horrible chill invaded her body, shooting icicles of death through her heart: this spell was killing him.

"Jak!" She clasped his face in her hands, still wet from her tears. "Jak, you can't leave me. You can't."

She was babbling, and tears were streaming down her face, clinging to the edge then falling down to his cheek, but none of it was stopping his eyes from glazing over. None of it kept his face from going slack in her hands as his eyes drifted closed.

"Nooo!" she screamed. Hands were on her, strong hands, lifting her up and away from Jak, whose face went still as soon as she lost her frantic hold on him.

"No!" Arianna fought to stand on her own unsteady legs and wrenched herself from the hands holding her. They belonged to her brother Marco, whose face was twisted in pain as well, but it was the emotional kind: the kind where he was already trying to comfort her for Jak's death while his body was still warm on the floor.

No. He couldn't die. She refused to let that happen.

She whipped around to Circe, the witch who had cast this godforsaken spell, tearing Mace's wolf magic from Arianna's body and putting it into Jak's. Circe *had* to know it would kill him. And the look on her face—sorrow laced with guilt—there was no question she knew.

Raging against a witch might be one of the stupidest things Arianna had ever done, but she didn't care. In fact, she barely gave it a thought as she lurched toward Circe.

"Stop it!" Arianna demanded, halting just short of grabbing hold of Circe's shoulders and shaking her. "Stop the spell. You're killing him!"

Circe frowned, and her expression was filled with pity, but she didn't move a muscle, just flitted a look around the barren concrete-and-girder construction site she had picked as a good place for Jak to die. Then she glanced at Marco, who had come up behind Arianna. He put a hand on her shoulder, which she batted away. Her brothers had to be in on this, too—a quick glance at her younger brother Kalis showed his face heavy with guilt as well. Only Sarra was frothing at the mouth, kicking the concrete flooring and swearing up a storm, the same rage animating her that was boiling inside of Arianna. Her fists curled up, and she felt like she might explode.

"Ari, he wanted it this way," Marco said softly.

"No!" It was a guttural thing wrenched from deep inside her. Arianna swung back to the witch, leaning in until she was practically nose-to-nose with her. "You do whatever dark art you have to do, but *you save him.* Or I swear to god, I will make you pay for this." Her lips trembled with fury. What

could she do to force a witch to undo her black magic?

Circe seemed unconcerned with Arianna's threat. If anything, she looked at Arianna with even more pity. She glanced at Jak's form on the floor. Arianna could barely look at his motionless body without losing it altogether, so she kept her glare on Circe's face, willing her to change her mind and withdraw this horrible spell.

Circe faced her again, her expression full of compassion. "The wolves inside him are almost finished with their battle. When they have destroyed each other, they will have destroyed Jak's body in the process. There's nothing that can stop that now."

"There *has* to be!" Arianna refused to believe it was hopeless. "Stop the wolves from fighting. Reverse the spell before they destroy him. Then his normal shifter healing can bring him back." She forced herself to look at Jak… he was nearly as pale as death already. "Pull Mace's wolf out of him and put it back in me." A shudder ran through her with that thought, but she would rather have that than let Jak die for her.

"You're no longer mated to Mace," Circe said softly, a hand landing like a small bird on Arianna's shoulder. "And an unmated female *is* the only thing that could draw Mace's wolf out of Jak's body at this point, given the death battle they're engaged in… but I will not undo the spell."

Arianna's whole body quivered with the need to make this happen. "Please." It was a whisper. She would fall on her knees and beg if she had to. "Please don't let him die."

"He's given his life to free you, Arianna," Circe said gently. "I will not undo such a precious and costly gift."

Arianna's vision blurred with a fresh round of tears that felt like they might drown her. This couldn't happen. She couldn't let this happen. She held her breath, hoping against hope that something, some thought, some idea, would suddenly materialize and give her something to cling to, some way to save Jak. She didn't notice Sarra raging up to Circe until she shoved her way in between Arianna and the witch and glared up into Circe's face.

"What did you just say?" Sarra demanded.

Circe cocked an eyebrow like she thought Sarra was slightly insane. "Jak is giving his life for—"

"No," Sarra cut her off, her voice low and

intense. "The other part. About the unmated female."

Hope surged in Arianna's heart. What was Sarra saying? *Would she… ?* Arianna swiped her eyes clear of tears. "Sarra—"

She held up a hand, practically shoving it in Arianna's face. "Let the witch talk."

Circe was frowning and shooting uncertain looks between Arianna and Sarra. "Mace's wolf is mourning the loss of its mate. The wolves in Jak's blood are pure magic, but Mace's wolf also carries his essence—an essence that was forcibly torn from its female half and which would be drawn instantly back again to any unmated female if…" Circe tipped her head to Arianna. "If I were to allow a conduit between them. Which I will not."

Arianna's heart thudded in her chest. She knew where Sarra was going with this. "Sarra, you can't—"

"Shut it." But Sarra's voice was quivering as much as Arianna's. She kept her focus on Circe. "Arianna's not the only unmated female here." Her words were slow and grave and steeped in a kind of iron-will that didn't surprise Arianna in the slightest. "Can you do it? Can you draw Mace's wolf into me before it kills Jak?"

Circe's perfectly manicured eyebrows hiked higher with each slow word from Sarra. "It can be done. But you would be unable to mate with any other wolf. Ever."

Sarra twisted up one side of her mouth in a smirk. "It's been that way for a while." Then she visibly swallowed. "Would I be his mate? The asshole. The one Jak rescued her from?"

Arianna's heart sank. She couldn't wish that on anyone… but at the same time, it was the only thing that might save Jak's life. And if Circe wouldn't do it for Arianna, but she would do it for Sarra… could Arianna say no to that? *Should she?* Her heart was tearing into pieces with this.

Circe frowned. Then she brushed past Sarra and Arianna and strode over to where Jak lay as still as a stone on the floor. The witch passed her hands over his head as if sensing something in the air all around him.

"His aura is extremely weak, but I can still feel it." She peered back over her shoulder at them. "The wolves are likewise near death. If you were to draw out Mace's wolf now, I do not think it would be enough to fully mate with your inner wolf, Sarra. It would depend on how strong the two halves are, male and female. The mating is a pairing of like with like." She bit her lip and frowned. "I'm honestly not sure what would happen. But if we're going to do anything, we'll have to work quickly. It may already be too late."

Sarra dashed over, plucked a hair out of her head, and offered it to Circe. "Then you better get busy."

Circe twirled her fingers in the air. The hair in Sarra's hand magically jumped into the witch's hand. Then she fluttered the fingers in her other hand, ruffling a magical wind through Jak's hair that liberated a strand of his. She quickly mashed them together and recreated the grayish, sparking spell-cloud she used on Arianna and Jak.

Arianna lurched forward, taking Sarra by the elbow and turning her. "Are you sure about this? If Mace doesn't feel the mating bond break, if he keeps coming after me…" She swallowed. How could she allow any other woman to fall back into the trap she had with Mace? When she knew full well how awful that life was?

Marco came up to Sarra's other side, taking her other elbow gently in his hand. Sarra gave him a quizzical look but didn't pull away. Arianna could feel her shake, and it was likely that she and Marco were the only things keeping Sarra's knees from buckling.

Marco dipped his head to peer into Sarra's eyes. "If Mace comes after you, he's going to have to go through me first." He nodded to Jak. "I imagine you'll have more than one wolf wanting to take a bite out of him before he can get anywhere near you."

Sarra quivered a bit, then sucked in a breath and let it out slow. Marco strengthened his hold on Sarra's arm, and Arianna could tell it was helping. Still… she was horribly uncertain about letting Sarra take the risk, but if it could save Jak… Arianna couldn't blame her for wanting to. She would do it herself in a heartbeat if the witch let her.

Circe smashed her hands together and blew the cloud of grayish spell on Sarra's face and then Jak's. Sarra stiffened, and Arianna and Marco both edged closer, making sure she was supported. Arianna's stomach writhed as she watched Sarra's face: eyes squeezed shut, mouth set in a grim line, small flinches as the spell took hold. Arianna knew exactly what she was feeling: the slow drip of blackness that was Mace's wolf, creeping into her body. Into her *soul.* The moment Arianna had been liberated from

Mace's wolf had been the most glorious, heart-lifting moment of her life… until she saw Jak writhing on the floor because of it. And now Sarra was taking back what Arianna had finally worked free of… only diluted, weakened maybe. Less by some measure.

Still… Arianna felt the guilt of that weighing down her heart.

But all of that was forgotten when Jak sucked in a breath, his pale face springing to life. He moaned, eyes still shut… and then even that small sign of life faded. Sarra rocked back, away from Jak. When she sagged, Marco caught her. Her eyes were still closed.

But it was the return of lifelessness to Jak's face that riveted Arianna's attention. "Circe?" Her voice was hushed, more of a gasp than a question.

The witch scowled, her hands floating again around Jak's head. "He's too weak. Mace's wolf is gone, but there's hardly any magic left in Jak's blood." Circe whipped her head to Arianna. "Do you want to save him?"

"Yes!" Arianna cried and dropped to her knees next to Circe and Jak's body. "Just tell me what to do."

"He needs blood. Magical blood. A lot of it."

Arianna thrust both wrists, upturned, toward the witch. "Take it."

"I'll only take the magic," she said quickly. "But it will be painful, Arianna."

"Hurry!" she said, tears springing to life again.

Circe clamped one hand around Arianna's wrist and the other around Jak's.

Then the world turned to white-hot pain. Arianna's vision blanked out, but she felt her body jerk back, falling to the concrete floor next to Jak's until she was lying prone next to him, still tethered to Circe by the iron-clad grip she had on her wrist. Before, cleaving Mace's magic out of her blood had felt like a twisting pile of snakes worming their way throughout her body… this bleeding of her magic into Jak felt like her soul was literally being torn in two. *Save Jak. Save Jak. Save Jak.* She focused on the words like they were a mantra, clamping her teeth against the scream that wanted to wrench loose and trying to breathe through the pain, even as her back arched up from the concrete with it.

Suddenly it was gone, along with Circe's hold on her wrist. Arianna's body slumped back to the ground, and the chill of the concrete floor seeped into her fevered skin. She blinked away the black spots swimming in front of her eyes, but the pain was completely gone now. Echoes of it still shuddered her body, and she was still gasping from it, but she ordered her body to obey her commands and roll over so she could see Jak.

He was stirring to life again. This time his face was twisted up as he fought through something, his eyes still closed. Arianna held back tears as she edged closer to him. She didn't know if he was in pain, or if he was just struggling to come back from the near-death precipice he had been hanging over. Arianna laid a hand on his chest, but he didn't seem to notice, still moaning and grimacing and shaking his head back and forth, like he was fighting something inside. Was there still some trace of Mace in his blood? She could feel Jak's heart beating under her hand, and he was obviously alive. What was happening?

Circe was still hovering over him, her hands held out as if in benediction, but clearly doing something very different: reading his aura? She mentioned it before.

"Does he need more?" Arianna asked her. "I can give him more." The truth was she felt lightheaded from the pain, but also weaker in another way… she wasn't sure how much of her magic the witch had transferred to Jak, but her hands trembled against Jak's chest as she held him. But whatever she had, she would give him.

"You can't spare any more," Circe said without looking at her. "And this should be enough. The question is whether his body will reject your magic… or if it will be enough to spur his blood to regenerate and rebuild his own magical supply."

Arianna hadn't thought of it that way: that her magic was different than Jak's. Unique to her. In a way, they were now mated, only in the most unusual way possible: *her magic in his blood,* instead of the other way around. It was amazing and beautiful to be joined to him this way… as long as his blood accepted her.

"How long until we know?" Arianna asked, her heart squeezing. She knew it was his magic and not *him.* She knew that Jak would never reject her, but his wolf… his inner magic… she didn't know.

"Very soon," Circe said, her face still grim with concentration, her hands still slowly stroking the air around Jak's head. "He was very near death, Arianna. If he rejects your magic, he will…" She stopped and glanced at Arianna. "We will know soon."

Arianna gritted her teeth to hold back her tears. Then she scooted closer to Jak, lying along the length of his body on the cold concrete floor. She ever-so-gently rested her head on his shoulder, her hand gripping his chest, her lips close to his ear. Her nearness seemed to calm some of his silent struggling, and his body stilled. She fought against the tears and the thought that maybe his body was growing quieter because she was losing him.

"Please Jak," she whispered, the words thick in her throat. "You were willing to die for me, but now… now I need you to *live.* For me." She swallowed. He wasn't moving at all, not even a breath moving in his chest. *"Please."*

Circe's hands move more rapidly in their examination of his aura, then suddenly stopped. Arianna's heart nearly stopped with it, but then Circe extended her hands over Arianna's head as well.

"Keep talking," Circe said, tightly.

Arianna's heart hammered back to life. She edged even closer, brushing her lips against Jak's cheek. It was still salty from her tears spilled on him before.

"Jak," she whispered against his skin. "You belong to me, and I belong to you. You're my alpha, and you promised… you *promised* everything would be all right. But nothing will be all right without you. Not ever again. Please… come back to me."

Slowly, Jak's chest rose as he pulled in a long breath. When he let it out slowly, Arianna was afraid he wouldn't take another one. But he did. And another after that. She looked to Circe for a sign that this was something… this was real…

There was a smile on the witch's face.

"Come on, Jak, you big baby," she said, lowering her hands. "Wake up." She snapped her fingers, and his eyes slowly opened.

Arianna let out a gasp. *They did it.* She lifted up from the floor and grabbed Jak's face with both hands, barely believing it.

He squinted up at her like he wasn't quite sure what he was seeing. "Arianna?"

She laughed a little, grinning like a mad fool.

And then kissed him thoroughly.

Chapter Twenty-Seven

Arianna is kissing him.

Jak was convinced he must be in heaven—not only did this kiss feel otherworldly, like he was closer to her now, in this mere locking of lips, than he had ever been before, even when buried deep inside her, but… *he was kissing Arianna.*

He had to be dead.

God had given him a reward: somehow Jak had died and stayed in some dark, unknowing place until Arianna could join him in the afterlife. And now they were together again. Only her lips were too soft. Her hair spilling across his face too real. And if this *was* real, if he was alive… then there was a witch who was seriously going to pay for it.

His arms were shaky and weak, but somehow

he managed to brush back Arianna's hair, gently cup her cheeks, slow the kiss, and lift her beautiful, smiling face away from his. The hardest part was that he didn't want to break the connection between them. He actually felt a physical twinge course through him as she leaned back, putting distance between his lips and hers. Her face glowed with happiness. Other faces swam into view: Circe, the witch; Sarra hovering over him with a troubled look; Marco and Kalis hanging back, but watching intently. The rest of the construction site sat in the background, just barely in focus with his still-blurry vision.

Dammit.

Someone had stopped the spell. The witch had gone back on her word.

A growl rumbled up from deep inside him, and he struggled up to sitting.

He glared at Circe. "What did you do, *witch?*" His fists were balled up at his side, and he was seriously contemplating raking a handful of claws across her too-pretty face. He would have done it already, except she could reduce him to ash without thinking.

The witch looked unimpressed. "Well, excuse me for saving your life." She sighed with elaborate patience then climbed to her feet, teetering on her heels. "You wolves really need to work on your manners." But there was a smirk on her face that didn't match the anger boiling in his chest. All of this was for nothing.

He ground his teeth. "That wasn't our deal."

"And what exactly *was* your deal, Jak Roberts?" Sarra asked, pushing forward and threatening to get in his face. But her face was contorting like Circe's as if she couldn't decide whether to smile or snarl at him.

Jak winced, realizing he really didn't want to reveal the details of his arrangement with the witch. Sure, they hadn't carried through with it, but the deal had been struck all the same. He peered cautiously at Arianna. What a disaster this was… she was still mated, Jak was still alive, and now he'd have to account for everything to her.

Only… the mile-wide grin on her face hadn't dimmed in the slightest. She threw a mischievous look to Sarra. "Should we tell him?"

"Naw," Sarra said, looming over him with her arms crossed. "Make him suffer a little longer."

They were teaming up on him. Jak had missed something, big time. "Would someone like to tell me what in the actual hell is going on here?"

Marco edged forward. He touched Sarra's elbow gently and had a quick, wordless exchange of raised eyebrows and nods that completely baffled Jak. When Marco seemed convinced that everything was fine by Sarra, which was extremely odd—when did the kid become acquainted with Jak's ex?—he turned to Jak.

"You owe Sarra your life," he said, solemnly. "Arianna, too. You're kind of recklessly stupid, so I'm not sure what they really see in you, but they seemed to think you were worth saving." The smirk on everyone else's face finally showed up on his.

And if Marco was okay with this… "What about the spell?" Jak asked. He was still confused as all hell as to what had happened.

Arianna's touch on his bare arm brought his attention instantly back to her. Her touch had always electrified him, but now there was something more… something literally electric zipped across his skin and enlivened his whole body with her nearness. His wolf was quiet, licking his wounds and still recovering from the spell, but this magic enervated him, too.

She was still beaming. "The spell worked, Jak. I'm free of Mace. I'm no longer mated." She dipped her head for a half second, then captured him with those gorgeous blue eyes again. "At least, not yet. Not the normal way."

Which confused the hell out of him again. He frowned. "What do you mean, the normal way?"

She reached out to touch the frown on his face, and the smooth caress of her fingertips was like a drug hitting him full-force. His body calmed. His confusion tempered. His wolf sat up at attention, rumbling for more.

He waited for her to explain.

A frown marred her pretty face. She glanced at Sarra then back to him. "You were dying. The spell would have killed you, but Sarra drew out the remnants of Mace's wolf."

He shot a look at Sarra, iciness gripping his heart, even with Arianna's soothing touch. Sarra looked unharmed, but if she had Mace somehow inside her… "What does that mean?" he asked her.

She shrugged. "I don't know, really. Maybe he'll be able to sense the connection? I don't feel terribly different. It was… unsettling at first."

She and Marco exchanged a look again. There was something there that wasn't before… Jak wasn't sure what it was.

"I'm fine now," Sarra said, looking back to Jak.

Marco's jaw worked. "Mace may yet come after her. If he does, I'll happily tear him to pieces."

"Yeah, well, you're going to have to get in line for that, kid." But Jak's heart was lifting. *The spell worked.* Arianna was free. And yet… somehow he was still alive. He turned his attention back to Sarra. "Looks like I owe you, again, Sarrabear. But I would have told you not to do it."

"Yeah, well, you're an idiot. I think we've established that." She smirked. "Besides, I didn't save your sorry ass. You're only alive because you've got a huge dollop of Arianna's magic swimming in your blood."

Jak turned to Arianna, eyes wide. "Is that true?"

Her smile had turned shy. "I wasn't sure if you would accept it. Well, your wolf anyway. I guess…" She glanced at Circe, who was smirking like the rest of them. "I guess your wolf thinks I'm okay after all."

He gaped at her a moment. Arianna had saved his life by donating her own magic to him. That was the connection, the electric feel between them. She was literally inside him… and his wolf yipped in excitement about what that meant. He'd never heard of such a thing, but he was in wonder of it. He was *bound* to her. Connected. *Forever.*

He reached for her, pulling her toward him. "Let me show you just what my wolf thinks about that." He brought her in for a kiss. The second her lips touched his, that electric feel danced across his body again. If he wasn't so damn tired, and weak from the spell, he'd be sporting a raging boner by now. As it was, he was back in heaven, her lips on his, her angel-soft hair billowing around him. Every part of him sang with the connection between them.

Damn, he wanted to get her alone. He couldn't even imagine how amazing it would be to have her naked in his arms, their bodies locked together… he pulled back from the kiss. Spell-damage or no, if he kept traveling down that line of thought, he would have the king of all hard-ons and no way to do anything about it.

He still held her close, caressing her cheek and peering into her eyes. "Tell me this is actually real. Because this feels like a dream I've had forever, and it's come true right before my eyes."

He'd never seen her smile so wide. "It's real." It dimmed a little as she glanced around their group. "I'm not sure exactly where we go from here. But I want to make sure everyone is safe. Sarra most of all." She turned back to Jak. "She's family now."

Jak nodded, happiness flooding his body with all those three little words contained. That Arianna had forgiven him for enacting the spell; that her biggest concern, now that everyone was alive, was Sarra's safety; and that they were all in this together.

Family.

It was something that only his pack with Gage had ever had a positive meaning for him. And here Arianna was, with a heart as big as the wide open sky, accepting him and Sarra both into her family without a second thought.

"Right," Jak said. "The first thing we need to do is get far away from here. Then we can sort out all the details." He tried to climb to his feet, but he only got about halfway up before the concrete floor started to tip up.

"Jak!" Arianna's hands were on him, trying to brace him, but it was Marco's shoulder under his arm that kept him from tumbling back to the floor. The smiles were gone, and everyone had concerned looks on their faces again.

Jak blinked away the dizziness and steadied himself. He waved off Marco and Arianna's help. "I'm fine."

Circe pursed her lips, looking him over with a

sharp eye. "You're not fine, little wolf. You were near death just minutes ago. It will take even your shifter powers a little time to recover from *that.*"

He held up his hands. "I'm good. Really. We should get moving." He lumbered toward the open center of the construction site. The truth was that everything felt weak like he'd been punched full of holes. It wasn't so much that any one thing hurt as *everything* ached. Like all the pieces of him were ready to crumble into a heap of dust. But he forced himself to stand straight and move steadily… as steady as he could. He didn't wobble… much. And each step felt stronger than the last. Arianna hovered on one side, Marco on the other, but both let him go under his own power. He was grateful for that.

"Where are we heading?" Arianna asked him as they neared Sarra's jeep.

"We need to clear out of Seattle," Jak said, holding in the grunts that wanted to escape as he negotiated the hard-packed dirt of the construction site. He glanced at Marco, who gave him a nod of agreement. Jak wasn't clear exactly who was in charge here—he was supposed to be dead, and Marco was supposed to take care of his sister. Now, with Sarra involved, their group was the size of a small pack… but without any clear hierarchy. Or an established alpha. It was as disorienting as the ravages the spell had worked on his body, but they could worry about all that later. Like he said, details. For now, Arianna had it exactly right: getting everyone to a safe place took priority over everything else.

When they reached the Jeep, Jak gingerly climbed in. It was harder to mask how difficult it was just getting his body to obey his commands, but he managed to keep the grimaces to a minimum. Arianna climbed over him, refusing to sit on his lap, opting to snuggle up next to him on the seat instead… which worked just fine for him. In fact, he was convinced it was helping him heal. Every time she touched his bare skin, it juiced his body with something between an electric jolt and a rush of pure love. A smile crept onto his face and stayed there. With her by his side, he literally felt like he was flying.

Sarra hoisted herself into the driver's seat and looked to him for direction.

Okay, so he guessed he was in charge. At least, for the moment.

"Arianna said you packed a few things for the road," Jak said.

"Clothes and toiletries," Sarra said. "Just enough for the two of you."

"Anything at the apartment you're going to miss?" He gave her a serious look. "We may not be back for a while, Sarra." Like, possibly a long while, but he didn't want to say that now. He hadn't thought it through well enough to have a handle on it, and his head was still a bit woozy.

She grimaced and gripped the steering wheel of the Jeep, staring forward at the unmoving cranes and empty half-constructed buildings. "No, I guess not."

"What about your paintings?" He knew they were the only things she would give a shit about. And he hated the idea of asking her to leave it all behind, simply because she felt compelled to save him.

"I'll paint new ones." But her jaw was working, and he knew her better than that.

"We can stop by your place. Just pick up a few things, whatever will fit in the back." He glanced at the back seat where Circe was once again perched between Arianna's brothers, smirking and enjoying the close quarters. Marco seemed to be gritting his teeth, and besides, he was focused on the back of Sarra's head, but Kalis was practically drooling on the drop-dead gorgeous witch. Jak would have to keep an eye on the two of them… but they should be getting rid of Circe soon enough. And there was plenty of room in the back of the Jeep for some of Sarra's works. Her paints and brushes, for sure. She'd been collecting those for a long time, whenever she could scrape the money together.

He looked back to Sarra, who hadn't said anything. Her knuckles were turning white where she clutched the steering wheel.

Arianna turned toward her. "Sarra, are you all right?"

Sarra shook her head as if warding off some thought. "Yeah." She peered around Arianna to Jak. "There are a couple things I'd like to get. To take with me." The way she said it… Jak could tell she knew. That they might not be coming back.

"You got it." He gave her a nod, and she started up the Jeep, gunning it and spinning out of the construction site. The momentum rocked Arianna into Jak's arms, which he didn't mind in the slightest. But a quick look back showed Circe draping herself over Kalis.

"God, Circe, give the boy a break," Jak said, giving her a full measure of disgust. "He's what, sixteen?"

"Seventeen," Kalis growled, obviously not pleased that Jak was trying to play Dad. And Jak really had no right to interfere—Kalis wasn't his family. *Not yet*, a small thought in his head said. His heart surged at that idea, and he snuggled Arianna closer to his side, debating if he should say something more.

Marco stepped in for him, growling out his words. "She's a witch, Kalis. Don't be an idiot." Marco paused. "No offense," he said to Circe. Another pause. "And thanks for what you did for my sister." He said it with a glare that said Circe wouldn't be getting any sexual favors in return for that act from him. Or from his brother.

Jak nearly laughed, but mostly kept it in. Only Arianna noticed the silent heaving of his chest, but she seemed perplexed about what he found so funny. And he'd like to keep it that way. He threaded his fingers into her beautiful hair, distracting her and himself completely. He brushed his cheek against hers, bringing her closer and dropping soft kisses on her neck. If they didn't have a car full of onlookers, he'd do more than explore her jawline with his lips. But every bit of contact with her seemed to strengthen him, so he kept it up. She didn't seem to mind, matching his every touch with another of her own.

No one interrupted them during the short drive back to Sarra's apartment.

As they climbed out of the Jeep, Circe scowled at the run-down neighborhood Sarra lived in. Jak hated sweeping Sarra into their mess, making her go on the run with them, but he couldn't say he was sorry to get her out of this dump. He'd been hoping for years that she would leave, but he could never convince her to go. Sometimes things worked out in the way you least expected. His luck had never been that good before, but now… he squeezed Arianna's hand, getting a fresh electric charge from that. Now it seemed like anything was possible, with her by his side. He kissed her quickly, barely taming the bright smile on her face, then followed after Sarra, who was unlocking the door on the stoop to let them into the building. Arianna's brothers and the witch were darting looks all around the trash-filled streets and crumbling façade… and keeping close behind them.

They didn't see anyone on the three flights up, but it was the middle of the day. The junkies were sleeping it off, and anyone with an actual job was gone for the day, trying to scratch out a living. Which was just as well.

"Let's grab what we can in one trip, eh, Sarrabear?" he said as they approached her door. "Between us, if we each carry something, that's probably all the Jeep will hold anyway."

She nodded in agreement, still tight-lipped and grim-faced. He would need to pull her aside at some point and really talk this through. See what the future held… for all of them.

Jak didn't realize something was wrong until Sarra was inside and he and Arianna were across the threshold with Circe and Marco and Kalis at their backs.

The apartment was trashed.

And it wasn't unoccupied either.

Chapter Twenty-Eight

ARIANNA'S FIRST HINT THAT SOMETHING WAS WRONG was when Jak shifted.

One moment, his hand was holding hers, reassuring and warm; the next, he was bounding across the room in wolf form, snarling and snapping at someone. Arianna stumbled back, stunned and confused.

Then she saw Jak's target: *Mace.*

A full-body shiver gripped her. Mace shifted to wolf just as Jak reached him, and they went down together in a bundle of fur-flying and fangs-gnashing. But Mace wasn't alone. His two betas, Beck and Alric, emerged from the kitchen and immediately shifted to wolf to join the fight. Marco and Kalis surged past her, already shifted, loping across the room to attack, one each going for the two betas. Sarra stood stock still in the middle of it, hands clenched, looking over the melee with shock. Terror seized Arianna's heart for all of them: Jak was too weak to fight, Kalis was too young, and Sarra carried Mace's wolf inside her.

Arianna leaped forward to pull Sarra back from the fight, but she shifted before Arianna's disbelieving eyes. *Since when could Sarra shift?* Arianna watched as Sarra leaped into the fight, teeth sinking into one of Mace's betas who had his jaws clamped into Marco's side.

Arianna stumbled back and whirled on Circe at the threshold of the door. "You need to do something!" she yelled to be heard over the growls and roars of the pitched battle raging in front of them.

The witch pressed her lips together, seeming uncertain.

"Please, just… stop the fighting," Arianna begged her.

Circe gave her a short nod and strode forward, but just then… someone else emerged from Sarra's art room. A female, tall and gorgeous. It took a moment, but Arianna realized she had to be a witch. The way Circe stalled out in the middle of the room, she must know who the woman was.

The witch scowled over the brawling wolves. "Circe," she called out, "I thought you were done with this business."

"Hecca, what are you doing here?" Circe said, her shoulders tense.

"Cleaning up your mess, apparently."

"It doesn't need cleaning."

The witches' bickering wasn't doing anything to stop the fight. Arianna braced herself, undecided whether she should shift and join them or keep trying to get Circe to use her magic to put a stop to it... then one of the wolves broke from the fray and shifted human. He was naked and skinny, and Arianna recognized him in an instant: *Mace.* He was diving for a pile of clothes off to the side... *oh no.*

"Circe!" was all she got out before Mace came up with a gun.

It fired.

The shot blasted through the air of the apartment, shocking everyone to stillness, including the fighting wolves. Mace swung his gun around to take aim again. Two blurs of fur leaped into action, surging toward him, trying to stop him.

"Enough!" Hecca's voice rang out, terrible and strong, like a lightning bolt through the air... then it was followed by some kind of actual lightning pulse.

It was a shock spell of some kind, and it brought everyone down, including Arianna.

She found herself on the floor, body twitching, immobile for a long, agonizing moment. She forced her body to roll over and crawled on her belly toward the other wolves, trembling from the after-effects of the spell and searching to see where the bullet had gone. With everyone down, it was hard to tell who was injured and who was just knocked flat by the witch's shock spell. The others shook it off, slowly rising, except for one wolf who was lying on his side. She recognized his shiny brown coat and flopped ears even before he shifted human in front of her: *Kalis.*

"Oh God no." She managed to get to her knees and scrambled across the floor to reach him faster. Blood pumped out of the gaping hole in his side, spilling over his naked body and onto the floor. "Oh, God. Oh, God." Her hands were shaking, but she pressed hard on his wound to stop the bleeding. He moaned and curled into her, making it harder to keep pressure. The blood was quickly covering her hands, and she could barely see him through the tears welling up in her eyes. She blinked them clear and looked up to see if anyone else was hurt. One by one, the wolves were shifting human again: they were all naked, their clothes left behind on the floor when they shifted the first time. No one else seemed injured. Jak stood face-to-face with Mace. Marco was holding Beck and Alric at bay with Sarra at his back. None of them were done fighting by the looks on their faces.

But the gun was no longer in Mace's hand—the witch had liberated it from him. It hovered in the air above her waiting hand. She looked at it as if it were a disgusting piece of trash, then twirled her fingers. The gun melted like metallic paint dripping from its place suspended in the air down to a pile of sludge on the floor.

Thank God. At least Mace couldn't shoot anyone else. Arianna prayed none of his betas were armed. But everyone seemed to be tensely holding their positions, waiting to see what the witches would do next.

"Why are you here, Hecca?" Circe's voice was tight.

Hecca stepped over the puddle of metal that used to be the gun, sauntering to the center of the room, near her sister. "Your pet has been naughty, Circe. He took something that didn't belong to him." She gave Mace a nod. "Our associate from the Red pack said your pet had been injured in the process and had a healer living nearby. I urged him to visit the healer first. I was hoping, dear sister, that you would be, shall we say, *finished* with your little pet before we found him. I was protecting your back and trying to clean up the mess you've made with your little obsession."

Circe threw a disgusted look at Mace, whose chest was heaving, red in the face, clearly ready to go again with Jak standing in front of him. "Your *associate* is an asshole. And I'm not in this for the reasons you think. I'm involved because I'm trying to right a wrong, Hecca. Once upon a time, you cared about such things."

"I care about our *business*… something you might take a moment to attend to at some point." Hecca sniffed. "Your little crusade is costing us, sister. What the wolves do with their mates is none of our concern. No matter how many of them you decide to circulate through your bed."

Circe's eyes narrowed. "If it's none of our concern, then why are you involved?"

Hecca threw a disdainful look at Mace. "When a son of the Red pack accuses my sister of helping a rogue wolf steal his mate, well, you forced me to get involved, didn't you? I thought maybe you were just having your fun and the two things were unrelated."

She gave Arianna a bitter look. "But I see I was wrong."

"*Steal* is not the correct word here. Rescue is more accurate. Besides," Circe said with an arched eyebrow, "she is no longer his mate."

Mace's glare jumped from the witches to Arianna, and she felt a shiver run through her… but nothing more. She was truly free of him. He frowned, confusion flitting across his face.

"That's right, asshole," Jak said, the growl in his voice full of satisfaction. "You have no claim on her now."

The rage on Mace's face reached epic proportions—Arianna thought he might actually have a heart attack, but he merely swung his fury to Hecca. "This is dark magic. *Witch magic.* Nothing else could break a mating bond like this. *You* are responsible for this. Undo it. *Now.*"

Hecca's voice went ice cold. "Take care, wolf. You presume too much."

Marco edged in front of Sarra, so he was protecting her from Mace's line of sight more so than his betas. Arianna knew him well enough to know the red in his cheeks was him being embarrassed. He was naked next to Sarra, and he studiously kept his back turned to her bare form.

But he stood ready to protect her with his life. Or at least shield her with his body. Mace would have to go through him to get to her. But that small motion… Arianna prayed Mace wouldn't notice, but of course, he did. He flicked his gaze to Sarra and narrowed his eyes, examining her. Then he flitted his gaze between Sarra and Arianna.

Finally, he raised a hand and pointed a furious finger at Sarra. "The bond has been… *transferred.* I don't know what dark art your witch has done, but this one… she carries the bond now. I can *feel* it." He turned back to Hecca. "Jak can keep his trash. I claim this one instead."

A jolt went through Arianna. *Oh no.* If somehow Mace got hold of Sarra and truly claimed her, he would find out she had little magic of her own… not enough for shifter pups in any event. And then Arianna could only imagine his rage. He would have no use for her, and he would kill her, for sure.

Arianna couldn't move—she was still trying to keep Kalis from bleeding out, and her hands were still steeped in his blood—so she threw her words at Mace instead. "You have no right to claim anyone! You're a sad excuse for an alpha, Mace, and if there were any justice in the world, you would be going to jail for the things you've done."

It felt amazing to say those words to his face, to feel the liberation of knowing he had no hold on her, not anymore… but her words just enraged him even further. He lurched toward Arianna, apparently forgetting that Jak was right in front of him. Jak shoved him back, his claws coming out.

"You'll have to go through me before you get to either of them," Jak growled.

Maces fangs came out. "With pleasure." He lunged for Jak. Arianna's heart seized up: fear for Jak, fear for Sarra, terror that her baby brother was bleeding out under her hands while her ex-mate tried to rip the throat of the man she loved…

"I said *enough.*" Hecca's voice jerked Jak and Mace to a stop.

They shoved each other away and stood glaring at one another.

Jak wiped the blood from his face. Arianna's body twitched. She couldn't tell if it was his or Mace's. Mace glared his hatred for Arianna over Jak's shoulder. Jak moved to block Mace's line of sight.

"Walk away from this, Mace," Jak said with surprising calmness. "It's over. Arianna's free of you. And no one here is going to let you claim Sarra. Walk away while you still can."

Mace looked like he wanted to take a bite out of Jak, but he held back and turned again to Hecca. "I *will* have a mate out of this." He was practically spitting the words out. "You promised to make this right!"

"I promised nothing of the sort." Her voice was cold again.

He shoved past Jak to stalk closer to Hecca, eyes blazing. "What would it take to ruin Morgan Media? A well-placed rumor? The fact that you've helped bury more bodies than I'm sure you would like dug up? I can make life as difficult for you as I like, Hecca."

"You are walking a very thin line, wolf." Hecca's voice glittered like ice. "I would take care, if I were you, not to step over it."

Mace's face was turning red again. "I want the female." Each word was underscored with anger.

Hecca glanced at Sarra. Marco had moved again, tucking her behind his back, shielding her from the witch, Mace, and even Mace's two betas, who were watching everything with sharp-eyed readiness. Jak edged between Mace and Sarra as well. The two of them were a wall of naked, brawny shifter muscle. They looked imposing, even if Arianna knew Jak must still be weak from the spell. Arianna felt completely helpless at her brother's side, but she prayed for this standoff to end quickly. She needed Sarra to stitch up her baby brother before he lost too much blood.

"It would appear the female does not want you," Hecca said with a voice filled with boredom. "And I'm tired of your wolfy games, Mace Crittenden. Be gone."

Mace's jaw worked. He stood, impotent before the witch for a long moment, and for a flash instant, Arianna thought he might actually attack her. Which was pure suicide. But instead, he growled and turned on his heel, stalking to where his clothes lay in a heap on the floor.

Arianna sighed in relief. She dropped her gaze to Kalis. His face was pale and sweaty. Her heart clenched. She wanted Mace to clear out quickly so Sarra could tend to her brother.

"If I can't have her..." Mace's voice was soft and dangerous. "Then no one can."

Arianna gasped and looked up. Mace had another gun in his hand, but it wasn't pointed at her. It was pointed at Sarra, straight through Jak and Marco as well.

An explosion rent the air, so loud and forceful that it knocked Arianna backward, flattening her to the floor next to Kalis. Her eardrums ached, and her body shook in response. That wasn't a gunshot… more like a bomb going off in the apartment.

A fine gray cloud hung in the air, like smoke curling in wisps up to the ceiling.

What in the world?

Arianna squinted in the haze. The only ones still standing were Hecca and Circe. They both had their hands raised toward Mace… only Mace wasn't there. The gun, Mace, the clothes he had been holding in his hand, that he must have retrieved the gun from—they were all gone. Only the smoke remained. And a small pile of ash on the floor.

Hecca and Circe exchanged an arched-eyebrowed look of surprise, then glanced back to the place where Mace used to be.

"Well," Circe said with amusement, "that was rather dramatic."

"We do have a certain flair when we work together, sister." Hecca had a smirk on her face. She shrugged. "I was tired of working with wolves anyway."

Everyone else started to stir, recovering from the explosive spell. Marco helped Sarra up from the floor, still keeping his eyes averted from her nakedness. Jak stood slowly, wide-eyed and staring at the spot where Mace had been moments before. Mace's betas stayed hunkered on the floor, but they had edged closer together, staring at the pile of ash, maybe fearing they were next.

"Well, then, Circe dear," Hecca said, brushing the dust from her finely tailored suit. "I trust you can handle things from here. I have actual work that needs doing back at the office. *Our* office, if you recall. Perhaps you'd like to show your face there sometime soon, once you're done playing with your pets."

Circe gave her a small smile and hooked her arm in a very friendly fashion around her sister's. "You know what, sister dear? I think I've had my fill of *wolf* for a little while."

Arianna stared, mouth-open, as the two witches sauntered out of Sarra's apartment together. They didn't even look back.

"How about you clear out, too?" Jak's words were directed at Alric and Beck. They hastily scooped up their clothes, avoided the small pile of ash that used to be their alpha, and scurried out the door. Once they were past the threshold, they checked their pace. Arianna guessed they didn't want to catch up to the witches on the way out.

She could hardly believe it. Mace was… dead. Vaporized really. With not a DNA snippet left to prove anything. And with him dead… Arianna scanned the room for Sarra. She was running off to her art studio. Which seemed strange—maybe she was getting some clothes? Jak and Marco were hastily retrieving their pants and pulling them on in her momentary absence. But Sarra returned just a few seconds later, bringing the black bag she had used to stitch up Jak. She was still naked as the day she was born, but she didn't seem to care. She knelt by Kalis's side and rolled him over to get a good look at his wound. His eyes went wide, and he struggled, unsuccessfully, to not stare at Sarra's breasts dangling above him.

"You can stare all you like, kid," Sarra said with a smirk. "But you're about to feel a bit of a pinch."

He gritted his teeth and closed his eyes as she probed his bullet wound.

Marco came up behind Sarra and handed her a t-shirt. She took a moment to slip it over her head but ignored the rest of the clothes he brought over as she went quickly to work, stitching up Kalis. Arianna stood, giving her room to work.

Jak was at her side in an instant. "Are you all right?" he asked, taking her hands and wiping them clean of Kalis's blood with a shirt he found lying on the floor. It was probably his.

Arianna managed a small smile. "I am now." She looked to the ash pile again. It made her shiver, and Jak pulled her into his arms.

He murmured into her hair. "He's never going to hurt you, or anyone, ever again."

Arianna nodded and huddled close to him, needing the comfort of his arms to tell her that all of this was real. When Sarra was finished stitching her brother, Arianna finally forced herself to pull away.

"Is he going to be all right?" Arianna asked.

Sarra stood, still naked from the waist down, but covered in so much of Kalis's blood that you could hardly tell. "He's going to be fine. Let's get him to the bed, though. I'd like to see him rest for a few hours before you try to transport him." She left unspoken where they might go or what they might do from here.

And, honestly, Arianna had no idea. All she knew was that she, and everyone she loved, was finally, truly safe. unoccupied either.

Chapter Twenty-Nine

THE LONGER THEY DROVE, THE MORE NERVOUS Jak got.

They'd left North Bend behind over an hour ago, taking Sarra's Jeep through the mountains on I-90. Now they were on the Eastern side of the slopes, with the sun starting to sink over the mountaintops and bringing an early dusk. Sarra was driving, and Marco was in the passenger seat, stealing looks at her, while Jak and Arianna snuggled in the back seat. Kalis was still recovering—he had slept for most of the ride, leaned against the window, snoring.

Marco was pointing out the sights… which consisted mostly of mountain peaks and the occasional deer. They were definitely in the country now, heading toward Arianna's family ranch, and Jak's one chance to make a good impression on her mother. Arianna nestled against him, her hands still touching him at every opportunity. He was doing the same. Her brothers didn't seem to mind, and Jak was still recharging from the spell that had nearly killed him just this morning… although it seemed like a lifetime ago. But every moment with Arianna by his side, he could feel the magic inside him growing stronger. Sarra had said it was his own magic, regenerating, coming back basically from the dead. Arianna's magic was bolstering him as he healed—that was why every touch from her felt like a new surge of energy—but soon his magic would be back to full strength again. Then he would have the magic of both of them inside him, and that made his heart soar. But every moment his wolf healed inside him, it insisted more strongly that he needed to claim Arianna for his own. Now that it was possible, Jak could hardly stand the moments between now and making that happen.

But first, he would have to win over her mother.

Marco edged closer to Sarra in the front seat, ostensibly to point out the exit from the freeway that she needed to take next, but Jak was no fool: he could see the way Marco was looking at her, watching her every movement, letting his eyes roam over her face when he thought she wasn't looking. There was definitely something going on there, and it wasn't a brotherly kind of interest. Jak was sure seeing Sarra naked hadn't exactly tamped down Marco's interest, but it had been there before the fight. From the moment Jak awoke, he could tell: there was something between them. Maybe because Marco swore to protect her from Mace? Jak knew full well how protecting a beautiful woman from an asshole alpha could excite all kinds of primal, lust-filled interest. Maybe it was simply that Sarra was one of the bravest, most selfless people Jak had ever met, short of his own Arianna? Sarra and Arianna were alike in the most basic of ways, even if they seemed nothing alike on the surface—and Jak wasn't at all surprised that Arianna's brother was falling hard for Sarra.

It didn't hurt that she was incredibly hot in her post-shift nakedness.

That had surprised everyone: *Sarra shifting.* She had tried to shift again before they left, but she couldn't. Whatever fleeting ability she had disappeared when Mace died—presumably he took his magic with him. And Sarra was back to her non-shifting, normal self.

Marco had to know what that meant, even if no one talked about it out loud.

Which brought Jak back to figuring out where all the pieces fit… he loved Arianna and wanted to mate with her as soon as possible. Assuming she was willing, but her every teasing, loving, impossibly sexy touch told him that she wanted this—and she had already said as much to his face. But now she was returning to her family's ranch in the countryside of Eastern Washington. That was Marco's domain—he was alpha of their small family pack. What were his intentions with all of this? Could Jak fit in somewhere in that scheme? And what would Arianna's mother think? Not to mention the issue of Sarra, who Marco was already trying to convince to stay more than just the night?

The nerves came creeping back into Jak's stomach, and he was glad when Arianna stirred against him, sitting up as they turned off a paved road onto a bumpy dirt road that took them even farther away from the lights of the highway.

Arianna stretched her beautiful body, and it was all Jak could do to keep his hands off her. "We're almost there," she said with a shy smile. "I can't wait to see my mom. She should be back from Robertson's ranch by now."

"Great." Jak winced internally at how awkward that sounded.

Arianna squeezed his arm and grinned. "She's going to *love* you, Jak."

"Right. I hope so." He swallowed.

"How could she not?" Arianna asked with a comical look of exasperation on her face. "You rescued me from Mace. You freed me from the mating bond—"

"And I'm bringing home her youngest son barely stitched together." Not to mention throwing a wild card into their whole family situation. But Jak didn't want to bring that up. Not yet.

Arianna slapped his arm playfully. "Marco will get the blame for that." Nothing could daunt the smile on her face, nor did Jak really want to.

"Hey!" Marco protested from the front seat. But then he quickly returned his attention to pointing out the long driveway Sarra needed to turn down. Kalis stirred with the commotion and rubbed his eyes.

Arianna scooped up Jak's hand, lacing her fingers with his, and holding the back of it to her lips for a kiss that went straight to low in his belly. He gave her a warning look, and she just smirked: she knew exactly what she was doing to him. Which only made him want to get her alone even more. He pulled her in for a kiss, but she put her fingers playfully against his lips.

"Time for that later," she said with a wicked grin.

He sincerely hoped so.

The driveway was at least a half mile long, but they finally arrived. The house was simple but spacious—two stories, with a big wraparound porch, wide planks for siding, and a peaked roof. Wood-rail fencing ran out from both sides and far behind the house was a barn as large as the house itself. Arianna had told them they were ranchers, but it appeared they were a dude ranch in the making with the number of horses they must have in there. There was a series of cottages in back as well, on the far side of the barn, maybe for guests? He had no idea. He'd grown up in a small country pack, too, but not this far out. Just in a small town like North Bend, which looked like the city compared to this.

Arianna held his hand and led the way, with Marco and Sarra helping Kalis out of the Jeep. He was already moving better on his own, but Jak could tell he was working the injury for all it was worth—the kid looked like he was crushing on Sarra almost as much as Marco. At least Marco was old enough not to be jailbait.

Arianna captured his attention again as she dropped his hand to throw open the front door.

"Mom!" she called, not waiting for him as she rushed into the house.

Jak hustled after her, not wanting to blow his chance before he even had it.

The spaciousness of the house continued on the inside—a wide entryway led to an open kitchen in back, stairs going up to the second floor, and a cavernous living area sprawled with couches. At the end was a rough-hewn table that could seat at least twelve, maybe more. It looked about a hundred years old, and the entire place was rustic, decorated with antlers, fur, and oil paintings of cowboys rustling cattle. It was like stepping back in time… and somehow the simple comfort of it ratcheted down Jak's nerves, just like being around Arianna had always done.

The love of his life was wrapped up in her mother's arms. Jak held back, not wanting to encroach on the moment: Arianna's mom held her tight, eyes squeezed shut with tears leaking from the corners. Even with her face contorted with tearful happiness, Jak could see she was as beautiful as her daughter: the same high cheekbones, same gorgeous, long black hair, only frosted with streaks of white that made her seem like an ancient sorceress, all wizened and powerful.

"Arianna," her mom whispered, still holding her tight. Then she pulled back and held her daughter's cheeks in her hands, looking her over like a mother worried her daughter wasn't as unharmed as she pretended to be. Then she peered into Arianna's eyes with the same brilliant blues that her daughter possessed. "My heart cried every day for you. Every day you've been—" She choked up, and her words cut off.

Jak was working hard not to choke up himself. Living to see this moment was all the reward he would ever need.

"I'm free now," Arianna told her firmly, even though she had already filled her mom in on everything on the ride over. Jak had listened to one side of that conversation, dying to know what was being said on the other end. "And I'm home." She hugged her mom again, hard but fast. Then she turned to Jak. "Mom, this is Jak Roberts." Arianna met his nervous stare and smiled. "He's the one who set me free."

It made his heart leap to hear those words, but

he forced himself to meet the steady gaze of Arianna's mom. She was inspecting him head to toe, taking her time, not speaking. Agitation was threatening to explode out of him, but he managed to keep it cool and step forward, extending his hand.

"Nice to meet you, Mrs. Stefan."

She took his hand in both of hers—her hands were soft but strong like he would expect from a woman who worked a ranch with only her two sons for help—and briefly held it. Then she dropped it and stepped closer, peering up into his face with a dead-serious expression.

"I cannot repay you for what you've done," she said as if he was expecting some kind of payment walking in the door. Her brilliant blue eyes bored into him.

Jak was nonplussed for a moment. When words finally worked their way to his mouth, he was glad they weren't completely idiotic. "I'm the one who owes your daughter." He glanced at Arianna then back to her mother's cool expression. "She's saved me in more ways than one."

The barest smile graced her face, then fled, banished by the serious look returning. "What are your intentions here, Jak Roberts?"

He gaped, then quickly shut his mouth. She was

as plain-spoken as her daughter. He should have expected as much. "I love your daughter more than my own life, Mrs. Stefan. With your permission, I would have her as my mate and protect her all the days I have left on this earth." He glanced at Arianna again, and the tremulous smile on her face made his heart swell. It gave him the courage to push further… for the thing he really wanted but wasn't sure was possible. "I've never had a family worth the name, Ma'am. I don't know if I'll fit into yours. But if you'll have me, I'll do everything in my power to pull my weight and keep all of you safe." Marco was technically the alpha, and Jak knew he'd have to submit to the kid to become truly part of their pack. But that kid was willing to lay his life down for his sister—he was the kind of alpha Jak wouldn't have to think twice about respecting. He could submit to him. And he didn't want Arianna to have to choose between him and her family. He wanted her to have *both.* Besides, he could easily vow to protect them like his own pack—his heart had already pledged to do that long ago.

Arianna's mom studied him a moment longer, blue eyes glittering. She flicked a look over Jak's shoulder, and he suddenly became aware that they weren't the only ones in the room—Sarra and

Marco and Kalis had joined them but had remained at the door.

Arianna was holding back her smile, and every second that passed without a response from Arianna's mom was a held-breath burning in Jak's chest. Arianna's mom lifted her chin, and Kalis gained a miraculous recovery as he strode over to give his mother a hug. She scowled at him, but only momentarily, before her face was taken over with a small smile. She took his cheeks in both hands and gave them a squeeze. He wrenched his face away with a horrified look that made everyone else in the room smile. Even Jak, although he hadn't missed the fact that Arianna's mom had completely dodged his unspoken question about remaining with them. Joining their pack and their family—it was a lot to ask, two seconds inside the door. His heart was pounding, hoping he hadn't screwed up already.

Marco waited until his mother was done embarrassing Kalis, then he brought Sarra over, holding her gently at the elbow. "Mom, this is Sarra, the shifter I told you about on the phone."

Jak liked how Marco called her a *shifter*—even if Jak suspected it was to win over Sarra more than his mother. For her part, Sarra looked more nervous than he'd ever seen her. Which was saying something, given she'd stared down more shifter gang members than he could count.

Arianna's mother beamed and took Sarra's hands in hers. "Welcome," she said with a wide smile. Then she gently took Sarra's cheeks in her hands, and the smile tempered to affection. "I heard what you did. Both the stitching and… the other part. Marco told me all about it. It's an honor to have such a brave wolf in our home, not to mention a healer. You are welcome here for as long as you wish to stay."

"Um… thanks," Sarra said. She looked a little lost, but in a good way. Like this was some kind of dream she was having—the kind she didn't really believe but didn't want to wake up from, regardless.

Jak was happy for her—he knew the hard road she had walked, and she deserved all the gratitude the Stefan family could dole out—but he couldn't help having his chest grow a little tighter. He hadn't quite earned the same warm welcome… yet. But he was determined to make that happen, for Arianna's sake. He resigned himself to the fact that it might take time, and that would have to be okay. He could be patient. He'd already given everything he had in this life for Arianna… he could give the idea of joining her family a little time to settle in.

Arianna's mom dropped her hands from Sarra's face and turned to Marco. Some kind of wordless conversation passed between mother and son. She gave him a nod that seemed like an order somehow, and Marco left her side to stand face-to-face with Jak.

Jak frowned, his heart sinking a little. Was this it? Time for him to leave already? He scrambled for some reason why he still needed to stay, at least the night—

"Jak Roberts," Marco said, his blue eyes staring steadily into Jak's. His voice was ridiculously formal, given what they'd all just been through. "My father was the alpha of our pack. When he died, I took on that role. I never thought I'd find a man I could respect as much as him, someone I'd be honored to be beta to. But then I never expected someone else to love my family as much as I do."

Jak struggled to keep the shock off his face, but he had absolutely no words for what Marco was saying. Then Marco shifted before him, and Jak couldn't keep his mouth from dropping open. Marco stood on all fours for a moment, staring up at him with wolf eyes, then slowly he stretched his paws forward and dropped his tail behind.

Marco was submitting to him.

It was so unexpected, Jak took a half step back. He flicked a look around the room: Sarra's face was shocked, but Arianna was smiling wide. She was in on this, clearly. Before Jak could say or do anything, Kalis had already shifted and submitted. Arianna's mother captured his wandering gaze and held it with a small smile. Then she shifted, too, followed quickly by Arianna.

The four of them were all submitting to him. He could feel the surge of their bond, tempered because he was still human, but bolstering him with an incredible energy nonetheless. He openly gaped at Sarra, who of course was still human.

She arched an eyebrow at him, obviously impressed. Then she tipped her head. It wasn't submission, but it was definitely approval.

Jak took a deep breath and shifted as well. In wolf form, he felt the full power of their submissions wash over him. It was a bath of magical energy like nothing he had ever felt. He was overcome for a moment… all the love and acceptance and respect built into this simple act… then, as the moments passed, he wondered why they were still bent in the submission position. Their thoughts twittered at the edge of his mind. Then he realized…

They wouldn't move until he commanded it. *Rise,* he thought, and as one, they lifted their heads and perked up their tails. Kalis bounded over to him first, bumping shoulders with him on his way out of the room and up the stairs. Marco likewise approached him, but in a more measured way.

We're straight shooters here, Jak. There was a laugh in his thoughts, probably because Jak's dumbfounded look was still on his face, even as a wolf. *Hope that works for you.*

I think I'll manage, Jak responded.

Marco ducked his head in acknowledgment, then backtracked to Sarra, who was waiting off to the side, still human. He nuzzled her hand and tilted his head to the kitchen. She followed after him. Before he trotted from the room, Marco scooped up his clothes in his mouth.

Arianna's mother approached him next. Her eyes were still blue, and her black coat was frosted with silver tips.

This is a burden we've placed upon you, Jak, she thought, holding his gaze. *You have us until the next moon. If the burden's too great, no one will begrudge you laying it down at that point.*

She was as kind-hearted as her daughter, something Jak should have also known would be true.

Nothing could pry this burden from my grip, Mrs. Stefan.

She dipped her head, then lifted it high as she passed him to climb the stairs after her youngest son.

He and Arianna were alone.

Shift for me, my love, he thought as he shifted to human himself. A moment later, she was naked in his arms. He had a sudden, fervent appreciation for the fact that everyone had vacated the room, leaving them alone. His hard-on was already raging. He kissed her thoroughly and was debating whether the hundred-year-old table could hold them when she pulled away.

A grin played across her face. "Not here."

"I'm the alpha of your pack now, Arianna," he said sternly. "If I want you in the middle of your family's living room, that's where I'll have you." He hoped she knew he was playing. He would follow her to the ends of the earth. All she had to do was ask.

She grinned wider and ducked down to the pile of his clothes on the floor. She looked up at him from there, her grin turning into a smirk. The fact that her lips were now so near his cock had him thinking that maybe he wasn't playing after all. He certainly wasn't going to last long in the *playful* stage if he didn't have her soon. But before he could act on that impulse, she popped up from the floor and shoved his clothes into his chest.

"I have a special place," she said with a shy smile. "Somewhere I've always dreamed of… being claimed."

His heart leaped, banging against his chest. Those words made his mouth ache with need for her. And if she had a special place for this most special of acts—something he never thought was even going to be possible for either one of them—then he damn well was going *there.*

He hastily shoved his legs into his pants. "I sincerely hope this place is nearby." His shirt was fighting him, but he managed to get it on.

Arianna was dressed just as quickly. "I've spent my whole life on this ranch," she said with a smirk. "And now everything I've ever dreamed of is here."

His body flushed with the love radiating from her. He was so tremendously smitten in that moment, it was all he could do to hold himself back. But he'd done much harder things… he could do this. Making Arianna's dreams come true was worth everything.

He held out his hand. "Lead the way, my love."

She grabbed his hand and towed him toward

the kitchen. It was big and rustic like the rest of the house, filled with massive copper pots and black iron skillets. They didn't slow down as she tugged him toward the back door. Outside, the light was waning, settling a warm amber glow on the rest of the ranch.

Jak didn't notice Marco and Sarra until he and Arianna had already passed them. Marco was half naked, just his jeans on, and he had Sarra up against the back wall of the house. That kiss was hotter than hell, the way he had her leg hitched over his hip and his mouth covering hers. The way Sarra had her fingers digging into Marco's back, she sure didn't seem to mind. Jak flashed a look to Arianna, but she seemed pleased as punch that her brother was making out with Jak's ex. Truth be told, he couldn't be happier for the both of them.

And pretty damn soon Jak planned to be in the same position with Arianna. His wolf growled his agreement, and Jak picked up the pace. Arianna's hand was clasped in his as they hurried toward the row of cottages beyond the barn. He didn't care if they were headed for a bed, a hay bale, or the forest beyond.

He was finally going to claim Arianna for his own.

Chapter Thirty

ARIANNA WAS SO FULL OF LOVE SHE FELT HER HEART might burst.

Jak was not only her alpha now, but the alpha of her pack. *Her family.* They had accepted him with open arms, just as she knew they would. Jak carried her magic in his blood, and she had submitted to him, but there was still one bond she craved between them: a true claiming. She had been free of Mace for less than a day, but she was already ready to give everything she had to Jak. He was literally her savior.

And now she wanted him to make her his mate.

She towed him toward the farthest cabin on her family's ranch. They were a small operation, but they had a steady stream of customers, riding the trails, living the ranch life, enjoying all the simple and earthy pleasures of the great outdoors. She'd grown up here, watching couples come and renew their love with a weekend of fun and relaxation… and she knew exactly what happened in the Bridal Suite cabin at the end. She always figured that one day, she and her mate would consummate their love there as well.

Life didn't always turn out the way you planned.

A fleeting sour thought of all the time trapped as Mace's mate passed over her like a cloud. But the bright smile on Jak's face as she pulled him up to the door of the cabin blasted away those thoughts like a clean wind dissipating the smoke of Mace under the witch's combined spell.

"Is this it?" Jak asked, a little breathless as he checked out the rough-hewn door of the cabin. It probably didn't look like much to a city shifter like him. And there wasn't much more inside. Mostly a bed and a tub. But it held her dreams, ever since she was a girl.

"This is it," she said. "It's not much—"

He cut her off with a kiss. Then he threw open the door and scooped her up, bridal-style, carrying her over the threshold.

"It's perfect," he whispered, eyes on her alone.

He hadn't even looked at the inside of the cabin yet, but the love in his eyes was all she needed.

He gave a quick look around, spied the tub, and carried her there. It was oversized, a whirlpool tub, meant for lovers. He reverently set her down, kissed her gently on the lips, and then slowly unbuttoned her shirt. The heat between her legs was already throbbing from the submission, their kissing just minutes ago, and the sight of Jak's naked glory, now hidden underneath his clothes again. But the gentle touch of his fingers on her chest as he unbuttoned her clothes just made the heat grow into an aching need to have him.

"I want to wash away everything that came before," he whispered as he pushed her open shirt off her shoulders, letting it fall behind her. He feasted his eyes on her breasts, now bare to him, before quickly moving to unbutton her jeans. "I want a fresh start for us, Arianna."

He knelt as he worked her jeans down her legs and lifted her feet free, one by one. Then he buried his face between her legs, and she gasped with the sudden touch of his tongue on her already throbbing nub. She grabbed at him, holding his head to her, but he was just teasing… and lifted away almost immediately.

His eyes were hooded with lust, and she just wanted him to take her *now.* Forget the bath. But he leaned over to start the water then started shucking off his clothes. She tried to be patient, but she couldn't help running her hands over his chest as soon as it was bare, letting her fingers revel in the fact that she could touch him like this… forever.

It was like falling into a dream and never waking up again.

As soon as his pants were gone, Arianna reached for his cock. It was so thick and at attention that it begged for her touch. She wanted nothing more than to pleasure him until he moaned her name.

She pouted when he pulled her hand free.

"Any of that, and we're not going to make it to the main event," he chided. But his smile was wide. He stepped into the tub and turned on the spray nozzle mounted on the wall. A gentle waterfall of rain-soaked his body, making it even more sizzling hot and tempting. She eagerly climbed in after him. He took her in his arms, but quickly turned her, so that she was under the water, not him. Then he reached for the bar of soap nearby and sudsed up his hands. Starting with her breasts, he soaped up her body. She clutched at his shoulders as his palms and fingers slowly worked their way over every square inch of her chest and arms, then down her legs and back up again. Far too briefly, he dipped his fingers between her legs.

She moaned. "Oh God, Jak. I don't know how much of this I can stand."

He grinned and turned her around. Then he slid his hands down her arms, lifting her hands and placing them on the wall next to the nozzle. "Just keep your hands there, Ms. Stefan, and let me do all the work." She groaned as he continued caressing her breasts from behind, rubbing his front against her back. His thick cock teased her, rubbing against her rear and sliding against her skin, their bodies slick with the soap and water.

She was going to come without him even touching her if he kept that up.

She bucked her hips back against him, making the contact with his cock even stronger. He let out a half-growl, half-groan, and picked up the pace in soaping down her back and legs and bottom. She was dripping wet between her legs by the time he pulled her back under the cascading water and rinsed her free of bubbles and soap.

"That's enough bath for you," he said, his voice such a low growl that she could barely hear it. But her wolf registered every syllable, whining and begging for him to claim her *right now.*

"Oh my god, Jak, I need you so badly." She was panting as he lifted her from the tub.

He didn't even bother drying them off, he simply carried her to the bed and laid her on it. Then he stretched her arms over her head and devoured her with a kiss. She wanted her hands free so she could run them over his dripping wet, hard-muscled body, but he wasn't letting her go. And his other hand, the one not holding her wrists prisoner, was between her legs, sending shocks of pleasure rippling through her body.

She gasped as he plunged two fingers inside. His teeth nipped at her breast as he pumped his fingers, bringing her crashing over the edge before she could even call out his name. When she did, it was as much a cry as anything. Her hips bucked against his hand as it wrenched pleasure from her, waves of it crashing throughout her body. She felt his fangs come out, grazing her breast as he worked it with his tongue.

He was breathing hard when he finally lifted his face to hers. "Arianna, my love, I need to be inside you."

"Oh god, Jak, *please.*" She was begging. She didn't care in the slightest.

He released her hands and caressed her face. His eyes were at half-mast, and she could sense his wolf raging beneath his skin.

"I want my magic inside you as well." His breath was uneven. "I'm not sure… I think I have enough. I think it's regenerated. All I know is my wolf is crying holy hell, he wants you so badly."

"I'm yours," Arianna panted. "And his. Take me. And give me all of you."

He growled in such a possessive way that she nearly came again with the way it made her quiver deep and low. He leaned back and roughly turned her over, lifting her hips and climbing behind her. She felt his cock, hard and ready at her entrance as she scrambled up on her hands, bracing herself. She wanted him to take her as hard as his wolf demanded as long as he could stand it. As soon as she was ready, he didn't hesitate, just slammed his cock inside her, taking her so hard from behind that it rocked her forward. She had to brace against the headboard, but each thrust shot thrills of pleasure through her body, making her arms weak and her head as light as a feather. If he hadn't been gripping her hips so tight, she might have collapsed under the pounding, but as it was, he just floated her higher and higher on a cloud of unbelievable pleasure.

This was more than they'd had before. Something about the connection between them, her magic in his blood, was making every touch more pleasurable, more intense. She was quickly climbing to the peak again, but then Jak leaned forward, gripping her hair and pulling her head to the side, exposing her neck.

He was going to bite her. He was going to finally claim her and make her his.

He leaned even more forward, still thrusting inside her, but bringing his lips closer to her shoulder where he would make his mark.

"You are *mine.*" His voice was ragged with pleasure.

"Yes," she panted.

"All mine."

"Yes."

"Forever mine." The last was a whisper.

God, if he didn't claim her *right now,* she thought her heart might literally die from beating so hard. But then the bite came, glorious and hot, piercing her skin and her soul. He kept thrusting and groaning, and her orgasm hit like a tidal wave, washing through her just as his magic spilled from his mouth, through his bite, and flushed throughout her body. It mixed with her magic, and they were intertwined in the most intimate way: body to body, blood to blood, soul to soul. They were completely one, completely belonging to one another.

It drowned her in happiness.

Jak kept pumping until he let out a long, guttural groan. It rippled through his bite and his cock and every square inch of skin touching her. The sound alone was so damn sexy it rippled fresh pleasure waves through her and nearly made her come again.

Eventually, the pulsing through her body slowed. Jak eased to a stop and pulled away from her… but only for a moment before collapsing on the bed next to her and pulling her down to lay sprawled across his chest.

"Holy mother of god," he breathed, staring at the ceiling. "Are you sure I'm not dead, Arianna? Because I'm fairly sure I just visited heaven."

She giggled like a small girl, a flush of embarrassment running through her at such a childish sound. But that embarrassment fled when Jak looked at her with marvel in his eyes.

"I am the goddamn luckiest man in the world."

She grinned and twisted around to climb on top of him, straddling him so that his cock, still swollen, pressed against her core, still tender from their lovemaking. She ground against him and grinned when his head tipped back, and he groaned.

"That's where you're wrong, Jak Roberts," she said, bringing his hands up to cup her breasts. That popped his eyes open again, and he lifted his head to watch. "I'm the one who's lucky to have you."

"You just keep thinking that, my sweet Arianna," he said, full wolf coming back to his eyes. "And I'll keep giving you reasons to think so."

She grinned. Then she started moving rhythmically, grinding at the contact between them. She smirked when she felt his cock growing firm again underneath her. She had every intention of wearing out every last bit of Jak's famous appetite.

And she had forever in which to do it.

Arianna and Jak have found their Happy Ending! Don't miss Lucas and Mia's Christmas story in…

A Christmas Wish (Dot Com Wolves 3)

Subscribe to Alisa's newsletter

for new releases and giveaways

http://smarturl.it/AWsubscribeBARDS

About the Author

Alisa Woods lives in the Midwest with her husband and family, but her heart will always belong to the beaches and mountains where she grew up. She writes sexy paranormal romances about complicated men and the strong women who love them. Her books explore the struggles we all have, where we resist—and succumb to—our most tempting vices as well as our greatest desires. No matter the challenge, Alisa firmly believes that hearts can mend and love will triumph over all.

www.AlisaWoodsAuthor.com

CPSIA information can be obtained
at www.ICGtesting.com
Printed in the USA
BVHW031249090720
583361BV00001B/35

9 781095 557990